The Riddle Of The Leviathan

Published By: Icon Press
Charnlea House
17 Oak Road
Matlock, Derbyshire DE4 3FJ

First published in 2004

ISBN: 0-9537502-2-1

Cover illustration by Bill Armstrong

Printed by:
ProPrint
Riverside Cottages
Old Great North Road
Stibbington
Cambs. PE8 6LR

Prologue

Captain Bill Stewart walked into the Coach and Horses with a hell of a headache. He decided that the swiftest cure was a double tot of rum. When he had ordered he sat down and took a speculative sip. Then he looked round and noticed that a man at the next table was reading one of the tabloid newspapers. The newspaper was open so that Bill could see the front page and the main headline. He sighed. Wouldn't the papers ever leave him alone? The headline which depressed him read, "**THE RIDDLE OF THE LEVIATHAN**".

Bill was in his mid forties. He had a good head of brown hair, now tinged with grey at the sides, and his face was chiselled square with a deep cleft in the chin. There were deep furrows on his forehead. He was wearing a lounge suit as he had just been to a court of enquiry. He was the subject of the enquiry because he had been the captain of a space ship which had gone missing. Nevertheless, he looked like a man who should be in uniform because he had a habitually straight carriage and a commanding way of speaking.

He took another sip at the rum and felt the warm liquid searching his toes. The man reading the newspaper folded it and left it on a table. Then he stood to put on his coat. He glanced at Bill. He then beamed and said, "Hell's bells! I don't believe it! It's you Bill. Man, I've just been reading about you. Such is fame, eh?"

Bill was stuck for a moment and then realised that the man was a school contemporary he hadn't seen for many years. He stood to shake hands and said, groping for the name, "Can I buy you a drink, er ...Carl?"

"I was about to go," said Carl, "but in the circumstances I'll be glad to sink another jar. I work in the stock market, you know, my snitch in the money trough and

1

all that. But there's no need to ask what you've been doing with yourself - but perhaps I should rephrase that, since the paparazzi are asking that very question. Still, perhaps you would prefer not to talk about it."

"I don't mind," said Bill. "But let me get you a drink first. What are you having?"

A couple of minutes later the two men were drinking and talking animatedly about times long gone and friends of their youth. Carl Britton was of slim build, but was heavy round the jowls from years of over indulgence. After a while he said, "I'm sorry you're in such a helluva mess, Bill. How did it all happen?"

"It's a long story, mate."

"I don't have to go back to the office this afternoon. How about you? Is the enquiry over?"

"In one sense, yes. All that has to be said has been said. The board needs till tomorrow morning to decide on their verdict."

"What does that imply, Bill?"

"I hope to be exonerated. But it depends whether or not they believe my story. The worst scenario would be a verdict of negligence, possibly combined with one of manslaughter, in which case I could be cashiered and even put in gaol for a long time. Not a pleasant prospect, I can tell you."

"We've had bits of the story through the media, of course. What puzzles everybody is where you've been for those five missing years. After all, it was two thousand and fifteen when you left. Then your space ship seemed to disappear from the face of the universe. I remember it well. There was even a memorial service at the old school. I was able to attend, as a matter of fact. I must say the old beak did you proud. He painted you as a twenty first century hero."

"Perhaps things would have been better left that way," said Bill. "I wish I'd never come back now."

"What really astounded everybody was the mysterious story about a sort of Messiah, Bill. How on earth did you come to swallow that? Or is it just a way of distracting the authorities?"

"I'll start from the beginning," said Bill. "It might do me good to get it off my chest. It was just a routine trip to the moon, you know. We were supposed to bring back a load of rare minerals for the Prospero Project. I remember the day we set out. Visibility was good in the northern hemisphere...".

Chapter One

It was a fairly ordinary trip, I suppose, that is until we came in to land after the return journey. My 2 ic, Andrew Whittle, was on the bridge at the time. I was in my cabin completing the log. When I had finished writing I glanced out of the porthole and saw the curvature of the earth coming up fast. Then, for some unknown reason the ship began to spin. It was a slow spin for a start. The home planet showed up through the glass, all green and white on the light bit. Then the ship turned and the moon came into view. Another turn and there was the earth again.

At first I concluded that this was nothing to worry about. I thought that Whittle would use the stabilisers and stop the spin. He told me afterwards that he had done that, but that it had made no difference. Anyway, the spinning grew faster and faster until all I saw out of the window was a blur. It was just as well that everything in the cabin was battened down. I thought it wise to strap myself in. I then picked up the intercom, but it didn't seem to be working. To be honest I thought my last moments had come. I was furious that I wasn't on the bridge of my ship, but there was no way I could get there while the ship was in a fast spin.

I don't know how long the spin lasted. I think I passed out for a while. When I came round the spin had slowed down. Yes, there in the porthole was the familiar configuration of the earth's surface. Then, yes, there was the moon again. But bloody hell, there were two moons. I watched for the spin to bring the moon back into view again. Yes, there again were the two moons. Naturally I concluded I was dizzy with the effects of the spin. However, the spin stopped a few seconds afterwards and I was able to unfasten my belt and make my way to the bridge.

I wasn't surprised to find that the crew were all still strapped in and that the ship was on automatic for landing. I went up to Whittle and said sharply, "A report, lieutenant, if you please."

Andrew Whittle unfastened his belt and stood beside me. I examined the controls carefully, but all the dials seemed to be behaving normally. I turned to look at Whittle. He was a swarthy man with black hair, of medium height with broad shoulders. I had seen him box and he was very useful with the gloves on. In fact, he had boxed for his native country, which was South Africa.

He said, "Nothing to worry about, sir. We've been in a spin but it seems to have righted itself."

"I know that Andy," I said irritably. "But what caused it?"

"It must have been the way the cargo was stored," he said smoothly. I recognised the tone of voice. It was the kind of voice a second in command used to his boss when he didn't really know the answer to the question.

"Rubbish," I said. "The laws of physics are consistent. We loaded the way we always load."

"That's the only explanation I can think of, sir."

"That, at least, is honest," I said. "We'll leave the controls on automatic. We should land within four minutes I guess."

"I hope so," said Whittle, smiling. "I have a really hot date tonight. She's special."

We then fell silent and waited for the completion of the landing procedure. Unfortunately, things did not go smoothly. The electronic beacons at the space port did not latch onto us and I had to put the ship back onto manual control. I then tried to get verbal contact with the landing base but there was complete silence. I locked our radar onto the base. However, the resulting picture showed merely open fields in the exact location where the base should have been.

It was then I had to make one of those awkward split second decisions. Still, that's what I'm paid for, I suppose. I concluded that the location was the correct one, but that the radar and radio control had been knocked out by the spin. I moved to a position where I could check the landing visually. Although it was coming up dusk there were no lights to be seen on the ground. It was then I saw that there were no air base buildings within sight. However, by that time I was committed to landing. I cursed myself roundly for making the wrong decision. It was not surprising that we had a very bumpy landing. Nevertheless, the ship was still in one piece.

I spoke to the crew over the intercom, explaining what had happened. I ordered everyone to stay put until I had contacted the base by the emergency 'phone link. However, I had no luck there. It was at that moment that I heard Whittle's voice saying, "Bloody hell, skipper, what's going on? There are two f...ing moons in the sky."

He didn't know that the Reverend Professor Cherrington was right behind him. He apologised immediately for swearing. However, the Professor was too busy admiring the twin moons. I heard him saying half aloud, "Wonderful! Absolutely wonderful! It's like a new act of creation."

Actually, we don't normally have a clergyman on board, but Anselm Cherrington was head industrial chaplain for the whole of England. He was with us on this occasion to gain some practical experience, and I must say that he had been very unobtrusive up to that point. I had never up to then been a great believer in providence and that sort of thing, but in retrospect I think it was some special providence that placed Anselm on board for that particular voyage, even though it turned out badly for him.

I gave the order to switch off all power systems and asked the crew to meet in the mess room. When they were gathered I explained that we were lost. The youngest officer, Joseph Blenkinsop, piped up, "We aren't far from Derby, sir. I saw the lights of the city in the distance as we were coming down."

I liked Blenkinsop. He had the makings of a good space officer. He was tall and blond with fresh features. The girls on the staff in the space port usually made a fuss of him. He had been brought up in Derby, so I assumed that he had correctly recognised his native city.

"Thank you," I said. "That remark does help, but it doesn't alter the fact that we're lost. We seem to be miles from the space port and I can't get contact."

The chief engineer, Bernard Rawlins said, "Shall I put the beacon light on, sir?"

Rawlins was a stocky, dark haired man from Tyneside. He was a very useful man to have around and was a genius with computers. I said, "Not just yet, Bernard. I'd like to look around first."

Rawlins said, "What's worrying you, skipper? Would you like to share it with us?"

"I just have a gut feeling that things are not quite right," I said.

"Is it the two moons?" said the Professor.

"Not really," I said. "It's more of a gut feeling. And I think the twin moons are some trick in atmospheric conditions. The same conditions may have induced that bad spin. I believe all our instruments are out of true."

Rawlins went to the window. He looked upwards at the sky. Then he said in a slightly worried voice, "Those two moons are not precisely the same, sir, and they look smaller than they should be."

"That is a bit odd," I said, "but don't let's panic. There's bound to be a scientific explanation. Andrew, you take charge. I'll have a reccy outside with Bernard. Bring a gun, Bernard. And Andrew, follow the X10 procedure, including an armed watch."

The steps were lowered and the chief engineer and I descended cautiously to the ground. It was now quite dark, but I had a torch with me so I shone it around to get my bearings. We seemed to be in the middle of a huge field. Way in the distance I heard some cows lowing. In those circumstances it was a very reassuring sound. I looked up at the sky. Yes, the Great Bear was there. Many other constellations I recognised. But standing well apart, two half moons gleamed brightly and gave a dim light, now that my eyes were used to the change of focus.

"They're very strange, aren't they," said Bernard, obviously awestruck. "I could have sworn the moon was still in one piece when we left."

"I still think it's an optical illusion," I insisted, but less vehemently than before. The two moons were slightly different and that could only be due to the angle at which the rays of the sun reached them. And yes, they were smaller than our old familiar moon.

"I've got it," said Bernard, his voice full of excitement. "I know what's happened, Bill. It explains the spinning of our ship and also our disorientation."

"What then?" I said, slightly irritated by his apparent grasp of a situation which was still puzzling me.

"After we left the moon it must have been struck by something from outer space which has split it into two pieces. The force would be tremendous. It must have caused a lot of damage on Earth. That may be why the space port isn't where we expected. Perhaps the poles have moved or something."

I took in this statement and thought about it for a moment. Then I said, "Bernard, you've been watching too many space films. Think about it. The force would have been so great that the tides would have swept the oceans right across the face of the earth. The world would still be rocking. And those cows wouldn't be so peaceful. No, something is definitely wrong, but I don't know what it is."

"I still think I could be right," said Bernard. The cataclysm would be on the moon, not on earth."

"Then why are the two moons so perfectly round?" I said sarcastically.

He thought for a moment. Then he said triumphantly, "What ever hit the moon split it down the middle, just like cutting an apple in half. The two halves are still close enough together not to have affected the earth's gravity too much."

"Then why are the two halves smaller?"

"Because they're further away," said Bernard triumphantly.

"Bernard," I said, "you may be a wizard with computers but your knowledge of basic physics leaves a lot to be desired. There is no way that those moons have been split recently. If they are the result of a split in an original single moon it must have happened thousands of years ago."

"I've got it then," he said. "We must have moved on in time. It stands to reason."

"Don't be bloody silly," I said. "I tell you it's an optical illusion." However, there was even less conviction in my voice than previously. "Anyway," I continued, "there's a light over there. Look, just to the right of that tall tree."

"Yes, I see it. Shall we go and enquire where we are?"

"Yes, but we'd better have a couple of men with us. Let's go back into the ship and plan for a night's stay here."

"Aren't we going to investigate now, skipper?" he said.

"Of course, but there's no way we can get off the ground before morning. And anyway, I expect we shall probably have to suffer the indignity of being towed by road back to the space port."

....

The chief engineer and myself, accompanied by two crew, walked smartly towards the distant light. I had chosen

Kirkbride and Stevenson to go with us because they were both useful men in a tight corner. Kirkbride was a red haired Irishman with a quick temper. Stevenson was a Cornishman who was built for wrestling, but was yet light on his feet. Both men had strong regional accents.

As we were walking along Kirkbride said cheerfully, "What do you think, then, sir? Are we really on Mars?"

I laughed. "Hardly, Kirkbride. What does everybody think? Do they really think we're on another planet?"

"Oh, no sorr," said the Irishman. "It's just my little joke. But are you sure you didn't put rum in our coffee this morning? That would explain why we're seeing two moons."

Stevenson laughed. "We're moon drunk. That's what it is. You know the old saying sir, 'A day on the moon and you'll play a new tune.'"

"We shall see," I said calmly. "Don't go asking silly questions at this house. And whatever you do don't mention the moon. Let them mention it first. Otherwise they'll think we're crackers."

We tramped on in silence. As we got closer to the building we could see that there were several windows lit. In fact, it seemed to be quite a large, sprawling building. As we were approaching our destination we came upon a metalled road. Its surface was incredibly smooth. The road seemed to be leading towards the house, so we followed it, our boots clicking noisily. Without thinking about it we found ourselves automatically walking in step. But then, like most space crews, we all had a military background.

At length we came to a huge metal gate which was firmly closed. However, there was a light on the archway above the gate. It was not a type of light I had observed before. It was a sort of neon light, I guess, and it glowed green in the darkness. In fact, it was just a little unnerving. There was a control panel on the wall at one side of the gate. One button was marked NIGHT BELL, so I pressed it firmly. However, we couldn't hear any bell ringing.

After about a minute we heard footsteps. Then a shadowy figure approached the gate on the inside. This person seemed to be wearing a hood. He came right up to the gate and said in a slightly quavering voice, "This is a strange hour for visiting. May I help you?"

"We're lost," I said confidently. "I wonder if you could give us some guidance."

The man threw back his hood. I saw a strong, kindly face and felt immediately more relaxed. The monk, for such he was, said with a smile, "We usually offer spiritual guidance. But what am I thinking about? You'd better come in, my brothers."

He seemed to press a button on his side of the gate and the gates opened silently.

"I didn't know there was a monastery in these parts," I said.

The monk said, "We've been here long enough. You're obviously from another part of the country. But you'd better come and meet Father Christophoros. I'm Brother Cuthbert, by the way."

Brother Cuthbert led us along a garden path and then through a wide door into a large building. "I'm sorry the gate was locked," he said apologetically. "It's really to keep the cows out of the garden as much as anything. And boys out of the orchard, of course."

Brother Cuthbert led us into a comfortable sitting room. We were invited to sit down and wait while our guide went to get Father Christophoros. The chairs were of a material resembling leather, but I'm sure it wasn't leather. The room was warm and well lit, but for the life of me I couldn't tell where the sources of heat and light were. On the walls were several pictures. I can only describe them as three dimensional landscapes. The strange thing is they were moving, much as a television picture moves. One showed a sea scene in which a boat was moving and rocking and seagulls were swooping and diving in the foreground. I stood and walked over to that particular picture. As I approached the picture blurred and all I could see was a recess in the wall with rays of light of various colours crisscrossing. To my embarrassment Brother Cuthbert came back with another monk just as I was putting my hand into the recess where the picture was - or had been.

Neither monk mentioned my rudeness. Instead Father Christophoros smiled warmly and said, "I'm the Prior here. May I offer you a meal? Have you come far?"

I noticed that his accent was faintly Scottish.

"That's very kind of you," I said, "but our space ship is only just across the fields. We had a kind of crash landing, I suppose. No damage, but I want to get in touch with my firm. And really I want to know where we are."

"You're well away from the usual flight paths," said the Prior. "To be more precise you are about eight miles east of Derby."

"That's not too far from where I thought I was. I can't imagine how I missed the space port."

"But there isn't a space station within a hundred miles from here," said Father Christophoros. "Oh, I see what you mean. You would be moving so fast that a hundred miles would be neither here nor there."

My three companions looked at me questioningly. I gave them a steely gaze to shut them up.

Father Christophoros continued, "How many are on your ship? We could probably put you up for the night. Or for longer if necessary."

"How kind," I said, wondering whether it would be wise to accept. "Actually, apart from myself and the chaplain there are twelve men on board. But I wouldn't dream of putting you to any trouble. We have plenty of supplies. And we don't wish to leave the ship unguarded. You know what villains there are around."

"I don't know what you mean," said Father Christophoros. "The only villains on this planet are in history books. Oh, I see, it was meant to be a joke. But come, why don't you bring your men over. And I would especially like to meet the chaplain. What is he doing on a space ship?"

"Professor Cherrington is the Chief Industrial Chaplain in the whole of England," I said. "He's getting some practical experience."

"At which university is he professor?" said the Prior, his face unreadable.

"Durham University," I said.

"But there hasn't been a university there for a hundred years. It was moved to Edinburgh. Oh, I see what you mean. He must be at Edinburgh, but he'll be in the so called Durham Faculty. I know it quite well. By the way, would you like me to walk to your space ship with you? I can bring a bright lamp."

"It's moonlight," I said. "We can manage."

"Oh, yes," he said, "the moons are lovely tonight, just like two ships on the ocean of the sky."

I had been trying to weigh up Father Christophoros while he had been talking. He was several inches above six feet in height. I guessed he would be about sixty five years old, or thereabouts. He had fine features and his skin was almost transparent. His fingers, I noticed, were very long, and his hands moved as he talked as if he were conducting an orchestra. He was the sort of person you could instinctively trust.

At that point Kirkbride asked a stupid question. He obviously couldn't help it, because like the rest of us he was eaten with curiosity. What he said was, "How long have we had two moons, sorr?"

Father Christophoros turned to look at Kirkbride. "Is that a catch question from Hibernia, young man? Tell me the age of the earth and I'll tell you how long we have had two moons."

I realised at that point that we were in deep, deep trouble. I have always been a forthright person and I decided there and then that there was nothing for it but to tell the truth. "Listen, Father, I began, I think it is time I told you our story."

The man's eyes seemed to glow with friendliness. "I'm pleased you have decided to be open with us. It has been obvious to me for some time that something strange is going on here. But why don't you introduce yourselves. And then, why don't you go and bring your comrades. I shall assemble my brothers in the morning and we shall all listen to your story then. In the meantime Brother Cuthbert will see to all your needs."

"I introduced myself and my three companions and then said, "Don't you want to know more about us first? We could be thieves or murderers."

Father Christophoros laughed aloud. "You certainly aren't, Captain Stewart. Your mental vibrations give a very balanced picture."

"Father," I said, "before you go, may I ask just a couple of questions."

He nodded and said courteously, "Of course. Go ahead."

"Is this the Planet Earth?" I said.

His face became quite still. "The problem is deeper than I thought. But yes, this is the Planet Earth."

"What year is it?" I said. I noticed that my three companions were sitting on the edge of their chairs.

"It is the Year of Our Lord two thousand and fifty nine," he said calmly. "What year did you think it was?"

"When we left our space station near Derby it was the year two thousand and fifteen," I said.

"Very strange, captain," he said. "But let's talk about it in the morning. In the meantime I shall pray for divine guidance. I shall be in the chapel all night, Brother Cuthbert, if you need me."

"How do you know we'll come back?" I said.

He smiled benignly. "My dear Captain, you haven't really any choice, have you?"

On the way back to the ship we talked excitedly about what we had learned. It was Bernard who hit the nail on the head when he said, "Skipper, I think we're on a different Planet Earth. We have crossed some kind of time and space barrier into a different dimension."

As usual I was cautious. "We can't be sure. Let's enquire a bit further before we start jumping to conclusions."

But my chief engineer wouldn't let the matter drop. "It stands to reason, doesn't it. We are definitely on Planet Earth. But it is definitely not the same Planet Earth. The monks know what we're talking about when we talk about Derby and Durham and so on. But the two moons have always been here. Therefore, it's not our planet, but yet in a funny sort of way it is."

"Suppose it's the same planet but on a different cycle," said Kirkbride. "I once read a book about recurring cycles. The theory is that it's all happened before and that it will all happen again."

But we hadn't time for further chat because we had reached our space ship.

Chapter Two

When we had breakfasted on a range of vegetarian foods, including cereals with milk, the Prior invited us to meet in the main hall at ten o'clock. Further introductions were postponed until then, which meant that Professor Anselm Cherrington was jumping up and down with curiosity. I persuaded him to wait until the meeting before he started to ask the one hundred and one questions which were bubbling to the surface of his agile mind. The Professor was just short of sixty, I guess. He was bald except for a grey fringe. His face was plump and cherubic and normally radiant with kindliness. However, he could be very angry in the face of injustice and a terrier for pertinacity when he was pursuing a righteous cause.

There were twenty two monks altogether and three guests on retreat. One of these was a woman. All of my crew, and the monks with their guests, assembled in the main hall at ten. The chairs were arranged in a circle, but all my men sat together, which was natural enough in the circumstances, I suppose. I glanced round the room at the decor. The ceiling and walls were covered with paintings which seemed to show Biblical scenes. On seeing these pictures I was curious to know whether the monks' view of Christianity was the same as ours. The idea of having two Christs on two different Earths seemed to me to be mind boggling, though later it was explained to me how such an apparent dualism could be possible.

Father Christophoros joined the circle like everyone else. However, it was clear from his demeanour that he was the authority among the monks. When all the fidgeting had stopped he said quietly, "To our visitors I extend a warm welcome to Mount Zion. I suggest that we all sit in silence for two minutes and wait for the Spirit to descend upon us."

I hate these artificial silences. My mind always wanders onto silly subjects. On this occasion I thought of the beautiful loo paper I had used half an hour ago. Each piece was decorated with a picture and it seemed such a shame to waste such artistic productions. On further reflection, however, I decided that the pictures were restful and productive in that context. The thought of everybody on the planet going to the loo to think beautiful thoughts was an amusing one.

At last Father Christophoros spoke again: "It is now time for introductions before our visitors tell us their story."

He named each of the monks one by one. As each monk was named he stood and bowed. Then the three people on retreat were introduced. I had already noticed the young woman. She was easy on the eyes but not exceptionally beautiful. She was tall and had long fair hair. She was wearing a long loose robe which concealed her figure. She was introduced simply as Fiona. When she sat down again I stared at her but couldn't get her to look in my direction. I was really wanting to see what her eyes were like. I feel I can learn a lot from people's eyes.

When the Prior had finished he nodded at me. I introduced myself and then the members of my party. There was a flicker of interest among the monks when I introduced the Professor. He said a few words in Greek which he later told me were a quote from the New Testament. After I had sat down again I looked over towards the mysterious Fiona. She smiled back and I could see that her eyes were blue as a cornflower. I think it was at that moment that I fell in love with her.

Father Christophoros then said, "Perhaps Captain Stewart would give us an account of how he and his friends came to be here. Please remain seated, Captain."

I gave a brief résumé of our story, explaining first why we had been travelling to the moon, and then how we had gone into a spin before landing. I mentioned our difficulties in orientating ourselves, including our surprise at seeing two moons. The monks seemed to find the idea of a single moon amusing.

When I had finished, Father Christophoros said, "I cannot pretend to understand what has happened to bring such interesting strangers to our door. However, in accord with our faith we must be generous in our hospitality to travellers. And I think it is fair to say that our new friends have travelled an extremely long way. No doubt they have many questions and no doubt we have too. But perhaps Professor Cherrington would like to give us a brief summary of his religious faith?"

The Professor didn't need asking twice. He gave a twenty minute talk which would have done justice to the Pope himself. I'm no theologian but it was obvious to me that the Professor was giving a very workmanlike description of Christianity. As he was talking there many oohs and ahs from the monks. The greatest surprise was shown when he mentioned the word "incarnation". At last he sat down and everybody clapped.

Father Christophoros was as inscrutable as ever. He said placidly, "I suggest we continue until lunchtime and that we have alternate questions, first one from our visitors, followed by one from ourselves. How about you, Captain Stewart?"

"It may sound like an elementary question," I said, "but do you have a city in the north of England called Carlisle. The reason I ask is because it is my native city."

Christophoros smiled and said, "I have visited the place several times. It is a very beautiful city. Shall I set the ball rolling for our side. I'd like to ask if your Earth is a united planet like ours?"

I looked at the Professor and nodded. He said, "I'm not quite sure what the question means. Perhaps you could explain it to me."

Christophoros said, "Our political system has evolved into a kind of unity with a royal family at the head. All the nations are bound together in a covenant of unity."

"I see," said the Professor. "We have tried systems like that. The League of Nations, for example. And after that the United Nations. But I cannot honestly say we have achieved political unity. We have wars sometimes."

The monks looked very serious when the Professor mentioned war. Christophoros said, "We have not had a war on our planet for a hundred years. The Second Planetary War was the war to end all wars."

"It was supposed to be for us," said the Professor, "but it didn't quite work out that way. May I ask a question that logically follows on from that one? What I should like to know is do you have religious unity on your Earth?"

Christophoros said, "We are going to be confused if we do not distinguish carefully between our world and yours. I suggest we call your home world Transworld because you have crossed over from your world to ours. And let us call ours This World because we are here. Now to answer your question. I must be brief now, but you will be able to learn more later. On This World we have a united Christian Church under a papal royal family. Just as the various countries are united in a covenant, so the churches of different traditions are united by a religious covenant."

"What about other faiths?" said the Professor.

Christophoros smiled. "That is two questions, Professor. However, the main religions have several ways of getting together. One of them is through the Temple of All Nations, but it would take me a long time to describe it. I have a video which you can see later. It will explain the religious system of This World. Now it is our turn. Would any brother like to ask a question of our visitors?"

An old monk said, "Transworld seems to be very uncivilised. Why do you still have fighting?"

The Professor looked at me and I looked at him. It was obvious that we were both in difficulties. I decided to pass the buck and let the Professor speak. He said, "It is a question of human sin. Surely people are sinful in This World just as they are in Transworld?"

Christophoros smiled. "We have an education programme to deal with immature people. People do have to return for treatment from time to time. It is a spiritual process. I think that needs further explanation later. I hope my answer will suffice for now. It is the turn of your party to ask a question, Captain."

I looked round. Whittle was obviously wishing to speak so I gave him a nod. He said, "You don't appear to need an army in This World. Do you have a police force?"

"The Peelers and the Coppers are part of our history," said Christophoros. "We don't need a police force as such. What we have is a group of men and women called rangers. People may get into difficulties when climbing a mountain, for example, or when sailing the oceans. The rangers are the people who deal with that sort of emergencies."

"Do they carry weapons?" said Whittle. I butted in at that point because I didn't like the way Whittle's questions were going. I said, "You've had your question, Andy. Let somebody else have a turn."

The questions went on for an hour and a half. As I learned more about This World I realised they were streets ahead of Transworld in almost every conceivable way. It was an odd feeling. I suppose a fair parallel would be if an uneducated Indian from a South American village was brought to London and was taken round the city. I could only hope that the people of This World wouldn't regard us as ignorant savages. I was certainly a bit worried about several of my men, not least about Andrew Whittle, my second in command. Some of the men liked wine, women and song, with the occasional fight thrown in for good measure. Whittle,

I suppose, was slightly more civilised than that, but essentially he was a selfish, ambitious egotist, and I knew that if he had half a chance he would cause trouble. I made a mental note to ask Father Christophoros to hide all our weapons in a safe place.

....

I sat beside Fiona at lunch time. This was no accident. I manoeuvred shamelessly to get a seat next to her, much to Father Christophoros's amusement. I learned that she was from London and that she was considering a Christian vocation. I guessed she was in her early thirties. She was very easy to talk to and the more I talked to her the more attractive I found her. She expressed an interest in seeing our space ship, so I offered to show her round that afternoon. This I was able to do, after checking with Father Christophoros. At the same time I mentioned the problem of the weapons to him. He agreed to lock them away, so I assigned a party to bring the weapons over to the monastery.

When we reached our craft she expressed surprise at its compactness. I was astonished to learn that she had had several voyages in space. One voyage in particular she said she had enjoyed, and that was a sight seeing trip round Venus.

We were soon on first name terms. I learned that she was a graduate of London University and that she spent much of her time playing in an orchestra. I was quite curious about this so I said, "How can you afford to spend so much time on your music. Don't you work?"

"That is my work, but I did some hospital training as well," she said.

"You mean you get paid for following a hobby?" I said.

She laughed aloud. "You seem to have some misconceptions, Bill. Still, that's not surprising when you have just arrived here. Nobody works in This World. We don't need to. Everything we need is provided by the automated factories which are underground."

"Suppose I want a record player, then?" I said.

"That would be difficult. You would have to go to a museum. But if you wanted an electronic music maker you could go to any of several outlets near Derby."

"What exactly is an outlet?" I said.

"I suppose I could show you one, but essentially what they provide is material things for all our needs."

"Who pays?" I said.

She looked slightly blank. Then her face cleared. "I see what you mean. In Transworld you obviously still have financial arrangements. We regard that as fairly primitive - sorry, I didn't mean to offend you - but your financial system is just a system of tokens really. And if my history is accurate the tokens are given to people for producing things. Is that how you do it?"

"Something like that."

"Well, as I have already said, the production of material things is all automated, so nobody has to be a producer."

"Doesn't the system need engineers to keep it going?"

"Practically no maintenance is required. But we do have volunteers who acquire the skills necessary to alter the machines or to mend them. People do work at things, but only if they wish to. A person can spend his or her time in whatever way seems appropriate."

"So if I wanted to spend my time lounging on a beach and generally loafing around that would be OK, would it?"

"In our experience people soon get bored when they do that. We have what we call All Age Universities. people can learn to do all kinds of things. They can also do adventurous things like climbing mountains. Or they can challenge each other to contests of skill."

"Like football?"

"Most people in This World would think that a childish pursuit. I have played myself though, and it is good fun. We have many schools of philosophy and one of them promulgates a theory that play is really a very creative thing."

I thought of Arsenal playing Tottenham and I decided to keep my counsel on the idea that play is a creative philosophy. Instead I said, "What is the expectation of life here?"

She smiled mischievously. "How old do you think I am?"

Whenever I am asked to play the age guessing game by a woman I always give an age ten years less than I judge to be accurate. I said, "About twenty five."

She laughed. Her laughter was a very beautiful sound, rather like a musical instrument playing a merry tune. Then she said, "Really, Captain, you are an idle flatterer. I was fifty five earlier this year."

My mouth must have fallen open. She said, "That seems to surprise you. Let me guess how old you are. I would say about sixty."

My mouth must have fallen even further open. I gasped, "You must be joking. I'm just over forty. In Transworld people live until they're about seventy or eighty."

"I'm sorry," she said. "I didn't mean to offend you. In This World the average expectation of life is one hundred and twenty, but sometimes people live until they're one hundred and fifty."

I relaxed slightly when I realised that I hadn't suddenly put on twenty years. She said, "I expect my age has changed your view of me?"

"Not really," I said. "Age is how you feel. And you look as if you feel about twenty five."

"Flattery again, Captain. But aren't you going to show me round your ship?"

It didn't take all that long to show her round. I must say she asked some very intelligent questions about the workings of the ship. While we were there the party of men assigned to take away the weapons arrived. She looked with interest as they tied the rifles into bundles and loaded them onto the electric buggy.

"What are those for, Bill?" she said.

"I assume you know what they are," I said cautiously.

"Of course, but why do you need them?"

"We don't," I said. "I'm just storing them in a safe place."

I didn't mention my worry that some of my men might do something drastic with the guns.

I was quite touched when Fiona innocently took my hand as we walked back to Mount Zion. I couldn't make up my mind whether she felt the same physical attraction for me as I felt for her. The fact that she was older than I didn't seem to matter all that much.

....

That evening the Prior gave me some unwelcome news. He had invited the Professor and myself to have tea in his study. This we were delighted to do because we wanted to learn more about This World. However, as soon as we were seated Christophoros said without smiling, "I have had some decisions from the authorities concerning your party, Captain Stewart. It seems you will have to be quarantined for six months until doctors can assess the dangers to the health of the people of This World."

"We're all healthy," I said. "Nobody can travel in space without a health clearance."

"I'm sure that is true, Captain, but your body systems may carry viruses which are strange to us. Do you see what I mean?"

"I guess so," I said. "But I'm a bit worried about the reaction of my men. They won't like being cooped up for six months."

"There will be a programme arranged," said Christophoros. "I think they will find it interesting. It will have elements of physical exercise, some spiritual development, intellectual challenges, and above all, it will be designed to help you to adjust to This World which does seem to be rather different from Transworld."

Christophoros was a nice bloke but he didn't really understand the needs of a space crew. My lads were a good lot, on the whole, but they were very earthy. The idea of some of them being interested in spiritual development was laughable. However, I decided not to prejudge the issue, especially when the Professor said heartily, "What a wonderful idea. It will be like being a student again."

"By the way," said Christophoros, "you might like to know that the visitors from Transworld are headlined in all the media. I'm flattered that my names for the two worlds have been universally accepted."

"Going back to the question of adjustment," said Professor Cherrington, "I don't think it is going to be easy. I have noticed some very significant differences between the two worlds already."

"So have I," I said. "But don't you think the question of our return to Transworld should be explored? After all, we do have responsibilities back home."

"You are married, are you, Captain?" said Christophoros. His voice had a slight edge to it and I supposed he was thinking about my interest in Fiona.

I said quickly, "Only to my space ship, Father. But going back to the matter of our return, the trouble is I'm not really sure how we managed to get here. It seems to me that there are some areas of science where we are completely ignorant, at least in Transworld."

"Are you sure we are dealing with scientific laws, Captain?" said Christophoros, with a faint hint of a smile. "In This World we believe that everything is ultimately subject to spiritual power."

"What an interesting idea," said the Professor. "However, in this context you seem to be implying that spiritual powers brought us here rather than a chance collision with a physical force. Do you have any definite reason for thinking that?"

"There is an ancient prophecy which suggests that strangers will come from an alien world before the Messiah comes," said Christophoros.

"I thought you told me that Christ was regarded as the Messiah in This World just as in Transworld," said the Professor.

"That's true. But it is our belief that Christ will come again."

"So it is with us," said the Professor. "But the idea does pose a lot of problems."

"We have to live with events as they happen," said Christophoros. "If Christ is born again as a man or a woman then what we have is a second incarnation."

"Which would mean that God had two sons," said the Professor, "and that would contradict the doctrine of the Trinity."

"Not necessarily," said Christophoros. "If you know anything about Hinduism or Buddhism the explanation should come to you."

"Got it," said the Professor. "The idea of the Son of God as part of the divine being is eternal and unchanging, but this Word or Logos can be expressed in human form more than once, just as a second Buddha or another avatar can be an incarnation of an eternal principle."

I must have looked a bit lost. Christophoros and the Professor both looked at me and burst out laughing. The

Professor said, "I'm sorry, Bill, we are getting a bit technical. And when theologians get together they do go on a bit."

"It's all very fascinating as I understand it," I said, "but what's puzzling me is the idea that we could be a sign of the Second Coming of Christ. I used to go to church, you know. You seem to be suggesting that some divine power has deliberately brought us here as a sort of prophecy. Does that make us angels?"

I said the last sentence in a humorous way, but Christophoros took my remark seriously. "Yes," he said, "in a way it does. An angel is a sort of messenger. And incidentally, I ought to say that the strangers from the alien world are supposed to pay homage to Christ the King just after his birth."

"Like the Three Wise men," I said. "I'm sorry, Father, but I'll need some convincing."

"There's a bit more to it," said Christophoros. "I have had several dreams lately and they suggest that the birth of Christ will take place in the year when Halley's Comet reappears."

"When will that be?" said the Professor excitedly.

"In two years time," said Christophoros, "that is, in the year of Our Lord two thousand and sixty one."

"I want to be back home long before that," I said.

Father Christophoros looked at me in a strange sort of way. "I don't think that will be possible, Captain. It will take a long time for our cleverest people to discover how you came to be here in the first place. And I ought to tell you another part of the prophecy which has just occurred to me. It says that the planet will be torn by conflicts at the time of the Second Coming."

"Our prophecies say that," said the Professor. "But surely that is a symbolic statement. It doesn't mean there will be a planetary war."

"I hope you are right," said Christophoros.

For some reason I couldn't identify, my heart was full of foreboding at the prophecy concerning world conflict told to us by this very holy man whom I was beginning to admire greatly. Christophoros himself looked just a little less calm than he had done previously. I dismissed my feeling of unease fairly quickly. After all, how could a handful of people cause a world conflict?

Chapter Three

I was a little surprised that Mount Zion hadn't been inundated with media reporters, but I was told that worry about the health risk had been paramount and people had been ordered by the Supreme Council not to come anywhere near the monastery. An exception was made for a team of doctors and psychologists who had all had about twenty different injections before coming. Moreover, they were to stay with us until the quarantine was over. They brought their own accommodation with them in the form of a prefabricated building of a type I had not observed before. I watched them erect this structure. It was made, I discovered later, of a plastic material which was very durable. The pieces slotted together and then the whole thing was sprayed with a liquid which bonded and waterproofed the whole building. The window panes were of the same material, though obviously transparent. The heating system, I discovered, was built into the walls and was run by electricity.

Within a month the visiting team had decided there was little or no risk of anyone in This World being infected with any kind of disease or illness. I suppose this is what encouraged Whittle and several others to feel it was safe to take French leave.

The disappearance of four of my crew was first noted at breakfast one morning about two months after our arrival. We had all got into the habit of being on time for breakfast because if you missed it there was nothing else available until lunchtime. That's why I took the trouble to go to knock on Whittle's door when he was not at the table. When I got no response to my knock I opened the door and found that his bed had not been slept in. Further investigation showed that, in all, four of our people had not spent the night in Mount Zion. Several innocent explanations occurred to me for a start.

I wondered if they had gone for a walk and got lost, for example. While I was pondering what to do Father Christophoros came into the dining room and buttonholed me. He said, "Captain Stewart, I am very disturbed to find that one of our store rooms has been broken into during the night and some of your guns are missing."

I went along to the store room with him to check what had gone. I found that four machine pistols and some of the ammunition had been lifted. I then knew that Whittle and the other three had deliberately left the monastery, against my orders, and that they were the only armed people in an unarmed world. I must admit that I was not only horrified, I was also afraid. I immediately explained my fears to Christophoros.

He said, "I will telephone the Rangers at their HQ. They will know what to do."

"Will they be armed?" I said.

He smiled briefly and said, "Of course not."

I went with Christophoros to his office. The telephone fixture had a television screen on which the person at the other end appeared. In fact, he simply spoke to a girl who took down the details. She said she hoped action would be initiated right away because there was a helicopter team on standby. I didn't feel like finishing my breakfast so I asked Christophoros what I could most usefully do. He suggested that I go into the chapel to calm my thoughts. I said to myself, "When in Rome do as the Romans do," and off I went.

Any time I had been in the chapel previously had been to attend a service. Several of my crew had also worshipped there, though Whittle was not one of them. However, there was a different feel to being alone in that chapel compared with attending a service. It was a strange experience.

Certain parts of the furnishings were fixed. These included a circular altar in the middle of the octagonal floor space. The altar had a bowl cut into the marble of which the altar was made and a light burned there constantly. All the chairs had disappeared except for a few armchairs placed here and there beside large potted plants. On one wall of the octagon shaped chapel was carved a statue of Our Lady. There was a prayer desk in front of the statue. On the opposite side was a carving of Christ on the cross. Again, there was a prayer desk in front of the statue. The other walls of the octagon had stained glass windows which were in motion. I had never seen anything quite like them before. I suppose there was some kind of a video behind each window which threw the moving pictures onto the glass. The motion was very slow and restful. One of the windows in particular attracted me. I'm sure it was an illustration for the twenty third psalm because it showed a lake beside which sheep were grazing. A stream flowed gently down a hillside into the lake. A shepherd was sitting on a rock, a crook in his hand.

I sat in one of the armchairs and tried to gather my thoughts. I pondered on the problem of the four men who had gone. For Whittle to do something like this was unforgivable. I decided that his file would have to contain a report of his behaviour. Then I thought how silly such an idea was when we would probably never be able to go back to Transworld. I smiled wryly to myself. I had even got round to thinking of our own world as Transworld. Then it struck me for the first time that the two worlds might be in different universes. My mind couldn't cope with that thought and I allowed myself to think one by one of the three men who had gone missing with Whittle.

I suppose young Blenkinsop could be excused. Apart from his sexual adventures, which were generally thrust upon him, he was an ingenuous youth who knew little of the worldly guile and diabolical plotting that went on in most large commercial concerns. I could readily accept, even though he was an officer, that he had been drawn into what he thought was a kind of schoolboy prank. I felt confident that he would come to heel when the error of his ways was pointed out.

The two non-commissioned men who had gone missing were to some extent an unknown quantity in this sort of situation. They had always given satisfaction in their work and were often chosen to do tasks which contained an element of danger. Kirkbride, the red haired Irishman, had an unpredictable element in his character which in the past had only shown up in off duty activities. I was certainly worried about what he might do if he felt he had real power in his hands.

Stevenson, on the other hand, was a much stronger character and less mercurial in his ways. Yet, if he had an opportunity to achieve a goal he was very determined. He had been turned down twice by an officer's selection board and I was worried in case he felt he could become a real power in This World.

Whittle, of course, was the true villain of the piece. He knew what he was doing all right. The one consolation I could find in his behaviour was the thought that he was only carrying out an experiment to see what the reaction would be to a minor act of rebellion. The ultimate concern was what he would do if he found he was faced with indecision and weakness. I knew my man. I just had a gut feeling that he was going to go all out to make a mark on This World history. Yet, I felt I still had time to influence events if only he would come back to Mount Zion without too much fuss. I might be able to convince him that he could do great things, but in a positive and helpful way.

Gradually my stormy thoughts began to subside under the influence of the peace and quiet of the chapel. I looked up at the dome in the roof. It was called the Four Seasons Dome. This was because the three dimensional picture produced by moving rays of coloured light portrayed the different seasons in turn. At the moment it showed a blue sky fluffed with small white clouds. Across this skyscape flew a flock of wild geese. It was such a beautiful picture that an old poem I had learnt at school came into my mind, words to the effect that 'God's in his heaven and all's right with the world.'"

However, that feeling was soon lost when Father Christophoros came into the chapel and whispered in my ear, "Your colleagues are on television. Would you like to come and watch?"

We went along to the lounge where several monks and several of my crew were watching the three dimensional television. Apart from the three dimensional aspect it was very similar to the sort of television I was accustomed to in Transworld. I supposed that the commentators and photographers were enthusiasts for that kind of activity. What I saw first was a helicopter hovering above some wooded land. Then the view changed to show my four missing crew members on the ground waving the helicopter away. The commentator, who must have been in another helicopter was saying, "The aliens seem to be unwilling to take any notice of the Rangers at the moment. Their helicopter is now moving away slowly, though I'm sure the Rangers will not go too far away. Another shot of the helicopter was shown. I noticed that it had three propellers all mounted on the same stem. I guessed that this would give the machine tremendous power and uplift if required. I caught a glimpse of the woman pilot before it swung away.

The commentator then said, "Our helicopter is going to land in a moment. I hope to meet the Aliens and to interview them. This will be the first opportunity the world has had to see any of these people close up and I am sure it will be an interesting experience. Stay tuned and listen to some music while we go down. I'll be back with you in a couple of minutes."

I groaned at the thought of Whittle speaking on behalf of the whole of Transworld. However, there was little I could do about it. Several more people came into the lounge to watch. Most people were chatting about what might happen, but personally I didn't feel like talking. Christophoros seemed to sense my reluctance to speak and he too remained silent. Meanwhile some music was played. It was rather bland for my taste, but it was restful enough I suppose.

Soon the holding picture on the television changed and a view of a forest clearing was shown. A tall man dressed in a leather jacket appeared. It turned out he was the man we had heard speaking before. He said, "The Aliens have disappeared for the moment. I understand they have primitive weapons, so a measure of caution is needed. But I will try to approach them to see if I can obtain an interview. He walked through the trees, the camera team following. He had only walked twenty five yards or so when Whittle appeared from behind a tree. He had his gun in one hand and he held up the other hand like a traffic policeman. Then the sound came through. Whittle said, "Will you kindly stop there, please. Now what is it you want? We are on a hunting expedition and you are disturbing the animals."

"Sir," said the commentator, "I just wanted to interview you. Many people throughout the world are curious about you and your friends."

"Are we live on television now?" said Whittle suspiciously.

"Yes, sir. We are indeed. May I ask you a few questions please."

Whittle immediately became full of bonhomie. He smiled broadly and said, "Of course. I shall be happy to speak to the people of This World. I have been so much looking forward to this moment, but as you may know we have been in quarantine and haven't been able to get out and about since we arrived. You're quite safe though. The doctors have given us a clean bill of health. May I introduce myself. My name is Andrew Whittle and I used to be the second in command of the space ship Leviathan. However, as we seem to be stuck in This World for the foreseeable future such titles are meaningless. I believe I am the natural leader in our party and I am anxious to promote good relationships between ourselves and the people of This World."

Whittle's sheer impudence amazed me. The man had talents I had never dreamed he had. For a start he was an accomplished actor. He was also a consummate liar, though I had guessed he might have talent in that direction. I looked at Christophoros and he looked at me. He smiled and said, "Don't worry, Captain, I shall see that you and the Professor are also interviewed on world television. Your second in command obviously has big ideas and lots of ambition. I'm sure we shall be able to channel his energies creatively once he has adjusted."

We turned back to look at the screen. The commentator was saying, "Tell me, Mr Whittle, what do you think are the chief differences between your Transworld and This World? Have you been able to adjust to the differences?"

Whittle said, "In many ways your civilisation is more advanced than ours. However, I think our world can possibly teach your world one or two useful things. As to adjustment, I suppose it will take time. Fortunately my language is the same as yours. And it is a tremendous advantage that This World happened to choose English as the main world language. This means I can communicate with anybody in This World quite readily."

"Haven't you disobeyed our rules, Mr Whittle? When are you going back to Mount Zion?"

"I suppose we have been a little naughty. We just wanted to try our hand at hunting."

"But that's what I mean," said the interviewer. "Hunting is forbidden in This World."

"I didn't know that," said Whittle. "But I think it is a pity. Human beings are natural hunters, just as they are natural fighters and survivors. But we plan to return to Mount Zion tomorrow. I suppose we'll get our fingers rapped for being naughty boys."

"May I ask you and each of your men what you wish to do while you're here, bearing mind that you may not be able to return to Transworld?"

"Certainly," said Whittle. "My own ambitions lie in politics but first I'd like to train to be a Ranger. I like adventure, you see. But let me introduce my men."

I could have strangled Whittle for the blasé way he talked about "his men". However, I was quite interested to hear what the other three would have to say for themselves."

Blenkinsop was very photogenic and I could imagine that the women in This World would find him just as attractive as the women in Transworld had done. When asked what he planned to do he said with a charming smile, "Perhaps I shall stay with Andrew and learn to be a Ranger. But after that I'd like to train in martial arts."

The interviewer made no comment, but Father Christophoros raised his eyebrows considerably. I learned later that even wrestling and boxing were frowned upon in This World.

Kirkbride's reply was cheerful and carefree. He said, "Well, to be sure, I want to visit Ireland first to see what the I.R.A. are up to."

It was obvious to me that he intended his remark to raise a laugh, but I was very worried in case he sparked off some kind of dispute in Ireland. However, the commentator said, "You do realise, Mr Kirkbride, that the I.R.A. stopped functioning as an organisation when the covenant of world unity was signed over a hundred years ago?"

I was fairly sure Kirkbride hadn't known that, but he gave no sign of his ignorance. He simply said, "Just my little joke, sorr."

He always emphasised his Irish accent when he was excited. He continued, "I'd really like to continue the work of the I.R.A. and start it up again - with appropriate aims, of course."

The commentator wisely left it at that. Stevenson's answer was non-committal. He simply said, "I'd like to settle in first before I make up my mind."

The commentator than said, "There you have it, folks. Four people from beyond This World. I'm sure we'll be hearing more about them. Of course, we wish them well and hope they will soon adjust to our ways. But it seems that there is no major problem here. The Rangers have accepted that the four men are just having a little fling. Nobody is in any danger and tomorrow everything will be back to normal at Mount Zion. And now back to the studio."

I immediately apologised yet again to Father Christophoros for the behaviour of my men. His response was characteristic. He said benignly, "As Confucius said, 'We cannot ultimately be responsible for another person, not even our first born child.'"

"I shall certainly speak to them strongly on their return," I said.

And so I did. I asked them to come to an office Christophoros had made available for me. To be fair to three of them, they did look a bit shame faced. Whittle, however, was unrepentant. He said, "You don't seem to realise Bill, that we are no longer company employees. Your responsibility for us ended when we landed in This World. We are in the same position as if we were off duty in Transworld. In other words we can do as we like."

"Wrong!" I shouted angrily. "We are guests in somebody else's world and what each of us does reflects upon the others. You've all behaved disgracefully."

"Are you speaking as the Captain of the Leviathan?" said Whittle impudently. "If you are, then you haven't accepted that your command has lapsed. The space ship is going into a museum, remember."

"Very well then," I said, "I'm speaking as a fellow guest who deserves a bit of consideration."

I wasn't going to stand on my dignity as the senior officer. I had to accept Whittle's point. Anyway, even as an officer, I have always taken the view that I would rather be judged on my ability than on any rank I might hold. So I decided there and then that I would defeat Whittle at his own game and get my companions to accept my leadership on merit, not on my position. However, I decided not to admit that my captaincy was completely defunct, so I continued with some asperity, "But just remember that if and when we return to Transworld I shall have to give an account of what we have been doing. And that you may find yourself under my direct command again."

Blenkinsop said nervously, "Do you really think there's any chance of us going back, sir?"

Whittle butted in before I could respond by saying, "Don't call him bloody sir, Joe. He's just the same as us now. And the answer to your question is that we haven't a cat in hell's chance of getting back and he knows it."

"I don't know anything of the kind," I said more calmly. "In fact, I'm going to make it my business to explore all the possibilities. It's my duty as Captain."

Whittle grinned and said, "Just wait till he gets Fiona into bed. He'll forget all about any idea of returning."

"You disgust me, Whittle," I said. "And I hope you're not going to disgrace us all with your womanising ways."

....

It was shortly after the escapade of Whittle and his comrades that the two emissaries came to see us. Both were men and they had come well briefed. Their main function was to organise an education programme for us. It had been brought forward because the quarantine period had been shortened, mainly as a result of Whittle's action. I must say it was a well organised and interesting programme and even the so called bits of spiritual development were presented in such a way that the men felt they were learning something of value. The programme was tailored to suit individual needs. Professor Cherrington, for example, hared away enthusiastically and was miles ahead of the rest of us.

The particular programme which interested me most was the historical one. It was as if the history of This World was a replay of our history but with different characters. Take Henry VIII, for example. I suppose you could say that he is one of the best known figures in British history. The odd thing is that there was a king of the same name about the time of the Reformation in This World, but he bore no physical resemblance to the Henry VIII I knew of. Instead of being stout and fat faced he was thin. However, he had a lascivious sort of grin in his portraits and he had been through seven wives, not six. He had been a right trouble maker by all accounts.

I came to the conclusion that many historical trends and a similar line of development were common to each of the two worlds. However, even taking into account the fact that I had moved on almost fifty years, it was clear that This World's development had accelerated rapidly in the past hundred years. I assumed that the history of Transworld would catch up, though I didn't expect to get back to see it. The thought did occur to me that if we did get back to our own world, our account of This World might possibly influence the history of Transworld.

On the other hand, it also occurred to me that we visitors to This World could influence their history. I wasn't quite sure what I had in mind in thinking this, but I certainly didn't expect the evils that came with us to change This World's history in the spectacular way that they did. It would be easy enough to blame Whittle, I suppose, but really the sort of conditioning we had all had in Transworld in terms of ambition and material success was what caused the catastrophe. Of course, it took time for these events to develop and in the meantime we were trying to acclimatise to what the Professor described as a living utopia.

I listened to a mind boggling conversation between the Professor and Father Christophoros around this time. It really concerned some of the religious and moral problems thrown up by the existence of two similar worlds. We happened to be having coffee together after discussing the progress of the education programme. The Professor remarked cheerfully, "I somehow have a feeling of déjà vu when I am reading about some of the personalities of your planet's past, Christophoros. Do you think some kind of reincarnation is involved?"

"You mean in the case of Jesus of Nazareth? I thought we'd already come to terms with that idea."

"No, that isn't what I meant. Take Darwin, for example who was a scientist in the 19th century Transworld. His theory of evolution is not quite the same as that produced by the Charles Darwin of This World, though of course similar enough for both theories to have the same principles behind them. What I meant was could our Charles Darwin be the same as yours mentally, though not physically. Or to put it in another way, could the soul of one Charles Darwin have migrated into the body of the other one, though in a new dimension. It's rather more complicated than the idea of reincarnation in the same world."

"I see what you mean," said Christophoros. "The process could, of course, go on in an infinite number of worlds. That might mean that Darwin just goes on repeating himself for ever. I feel that would not only be a trifle boring for the poor man, but also it would not be in keeping with our Maker's plans for the development of a soul."

The Professor said, "But he could repeat his life several times in different dimensions until he had learnt the lessons he was supposed to learn, just as if he went from one school to another until he was ready for heaven."

"That is a possibility," said Christophoros, "but suppose the different worlds produce Darwin simultaneously. What I mean is, he could be alive in both your world and in our world at the same time."

"That has its problems," said the Professor. "Unless of course one world is reality and the other world is a dream. So while he's asleep in Transworld he's busy in This World and vice versa."

Christophoros laughed heartily. "I'm wondering what I'm doing in Transworld at the moment? Perhaps I'm a parish priest. Odd things, though, dreams, and sleep is a kind of parable about heaven, I suppose."

Just at that moment the dinner gong echoed through the monastery. I said humorously, "I don't know what I'm doing in Transworld, but my empty stomach tells me what I'm going to do in this one. I'm famished. It's all this studying we're having to do, Christophoros."

Chapter Four

It was a shock when I learned that Fiona was engaged to be married. Foolishly I had looked for a ring on the third finger of the left hand and, not perceiving one, assumed she was free. I was walking round the gardens of the monastery with her one evening around dusk. There was a very heady scent from a range of flowers, some of which were similar to roses. The two moons were full and just showing white. I suppose I am a romantic at heart and my only excuse for my premature approach is that Fiona is very beautiful and I really had fallen in love with her. Like many people in the same position I assumed from all kinds of supposed signs that she felt the same way.

I took hold of Fiona's hand and she gave my hand a squeeze. I said, "This is one of those evenings sent straight from heaven."

"It's beautiful, isn't it," she said. "I really wonder how some people reject any belief in God when I contemplate such beauty."

"You aren't going to be a nun or anything, are you?" I said, alarmed at this statement in that environment.

She laughed gently. "No, my dear Captain, I am not. I hope to marry and have children. In fact...".

It was at that point I made my biggest mistake in interrupting her. She told me later that she had just been going to tell me about her marriage plans. I said, "So do I, my dear."

I turned to face her and took both her hands in mine. Again, I misinterpreted her efforts to communicate. Her face showed surprise, but not hostility. I took this to mean she wanted me to kiss her and I did so, or at least I attempted to do so. She pulled away quickly as soon as I planted my lips on hers. She said, "Please, Bill, don't."

"I'm sorry," I said. "It seemed the right thing to do."

I still didn't get the message. I thought perhaps I had committed some solecism by kissing her at the wrong time or in the wrong way. I stretched out my hands again to take hers, but she pulled away. This time there was no mistaking the expression on her face. She was quite angry. I must say, though, that this made her even more desirable. Fortunately I had the sense not to try to touch her again.

I was stuck for words. Then suddenly she burst out laughing. "You ought to see your face," she said. "You look as if you are completely devastated. It can't be as bad as that. You can kiss me if you like - but just remember that I'm spoken for."

I obediently gave her a chaste sort of kiss. She then said, "Perhaps it's my fault but I thought you would have seen my engagement bracelet."

She held up her left hand on which was a slim golden bangle.

"I'm not psychic," I said huffily. "Where I come from women wear a ring on the third finger of the left hand to show they're engaged."

"I'm sorry, Bill. But come, we have had a little misunderstanding, that's all. I do find you very attractive, by the way - and if I wasn't engaged...".

"I understand," I said, recovering my composure. "How long have you been engaged?"

"Ten years."

I must have raised my eye brows at that. She said, "You seem surprised."

"A little," I said. "Aren't you leaving it a little late to have children?"

"We can have children at any age. We have a sperm and egg bank. Every man and woman at the age of eighteen stores sperms or eggs as the case may be. This means we can have children even after the normal age. But I still have plenty of time anyway."

"I can see the concepts of age and development are different from those in my world," I said. "But I would have been prepared to marry you in any circumstances. If ever you change your mind...".

"You will be the first to know, Bill. You must meet Nicholas, by the way. He's much older than I, but that doesn't really matter. We were matched by the Cupid Machine, so it must work out."

"What on earth is a Cupid Machine? But let me guess. It's a computer which tries to match people's interests and hobbies. I've never believed in them myself. I think it's much better for nature to take its course. True love, I mean."

"We used to follow such customs in This World. But there were so many divorces that we moved onto the Cupid Machine. It matches all kinds of things, including interests. It analyses the genetical structure, the metabolism, family background, intelligence and lots of other things. It contains the statistics of people from all over the world. You would think the machine would identify about a hundred possible partners for everyone, but amazingly it usually comes up with one person of the appropriate sex. Not surprisingly, when the couple meet there is instant rapport. Take Nicholas and myself, for example. We are so together we are virtually telepathic."

"That must be slightly boring," I said, with just a slight edge to my voice. "Wouldn't a blazing row clear the air now and again."

She laughed merrily. "We have ways of dealing with such things before rows, as you call them, develop. There is another machine called the Tranquilliser. I have one in my pocket, as a matter of fact. Look."

She took out of her pocket an object which looked like a very tiny radio. She clipped it onto her collar and plugged a wire from the machine into her ear. "It isn't switched on," she said. "Would you like to try it? After what has just happened you could do with some treatment. It is slightly unhygienic but I'll clean the ear plug for you."

I fastened the machine to my collar and plugged in. I could hear a sound like the sea and the wind combined. It was certainly very soothing. After a minute I took it out and said, "I'm quite impressed. What's the sound supposed to be?"

She smiled. "It's what a baby elephant hears in the womb. A woman called Marie Curie discovered how soothing the sound is. If two people plug into the same machine when a quarrel is brewing, then the symptoms disappear and all is well."

"I still think nature means us to have a good row now and again," I said obstinately. "These machines take all the fun out of life."

....

Shortly after this disastrous episode with Fiona I managed, with great good fortune, to overhear some of my crew concocting a diabolical plot.

The garden at Mount Zion was very extensive. I was getting a breath of fresh air one afternoon after a particularly heavy session on the educational programme. It was one of those somnolent afternoons when only the bees are busy among the flowers. I could hear voices at some distance from behind a low wall. I was sure I recognised Whittle's voice.

I followed the walk I had planned which, in fact, took me closer to the chatting group. From the top of some steps I could see that six people were flaked out on the grass. As I had thought, Whittle was in the group and it was he who was doing most of the talking. I heard an occasional phrase when his voice rose slightly in his excitement. I heard the words, "We could easily take over the whole bloody world." I decided then it was right to eavesdrop. I manoeuvred myself into a position where I could hear what was said more clearly without being seen.

I heard Stevenson say sceptically, "I'm not so sure, Andy. These guys probably have the technology to stop us. Perhaps they have some sophisticated weapons hidden for emergencies."

"I tell you they haven't," said Whittle. "I particularly asked a lot of questions about this the other day in the seminar. They don't believe in violence and every single weapon on the planet has been destroyed or is in a museum. It's against the law to carry a knife, even. It's amazing. And they don't have prisons because you can do what you like."

"I don't believe that," said Kirkbride. "I'll bet they have some sort of establishment where they kill off all the naughty boys. That's why there aren't any around. The poor sods are all bloody dead."

"No," said Whittle, "not at all. They have hypnotic sessions when they're young and all aggressive tendencies are removed painlessly. That's why it will be a piece of cake."

"What would we get out of it?" said a voice I didn't at first recognise.

"You get power and wealth beyond all your imagination," said Whittle.

"But we've already discovered they don't have any money," said the same voice. Then it came to me. It was Ernest Clamp, the assistant engineer. When I heard what the plot was about I could see that he would be a very useful man for Whittle to have around.

Whittle said persuasively, "But that's only because everything is free. Suppose we gained control of all the supplies at the outlets. Or even better at the manufacturing points. Then we could regulate the food supplies and every single thing that people use. We could then print some money and make the blighters work for everything they wanted."

"I like it," said Clamp. "Yes, I definitely like it. We could control the whole planet. And we could train them to work for us."

"And we could train an army to fight for us," said Kirkbride. "I want to be in charge of the army, Andy."

"It's yours," said Whittle. "But you haven't heard the good bit yet. I'm working on a book that will change the political system. It's called The New Society. We'll print millions of copies and make it compulsory reading."

"What's it about, Andy?" said Blenkinsop.

"Quite simply, it's about making a master race to rule the world. Only white people will be eligible. All other races will be slaves. It has a simple beauty about it. It's like a concerto. I feel exalted when I think about it. And you men will be co-architects of the new world with me."

It was then I remembered that Whittle had been brought up in South Africa. What he was proposing was a cross between the outdated apartheid system and Hitler's theory of a super race. I knew then that my overriding responsibility must be to stop Whittle at all costs. Cautiously I moved away and returned to the house by a circuitous route.

....

I thought carefully before I talked to Father Christophoros about Whittle's Machiavellian scheme. The trouble was, after I had slept on the idea of the proposed plot, it began to seem very unrealistic and impractical. How could a handful of men take over a whole civilisation? I concluded that Whittle's chances of success could be rated at about half of one percent. But that tiny chance of his succeeding in his coup gnawed away at my conscience and I eventually felt I had to share it with the Prior. If he agreed that Whittle's scheme was completely ridiculous, then at least I could say I had done my duty.

I caught Father Chris (as we all began to call him) in his study one evening after dinner. As always he was extremely courteous, but his face became very grave as I unfolded the diabolical plot of my comrades. A knot formed on his forehead and his finely cut features looked as if they had been chiselled out of stone. When I had finished he said, "Give me a moment or two to think, Bill."

He put his head into his hands as if he were concentrating deeply. After a minute or so he straightened and looked at me. I was astonished. His face had become completely relaxed and there wasn't a line anywhere on his face. I learned afterwards that he was using a technique of meditation originally invented by Buddhists. I looked at him questioningly. He said quietly, "The most worrying thing about this matter is that somebody should conceive such thoughts. Even if no further steps were taken by Mr Whittle and his companions, their thought vibrations could contaminate others."

"Like a sort of telepathy, you mean?" I said.

"The human mind is a strange machine, Bill. All our minds are linked together by the spiritual power which binds the universe into one. It is for this reason that prayers by a large group of people can affect the thinking of a whole society. Unfortunately, the reverse is true. Ill thinking is also powerful, especially when motivated by strong emotions."

"So how do we deal with it?" I said.

"I think bad thoughts are defeated by good thoughts," he said calmly. "I shall start a prayer circle among my brothers and sisters."

He must have caught some hint of my thoughts from the expression on my face. He said, "I shall, of course, take some action at the same time. I have a friend in the Supreme Council. He is on the Supplies Committee. He will be able to tell me if it is possible to take over the manufacturing plants or outlets as Whittle is planning to do. In fact, I'll 'phone him now."

It so happened that his friend was at home. The face of a man with a van Dyke kind of beard came onto the telephone screen. He smiled broadly when Father Chris said,

"Hello, Carlos, this is a voice from the future. You will have a good week, I'm told."

"Still cracking your metaphysical jokes, Christophoros, I see," said Carlos.

"I have a problem, Carlos."

"I assume you think I'm wise enough to advise even you," said Carlos. "What's it about?"

"The security of the world," said Father Chris. "Let me explain."

After first saying that I was listening in, he explained the nature of the problem to his friend.

When he had finished Carlos said, "I have several reasons for thinking that it would be impossible for anyone to take over the production system, Christophoros, but I will institute a security check. However, I can assure you that anyone trying to take control would have to break through several security barriers first. Some years ago we had some larking teenagers trying to penetrate the system. They wanted to change the computing process so that they could produce some drugs."

"I remember the incident," said Father Chris.

"The thing is," continued Carlos, "that was when we made it almost impossible for anyone to change the manufacturing process to make dangerous things like drugs or weapons."

It was then I realised that This World was not quite the Utopia that Professor Cherrington thought it was. That frightened me a little, because if Whittle could bring out the potentially bad elements in society and enlist their aid, then chaos could be the result. However, I was reassured to some extent at what I had heard. It would not be easy for Whittle to carry out the particular scheme he had in mind.

Father Chris and Carlos exchanged a few pleasantries and then rang off. The Prior smiled at me and said, "Does that make you feel better, Bill. But do not concern yourself, my chain of prayer will still go ahead and we shall combat any bad thoughts that are around."

I was a little sceptical about this idea. It might work for the inhabitants of This World, but somehow I thought that Whittle's bad thoughts would not be susceptible to change by telepathic prayer.

....

It was shortly after that when Professor Cherrington and I were invited by the city fathers of Derby to attend a civic dinner of welcome. I have never been keen on official functions of that sort, but the Professor, as usual, was full of enthusiasm. We were both worried about what to wear, though. Eventually the Professor found an easy way out. He borrowed a cassock from Father Chris, being assured that clergymen always wore cassocks at civic dinners. I asked Father Christophoros what I should wear and he said that my uniform would be appropriate. We discovered later that we could easily have obtained formal dress by feeding our measurements into a computer. The women at the dinner wore gowns at ankle length, as I would have expected. The men, however, wore silk knickerbockers and buckled shoes. I must say I should have a felt a right clot dressed like that, especially if any of my men had seen me.

As we drove through the city of Derby in an open car I looked around curiously to see if the city was anything like its Transworld namesake. In fact, I concluded that the general street plan was similar. The market square was where I would have expected it to be. So was the cathedral, but instead of having a simple tower it had a lofty spire. The Professor remarked that this indicated that both worlds probably had a common starting point and shared the same general development, but that many variations had developed also. He said confidentially, "The main philosophical problem is the teleological one. In other words where is it all leading to?"

I said, "I think my main problem is more immediate. I don't particularly wish to make a speech."

His cherubic face lit up with amusement. "Don't worry, Bill. Once you're on your feet it will all fall into place."

Strangely enough he was right. Once we had eaten the sumptuous vegetarian meal and quaffed some very fine wine, I had a very rosy view of This World. The resplendently dressed mayor spoke first and bade us welcome to his city. Then it was my turn. I felt so light headed that I almost said, "Friends, Romans, countrymen," but common sense and the professional aura of my uniform prevailed and I started off in a very conventional way, thanking all and sundry for the welcome we had received. Then I made a few comments about how dazzled I was by their advanced civilisation. My speech didn't exactly raise the roof of the Assembly Room, but there was a good round of polite applause when I had finished.

What happened next was unscripted. Cameras appeared as if from nowhere. The mayor then announced that the guests would be allowed to ask the Professor and myself questions. Before I knew where I was I was on international television. However, the euphoric feeling induced by the wine continued and I managed to hold my own. I played the part of the common man very well, I thought, and acted as a foil to the Professor's learned responses.

While I was listening to the professor I gazed round at the glittering assembly. It was very impressive, but essentially it wasn't too different from any similar function in my own world. I was even ogled by one or two middle aged ladies. Uniforms always seem to attract the female eye. I didn't want to offend anybody so I surreptitiously ogled back.

Most of the questions were about what Transworld was like compared with This World. I think my most effective answer to a question was when I described my trips to the moon. Of course, I was on very familiar ground, but my description impressed them because their trips into space were usually for leisure. I also explained what the minerals were used for and I think they concluded that Transworld was a reasonably civilised sort of place.

I feel, however, that I ought to give credit where credit is due by recording several of Professor Cherrington's brilliant answers. He was asked about the Transworld education system. After describing the early stages of going through school he then embarked on one of his famous discourses about continuing education. "The world itself is a university," he said. "And education is for all and for life. We have a saying in Transworld that education should be for life, but I always say that life should be for education."

I could see that this statement had gone down very well. Then he continued, "But I'd like to take that a stage further, if I may. I believe firmly that education prepares us for eternal life. That is what it's all about, the ultimate purpose of God for pilgrim souls."

I knew by now that ninety percent of people in This World believed in God and a future life. It was not surprising, then, that there was thunderous applause at that point.

The Professor also made a comment on politics that went down very well. In response to a question on democracy in Transworld he said, "Of course, the British Parliament is the mother of all parliaments in Transworld, just as it is here. However, it has to be admitted that we have not yet attained worldwide democracy, as you have in This World. I can only say that if ever I should return to my natural dimension then my first care would be to try to start a world parliament just like yours."

Yet again there was rapturous applause, one person shouting, "Stop here and enter politics!"

On the question of war and peace he said, "I have been a life long member of an organisation which stands for world peace. Unfortunately we still have one or two lunatics who wish to start wars. There has been some progress in promoting a United Nations Peace Corps, but we have yet to find a solution as efficient as yours."

I suppose the Professor captivated his audience by a subtle use of the sincerest form of flattery, that is, imitation - at least in principle.

At the end of the evening I felt that the Professor had given a very good impression and I hoped that this would counteract the less favourable impression created by Whittle in his broadcast to This World.

....

Some months after our arrival I decided I should like to visit my native city of Carlisle. Strictly, I suppose, it wasn't my native city but it was the This World equivalent. I was quite curious to see how it would compare to my boyhood memories of Cumbria. Incidentally, the original name of Cumberland was still used in This World.

I was surprised when Fiona offered to go with me. There had been just a slight awkwardness between us since her rejection of my advances, more on my part than on hers, I must admit. She said, "You really need somebody who knows their way about."

I expressed my thanks and wondered whether a few days at close quarters would move her in my favour. I had made some discreet enquiries and had discovered that engagements in This World were sometimes broken, though marriages seldom broke down. I suppose it is really a credit to their system. I was still in love with her and it just wouldn't go away. I did say cautiously, "What will your fiancé think about your coming with me?"

She laughed and said gaily, "He goes out with other women all the time. We don't tie each other down, you know."

Fiona explained that we needn't do any packing because the hotel would provide all we needed. "But," she said, "I'll just take my favourite umbrella, knowing what the Lake District is like."

That remark was strangely comforting. It made me feel really at home.

One of the monastery vehicles took us to the underground station. It was a very plush and streamlined, electrically operated minibus. I knew by this time that I could travel to any country in the world by underground train. Within Britain it was possible to go to any sizable town by this method and in a very short time too.

Father Chris drove us to the station himself. He said he needed a little break from his routine and regretted that he couldn't go with us. I had invited the Professor but he had declined to leave his education programme.

There was a huge dome to mark the entrance to the underground. There was a spacious entrance hall where the system was completely automated. Fiona went up to a computer and tapped the keys a few times and within ten seconds she held two tokens in her hand. Each token was fitted with an electronic plate which could perform several functions, including opening doors and gates. I looked at my token curiously. On one side it had the words, "Derby to Carlisle reversible." On the other side it had a green circle and under the circle was the instruction, "Follow this sign."

Fiona explained that the station was fairly quiet that day because the weather in Derbyshire was good. In times of inclement weather people left everything and emigrated for a few days or weeks or months as it took their fancy.

There were a dozen different escalator ways to choose from. I noticed that a sign above one entrance said "The Americas" and above another "Australasia". We headed for the one marked "England only." After going down one floor we were in another spacious hall from which there were more descending escalators. We went onto one marked "North West". At the bottom of that flight we found another hall

54

where we found on offer a number of guiding symbols in different colours. We followed the green disc, of course, and after descending two more flights we came to a waiting room. On the wall was a large green disc with Carlisle written across it. A few other people were waiting. Some were watching a football match on television.

I looked around and saw a huge circular door at the top of a staircase. There didn't appear to be any rails that I could see. I concluded that we had to enter the train through the circular door. This proved to be correct. A green light above the door flashed. The door swung open. We all headed for this entrance. There was a short tunnel about thirty yards long and another circular door at the end. When the first door had closed behind us this second door opened silently. It led into a room where there were some comfortable armchairs. We all sat down. There was just the faintest sensation of movement and I assumed we were in transit.

Fiona had already explained that the trains ran through magnetised vacuum tunnels which kept the cylindrical carriages centralised so they didn't touch the walls at any point once the journey had begun. This made for very speedy travel and we were in Carlisle within twenty minutes. Fiona told me that intercontinental trains were quicker and that you could go to Rome in one hour and a quarter.

At our destination we went up a series of escalators until we came to a domed entrance hall similar to the one at Derby. I walked out eagerly to take my first view of Carlisle in This World. To my surprise the station exit was in front of the castle, which was fairly similar in structure to the one I remembered at my Carlisle. The cathedral was nearby, but it bore no resemblance at all to the one I remembered. I learned afterwards that a previous building had been knocked down two hundred years ago. It was at that time that the people of the city had erected a new structure in metal and a plastic material called colloid. The "new" cathedral was of a very satisfying shape, a square building with a dome at each corner.

I have to say that this visit was very disappointing on a number of counts. The greatest disappointment was that I could find no trace of any street resembling the one where I had been brought up. The second disappointment was that, apart from the general configuration of the land, I hardly recognised any place except for the castle. My third disappointment was that there was no Cumbrian dialect as such. Everybody had come to speak standard English with just the faintest of London accents.

On the other hand, there were some consolations. One joy was a trip to the Lake District. The only way to travel in that area was by electric bicycle. Other modes of transport, whether by land, sea or air were strictly prohibited. To explore the fells in this way was sheer delight, especially with Fiona.

Another interesting experience was to see some housing complexes. This World had developed the garden city idea to a fine art. About a hundred families lived in a complex. Each complex had a shared garden and a huge community centre. The houses in each complex had to be architecturally compatible. One I looked at was built of houses in the Tudor style. The interiors were very plush with every convenience that could be imagined. I learned that a complex could be destroyed and rebuilt on the same ground within a week. Consequently, when most of the residents wanted a change there was a great planning session which everybody enjoyed and the result was a completely new complex in a different style.

Perhaps the most enjoyable element of my visit was a walk along the banks of the River Eden with Fiona. I could easily have imagined then that I was in my own Transworld. The poignant part of that experience was that I had taken my first love along a similar walk. I knew without any doubt that I was hopelessly and permanently in love with Fiona. However,

I was careful to avoid any kind of physical contact. I did notice, though, that she was looking at me in a very odd way from time to time. I could have sworn she was in love with me when I looked at her, but she gave no sign of it.

Chapter Five

During my educational programme I discovered that a monarch called King William had been crowned king of the World Federation about fifteen years previously. Before that he had been King of the European Federation. His father had been the first king of the European Federation. These monarchs were descended from a royal line which had for several centuries ruled in a single European country. When the question of European unity had become politically possible it had been decided that a monarchy was needed as a symbol to mould the very varied peoples of Europe together. Within Europe each country had retained much of its former power and political structure, though a common language and a common currency had been created.

When the nations of the world had decided to make a covenant of unity the European pattern had been emulated. The European monarch had been invited to become the ruler of the World Federation. As in Europe, individual countries had retained much of their traditional power structure. To make communication easier English had been adopted as the universal language. However, for most people it was a second language because it was felt that each country should preserve its own distinctive culture, including its language.

King William lived in Rome for three months of each year, but he spent at least two months of the year in each of the other continents. He had no executive power, but because the royal family was highly respected by people of all races and creeds his influence was tremendous. I was very much looking forward to meeting him in due course.

Religious patterns, I discovered, were fairly similar in many respects to those in Transworld. However, there were some significant differences. One such difference was the unity of all Christian groups under a papal royal family which lived in Jerusalem. Despite this unity, I understood from the Professor that there were still great differences in practice. In addition, relationships between the major world faiths were supposed to be very friendly. I had been invited to go to Jerusalem after I had been to Rome. A meeting with the Pope was promised.

There were two buildings I was very curious to see. One was the World Federation Parliament Building. The other was the Temple of Religious Truth in Jerusalem. I had read descriptions and seen pictures of both buildings, but in my judgment nothing can replace first hand experience in assessing the value of things or people. From my reading I had discovered that both buildings were highly symbolic in their structure and they seemed to be different from anything I had ever seen before.

The Professor and I travelled together in the company of a guide. The remainder of the group had been divided into pairs and each pair was similarly assigned a guide. I had hoped that Fiona would go with us, but she claimed she was too involved in her work at the monastery. I was very sorry to leave behind the friendly atmosphere of Mount Zion and our farewell to Father Christophoros was quite painful because he had become a very good friend. The idea was that we should go on from Rome and Jerusalem to our respective pursuits. These had been decided with the help of counsellors. I was still set on being a teacher and I was due to attend Edinburgh University from the beginning of October.

The evening before we left I went for a walk with Fiona. On this occasion she deliberately avoided touching me in any way. She no longer held my hand in the natural way she had done when we first became acquainted. We talked about all kinds of things. Eventually we got round to the subject of when we might meet again. Fiona was very vague when I pressed for a specific date for seeing each other. She was equally vague about the date of her wedding. Was it my imagination, or did she seem less enthusiastic about her forthcoming marriage than she had been.

When it came to saying good night she looked very sad. For myself, I was quite devastated. The reason for this was quite simple. I had met the most wonderful woman I had ever known in the whole of my life and had fallen in love with her; but here I was shaking hands in farewell as if she were a business acquaintance. However, as she let go of my hand she gave me a quick kiss, not on the cheek, but fully on the lips. I had a brief sensation of roses and lilac and then she was gone. I made up my mind right then that I wasn't going to let her go without a fight. Nicholas might be as good looking as Apollo, but he was going to have to struggle to keep Fiona. I knew though, that I would have to use fair means. The old adage that all is fair in love and war would not wash with Fiona. However, if I felt sure could get away with a sneaky tactic I certainly wouldn't hesitate. After all, what was at stake was a life of supreme, conjugal happiness compared with a boring life on my own or with some other poor woman who would never be able to compete with my ideal of Fiona.

The Professor and I got on very well with our guide, I ought to say. Germanus was an American, though he said his family had originally come from Austria. He was six feet four in his socks. He had a good crop of blond, curly hair and his face was squarish, giving an impression of a strong character. He made a very striking figure and I was told later by someone else that he had won the decathlon in the Olympic Games. This did not surprise me, because Germanus excelled at all kinds of physical pursuits.

The day before our departure Germanus advised us not to clutter ourselves with luggage. "The monastery will send on your gear to Edinburgh for the autumn," he said. "And in Rome you will be able to get anything you want very easily."

I knew this was true from my visit to Carlisle. Underclothes, bathroom accessories, new shirts, shoes and sandals - whatever one's needs were - a trip to an outlet would provide them, even if the hotel did not. Disposing of them was equally easy at one of the many disposal points. It certainly made travel a lot simpler. We boarded the underground in Derby just as if we were off on a day's excursion. We were in Rome in very quick time, having left the monastery some time after breakfast and arriving in Rome in plenty of time for lunch.

I had found Rome in Transworld delightful. Rome in This World was equally delightful, though different in a good number of respects. For one thing the Romans in This World did not have a lot of respect for ancient buildings. They could recreate the original ones in their full glory at the drop of a hat - and often did, letting them stand for a few months and then replacing them with buildings from another period of history.

We called briefly at our hotel as soon as we arrived to make sure the arrangements were secure. Germanus said the Italians were a little sloppy about reservations because of the number of new people who arrived each day for a tour of some kind; and, of course, there was no commercial motive to concentrate the mind. We were offered a range of delicious dishes at the hotel before we embarked on a tour in an open electric car. Not surprisingly, pasta was a main ingredient in many Roman recipes.

The hotel was near what, I was told, used to be the Vatican City. The former city of the popes was now the centre for the secular royal family and their entire entourage. It had been thought appropriate for the Pope to live in Jerusalem. La Piazza S. Pietro was part of what was now the Royal City and our hotel was between there and the Castel Sant'Angelo. Germanus drove us along the Corso Vittoria Emmanuele II towards what I supposed would be the Piazza Venezia, but this square and the monument to the Italian king had been replaced by a huge mosque. Apparently the population of Rome was twenty five percent Muslim. I must admit that after that I completely lost my bearings. I know we crossed and re-crossed the River Tiber once or twice, but apart from that I didn't recognise any "familiar" landmarks.

However, Germanus pointed out to us a number of important places. What impressed me most was the number and variety of religious buildings. We saw several impressive mosques and Christian cathedrals, but we also saw a huge synagogue, a Sikh temple and perhaps the largest building of all, a Hindu temple. Buildings in metal and colloid were plentiful but so also were structures in more traditional materials. There was no overall plan, but certain quarters had been given a unity in their architecture. One very beautiful area was made up of buildings in classical Greek and Roman style. Germanus told me the area had only been completed two months previously. At one time that particular patch of ground had been the zoological gardens, but zoos as such had been replaced by more natural wild life parks, some of which were huge. I discovered later that many species of animal in the parks were extinct in the wild, and these included penguins and polar bears.

The Professor asked Germanus to show us round a church. We happened to be passing S. Lorenzo Fuori le Mure at the time, so we went in there. This recently built church, placed on the site of a very ancient building, had been planned by a woman architect called Angelina Mysteriosa. It was built entirely of glass, or at least various forms of glass, some of which were previously unknown to me. The walls looked opaque from the outside, but inside the church the effect of the light coming from all directions including the floor was very strange indeed. The floor itself was made of glass tiles in varicoloured patterns. The walls and roof were designed to show the theme of creation. Indeed, one could almost imagine one was in a forest glade because of the effect of the pictures on the glass walls. Different kinds of animals gathered round Saint Francis on one wall, while on another Adam and Eve were naked and unashamed. The roof was an amazing work of art because it showed the sky at night shading into the daytime sky. The great light and the lesser light from Genesis were there, of course, as well as the stars and a rainbow.

The altar was like a huge octagonal jewel in the centre of the church and there was an array of glass candle sticks on the upper surface. The "candles" were, in fact, electric lights. Round the altar were concentric circles of fragile looking glass chairs. Each chair was a work of art in itself. The back of each one showed a scene from the Bible, visible both from the front and from the back. The pulpit was suspended from the ceiling and it resembled a coruscating fountain of light, this being symbolic for the word of God as the light of the world. Apparently the preacher was hoisted aloft on a small platform which served as a lift. I looked at the platform and noticed that it was decorated with a picture of Christ ascending to heaven. The Professor thought the art work was a bit overpowering and that it might interfere with worship. However, Germanus claimed there was a completely different atmosphere when the place was filled with people. Unfortunately I was never able to return to that church to attend a service.

That was all we had time for during our first afternoon in Rome. The following morning we were due to have an audience with King William and other members of the royal family. All in our party were invited and we all got togged up in smart grey suits with high, stiff collars. Germanus was dressed the same way. In fact, so was everybody else at the audience. This was supposed to be democratic, but personally I didn't like my suit because it reminded me of the worst years of the Chinese Communist period in Transworld. Everybody looked like a conforming communist.

Before the royal party appeared we went into a large reception room decorated in a glittering baroque style. We were divided into small groups of two or three so that different members of the royal family could speak to each group in turn. I was astonished to see that King William was an ordinary looking, pot bellied little man of indeterminate age. I had become very cautious by this time of estimating people's ages in This World.

It so happened that the Professor, Andrew Whittle and I were in the same group. Prince Edward, the heir to the throne came to speak to us first. He asked us three questions and then moved on. I gathered later that he asked each group three questions and usually the same ones. First he wanted to know if we were settling in all right. Then he asked what our future plans were. Finally, he asked if we had families in Transworld. Of course, by the time we had all three answered his questions it was about time he moved on to another group.

The next royal to chat to us was Princess Anne, the wife of Prince Edward. I must say she was a charming girl. She had a less formal approach than her husband and just chatted away quite naturally. She made me feel warm inside - and I don't think it was just the sex thing. Having said that, I have to admit that she was attractive in every way, with her long black hair and shining dark eyes. Her most powerful attribute, though, was her inner tranquillity. It may sound fanciful, especially in the light of later knowledge, but that girl had a special aura of saintliness about her. When I next saw Father Christophoros he told me that she had lived for several years with a religious order, which perhaps explained the impression she made on me. She seemed to find the Professor's views on religion particularly interesting.

Eventually, King William himself came to our group, accompanied by the Queen. He was wearing the same kind of suit as the rest of us. However he was wearing a red sash so that everybody could tell at a glance who he was. The Queen was taller and very regal, but she left her husband to do all the talking. He asked me some very penetrating questions about space travel and addressed the Professor with respect. It seemed the King had had a university education and he believed strongly in encouraging academic pursuits, even more than artistic ones. Nevertheless, the king himself was an artist and produced some beautiful oil paintings. He seemed not to take to Whittle, but that was probably due to Andy's hostile attitude. He had a hang up about royalty. Indeed, I was surprised that he had agreed to come, but then it was probably a policy decision so that he could appraise the situation.

I asked the King if it would be possible for us to look round the World Parliament building. He said that it wasn't difficult because anyone could look round when parliament was not in session. He went on to make some very knowledgeable remarks about the political scene. I was interested to hear that political parties existed and that fierce debates often took place about such matters as free passage for all world citizens or the creation of new cities. As to the former, it was normal for a citizen to have free passage but this right could be forfeited if a person acted in an unbecoming way while travelling.

I was longing to ask the King further questions, but he moved on and the audience came to an end. I suppose I could consider myself lucky to have met four members of the royal family, considering I had never met any of the royals in my native country.

The following day Germanus took the Professor and me to look round the parliament building which was topped by the biggest dome I have ever seen. Round the building the flags of all the member nations were displayed. I asked which was the one for the U.K. Germanus pointed to a white flag with a crown in the centre and a symbol in each corner. I went to have a closer look and saw the the symbols were a rose, a thistle, a daffodil and a shamrock.

We stood for a while on of the extensive lawns to examine the outside of the parliament building. Below the dome the roof fell away in a series of huge steps and then finally sloped to the ground. The framework of the building appeared to be stone, but I was assured it was colloid. There were thousands of windows which appeared to be of different colours. Germanus told us that from the inside it was possible to follow the history of the world by going round all the windows, each of which depicted a scene from the past. It was difficult to take the whole of this building in at a glance. Perhaps the most striking feature after the dome was the long needle which thrust upwards from the top of the dome. It was made of a shiny metal and seemed to stretch up for hundreds of feet. I looked more closely and saw that there were very fine supports, rather like the struts of an umbrella, which came from a point halfway up the needle to the rim of the dome. Germanus said the needle acted as a radio and television transmitter from which waves were beamed to satellites. Anybody anywhere in the world could watch the world parliament at any time it was in session.

I said to Germanus, "I have seen a number of long metal projections like that one. Are they all transmitters?"

"That's a good question," he said. "Some of them in fact are transformers. There are satellites in space which store the heat of the sun. Each satellite is made of paravanes which turn automatically to face the sun. The heat is beamed down to earth and is transformed into electricity by similar needles to that one."

"So the needles must stand on power stations if they are transformers?" said the Professor.

"In a way, I suppose," said Germanus. "But it is all automated. Every building is connected with the system and much of the heat and light in buildings really comes from the sun."

"So that's why there aren't any chimneys," I said. "Don't you use coal and gas?"

"It all ran out ages ago," said Germanus. "We had to find another form of power. In fact, as well as the sun we use the tides. We have gigantic water wheels horizontally placed where tides are strong. These are connected to our underground manufacturing system and drive all the machinery. Only a few computer experts are needed to manage each area's production system."

"What about wind power?" I said.

"Yes, we use that too. We have a vast number of wind kites, as we call them. These are moored on mountains in lonely places where people rarely, if ever, venture. The winds have a high velocity at that altitude."

"How do they work?" I said.

"In the same way as a windmill or a wind pump, both now outdated, of course. But it's the same principle. Each kite is a metal structure which has a number of propellers. Not only do the propellers keep the kite flying, but they also generate electricity. This, of course, is fed into the system."

We then moved on into the building. Inside, the Professor and I were both impressed by the symbolism of the Round Table. In This World, just as in Transworld, King Arthur and the Knights of the Round Table were legendary. Some one, I believe a university professor in Chicago, had suggested that this symbolism would make a sound basis for a politically united world. Consequently, a huge round table inscribed with the names of all the covenanting nations had been placed in the centre of the great hall, right under the centre of the dome. The seats for the members were placed in concentric circles round the table. Each member was given a knighthood and even after he had stopped being a member of the parliament he was allowed to retain his title. The member for the United Kingdom, I noticed, was called Sir Walter Featherstonehaugh. Of course, each country still had its own parliament and, indeed, it was an essential part of the covenant that all member states should have a democratic senate or parliament.

While we were in the main hall the Professor said, "Surely nations disagree sometimes."

"Now and again," said Germanus, smiling broadly. "Of course they are just like families. But we have a procedure. A formal debate is set up in parliament with the opposing parties making the main speeches. When the debate is over a vote is taken and the decision is usually accepted."

"Suppose it isn't accepted?" I said, thinking sceptically of similar arrangements I had seen before.

"There are several other stages that the argument can go through. First there is the court of appeal. If one of the parties still feels aggrieved, then the matter goes to a court which is composed of fifty neutral people, each one from a different country. They are selected at random. The arguments are put forward again and a vote is taken by the fifty referees. That usually ends the matter, but if it doesn't, it can go to the Supreme Council for adjudication. If there is still no agreement it can go to the King's Council which consists of the twenty most senior national leaders. But no case has ever got that far within living memory."

The Professor said, "Two of the great scourges in Transworld are drought and famine. How have you managed to solve those?"

"Sea water is purified at huge plants all over the world and the water is piped to every region," said Germanus. In any case, we can control the weather if we wish to, but mostly we don't because we have a good weather system to start with. We only interfere in an emergency and only locally. The food supply is assured by our manufacturing processes and our mechanised farms. But just in case there is a food shortage we have vast food stores at both poles. These are reviewed regularly. All the work is done by volunteers, of course."

We next took a look at some of the picture windows and I must say I was very impressed. One that took my fancy in particular was an illustration of a twentieth century war. It showed the explosion of an atom bomb and the consequent destruction. It was like something out of Dante's Inferno. We were allowed to look round some of the committee rooms and the parliamentary museum. Each of the committee rooms was also based on the Round Table principle. Each such room was named after an illustrious personage, usually a former member. One room, for example, was named The Sir Adolf Müller Room. The museum contained only items of historical interest which had some connection with the world parliament. In one display a copy of the original covenant treaty was on show, together with a number of photographs of the ceremony. The trouble with museums, I find, is that there is never enough time to look round properly and vows to return later somehow never seem to be fulfilled.

All of our party visited the End All Wars Museum together, several days after our arrival in Rome. Germanus and one of his colleagues were in charge of the arrangements. Most of the exhibits were of modern weapons. I use the term "modern" loosely, because in fact they were all well out of date. What I mean is that they were all weapons that I had observed in use in my lifetime - and that is how most people would define the word "modern". Tanks and guns were very similar to their Transworld counterparts. I must say, though, that the techniques of display surpassed anything I had ever seen before. The Professor, however, insisted that he had seen displays equally as impressive in our own world.

Some of the displays were very realistic and quite extensive. For example, there was a scene showing a tank and infantry battle. The tanks weren't actually moving, though their gun turrets were revolving and their guns appeared to be firing blanks. Some quite convincing robots were dressed as soldiers who were shooting at each other from some dugouts.

The uniforms were a sort of camouflaged battle dress, I suppose, and the robots wore steel helmets rather like the ones I had seen in pictures from the first World War.

It took a lot of walking to get round the whole museum area of outside displays. There was also an indoor section which contained displays of smaller weapons and displays of different kinds of uniforms.

We were all fagged out after our tour of the museum and we went into a nearby piazza to rest our aching feet. That was one ailment they hadn't found a cure for in This World. I was near enough to Whittle's group of cronies to overhear some of the conversation.

I heard Whittle say, "What do you think, Ernie, do you think we could get those tanks and guns working?"

"I would have to look at them more closely," said Ernest Clamp, formerly our assistant engineer. "It's the working bits that count. But I would say from the realism of some of the displays that it shouldn't be difficult to get some of them working."

"I bet we could make some more, using them as a pattern," said Kirkbride. "Yesterday I was talking to a chap who was explaining the manufacturing processes to me. He's had a spell on the computer system. You can produce almost anything if you have the measurements and the right kind of material. It would be easy to start making armaments if we had a few experts on our side."

Just at that moment the Professor and Germanus rejoined me after a visit to what was euphemistically called a relief centre. In other words they had been to the loo. The Professor was talking excitedly about what different religions had in common. He went on and on so that I couldn't hear what the people in the other group were saying. I was, of course, concerned about what I had overheard, but after a while I decided that the men were only speculating. To be honest, I didn't wish to create a situation in which we would be regarded with suspicion. Later I much regretted my easy going attitude towards Whittle's dangerous ambitions.

After a while Germanus and his colleague gathered us all together. Whittle and his companions were chatting cheerfully and waved at some girls who happened to be passing. The girls obviously knew who we were. They smiled broadly and waved back. I must say they were very attractive. However, I was not interested. Instead I thought wistfully of Fiona.

Chapter Six

Before we left Rome we were able to look round several interesting places. For a start I had my first opportunity to inspect a manufacturing outlet, or what we would call at home a hypermarket. I had visited several of these before to pick up various items but I had never had the time to have a really close look.

The one I visited with Germanus was on the outskirts of the city and it covered approximately one square mile. It was all under cover. Crisscrossing the area there was a grid of roads on which small truck like vehicles were allowed. These belonged to the outlet. The range of goods obtainable ran from pins and needles to items of furniture. If anyone wanted anything bigger than a bed or a sofa he had to go to an adjacent place where larger items like boats, planes and electric motor vehicles were available.

We walked round slowly so that I could see what was going on. There was a food section, a clothes section, a furniture section and numerous other sections in which items were lined up in neat rows. At the end of each section was a lift. We stopped beside one of these and watched a load of wrapped items being automatically lifted onto a conveyor belt.

I couldn't see any operators around but Germanus explained that several enthusiasts were working behind the scenes making sure that all the systems were running smoothly.

I said, "Suppose I wanted something produced to a pattern of my own? How would I set about getting it?"

"For some items," said Germanus, "you would need to give a few days notice and enclose clear instructions with your application. Look, there's a postal chute for applications and there is a pile of application forms."

"Suppose I wanted a pair of socks with red and yellow stripes?" I said mischievously. "I didn't see any of that particular pattern on the stand."

Germanus grinned. "How many pairs do you want? The minimum is ten of any small item - otherwise it's not worth setting up the machinery."

I was a little outfaced because I didn't really want any socks to that pattern, never mind ten pairs. Germanus saw my embarrassment. "Look," he said, "let's do something that you really want. If it's something sensible we can leave the other items on the stand. What are you short of?"

"I could do with a pen."

"OK, let's order a silver stylus point pen with your initials on the top. We'll have to order ten pens, but we can instruct the computer to initial only one of them. We don't need to complete an order form for a small item like that."

He led me over to a desk where there was an order computer. He sat in front of it and tapped a few keys. His instructions appeared on the screen: "Ten silver stylus ball point pens. Black ink. Initial one pen WS." He then pressed enter. The screen showed: "Your order will appear on stand 132 in ten minutes."

We wandered around for a while and then when we thought it was time we went to stand 132 and arrived just in time to see the bundle of pens coming onto the conveyor with a number of other items. Germanus picked up the bundle and extracted the one with my initials on it. "There you are, Bill. Take that back to Transworld with you."

He placed the remaining pens on the stand and we wandered on. After a while I said, "Can we go downstairs? To the manufactory, I mean."

Germanus gave me an odd look before he said, "I don't think we really have time today."

To be honest I thought he was putting me off because he was suspicious of my intentions. Perhaps he had heard of

Whittle's half baked plans for manufacturing weapons. Then he disarmed me by saying, "But we could come back tomorrow. It would mean missing the school and the medical centre though."

I said, "Never mind. Perhaps I can see the manufacturing bit some other time."

The following day we went to see a school, as planned. It was, I suppose, a kind of community centre as well as a school. There was no given age for starting and no special age for leaving. Some parents preferred to educate their own children at home. It was a completely free choice and there were no checks to see what people did. However, the average intelligence of citizens in This World was very high, so most parents were very keen on the educational process.

There were almost as many staff at the school as students. Indeed, some of the staff also followed courses as students. This type of school was described as a Community College. If people wished to attend a university they had to attend a course in appropriate subjects at a Community College first. The head of the school called himself the Chief Learner which I thought was a bit twee till I met him. He was a huge man with bushy brown hair and a spade shaped beard. He had a booming voice and a laugh like thunder that echoed around him wherever he went. His name was Pete and that is what everybody called him, even the four year olds.

The campus was extensive and it included an airfield for those pupils who commuted from a distance. Pete took us first to the timetable room. It was an astonishing place, a bit like a railway station with revolving timetables. Pete explained that four people working on computers operated the timetable. When I saw the range of subjects I could see why it needed four people to organise things. Pete explained that every pupil's timetable was worked out from a physical and psychological profile. The pupil had a hand computer which told him where to be at any particular time. At the end of every half year the profile was brought up to date.

As we were strolling past a group of youngsters playing a game like rounders Pete said, "You know what the Romans said, don't you, 'A healthy mind in a healthy body.' Well I take that a stage further. Our aim is to have developing mind in a developing body."

"What about the spiritual side?" said the Professor curiously.

Pete laughed his thunderous laugh. "It's optional but I see that everybody opts. They all get a good grounding in morals and the principles of religion. Generally they follow their parents, of course, but at the age of eighteen a youngster can have the choice of changing his faith if he or she wishes to. They learn enough here to be able to make that choice. We have experts on most living faiths on the staff."

I said, "How does everybody come to be so intelligent? Has somebody been doing some genetic engineering?"

"That sort of thing is limited to righting nature's mistakes," said Pete. "For example, there used to be a hereditary condition called Charles's Syndrome, but that has been eliminated by discreet genetic engineering. So everybody has a good start. There are various tests for children, all optional, though most parents take advantage of them. These tests identify weaknesses and then the child can be given a seek-and-find course on the self learning computer. If you compared our system with a hundred years ago I think you would find that then there were many apparently unintelligent children. I think there are two reasons why that group no longer exists. One is the improved techniques of diagnosis and treatment. The other is the time factor. We all have leisure to do what we choose. Many people choose to be educators and we give the child who needs help a one to one relationship in the weak area. Mind you, some children have special gifts and these are encouraged. That's another of my educational planks. Find what you're good at and perfect it. And when you think you've perfected it think again."

I must say I liked Pete's approach. While we were chatting a twelve year old came up and obviously didn't wish to be rude, so she hovered instead of interrupting. However, Pete soon spotted her and called her over. He said, "This is Gretchen. She was supposed to report back to me today." He turned to the girl and said, "Did you find what you were supposed to find Gretchen?"

"I found there are more than twenty thousand ways to answer the question, Pete. Can you be more precise? I don't want to write a book, just an essay."

Pete roared with laughter. "Right! Right! Let's put it this way then. We'll restrict the area of research to the years 1840-1850. That should help."

When the girl had gone I said, "What was she supposed to find?"

Pete said, "A fairly simple thing really. She had to explore and explain the population trends in a particular century. Actually, I've conned her into answering the same question because if she concentrates on one decade the answer will be very similar. The only thing is the statistics will be more manageable, but she will still learn the method of research, which is what I wanted her to learn. It won't be as reliable, of course, but that is the next lesson."

Incidentally, I learned later that the population of This World was only a fifth of the population in Transworld. The number of people the planet could comfortably sustain had been worked out carefully. The population had been reduced a long time ago by limiting the number of children people could have. Now the number of people was kept stable by the willing cooperation of all concerned.

I was quite impressed I must say. I was even more impressed when I saw the range of teaching aids. I was allowed to play with a model of the solar system for a while and I was interested to find an extra planet on the very edge of the system. I wondered if it was in our world as well. If it was and if I ever went home I could make a name for myself by discovering it, I suppose. If it did exist in relation to Transworld our space probes must have missed it because it was fairly small.

I asked Pete before we left if he had behaviour problems with any of the pupils. He said simply, "No, of course not. Emotional problems are sorted out by the medical centre."

I did find that response rather strange. Germanus, however, explained that psychiatrists had developed their studies much further than I could ever have imagined. Many incipient problems were identified in the first year of life by a series of physical tests. Parents could also take advice on the emotional balance of the family so that any problems could be eliminated scientifically.

In fact we had an opportunity to visit a medical centre and I was able to verify what Germanus had told me.

....

At last the day came when we were due to travel to Jerusalem to see the Pope. I was quite excited about the idea of going to Jerusalem myself, but the Professor was jumping around like a two year old when we set off.

During the underground train journey the Professor asked Germanus a number of questions about the Papal royal family. He was obviously dying with curiosity. We had only been sat down for a minute when he said, "Tell me Germanus, when did you have your first married Pope?"

Germanus smiled as if he really wanted to frown. "My dear Professor," he said, "I became a Hindu last year so I'm not sure I am the best person to answer that question."

"You kept that dark," said the Professor. "If you'd shared that information with us I wouldn't have put my foot in it just now. Anyway, you told me you were brought up a Lutheran, so you must have an inkling when the first married Pope was, even if you were on the other side of the fence, as it were."

Germanus smiled with genuine amusement. "The present Pope is, or was, an American Lutheran. He married a Catholic lady before the churches were united. And after Saint Peter himself, he is the first married Pope."

The Professor didn't often look stunned but this information seemed to surprise him considerably. "I must have missed that in my reading," he said. "Am I right in thinking that the Pope has been ordained as a priest or minister in all the main churches so that he can be seen as impartial."

"Perfectly true," said Germanus. "Even a Hindu can see the wisdom of such a move. But of course, in Hinduism we embrace all faiths and creeds readily enough, so there is not a problem."

"And I understand the Holy Father is interested in Hinduism," said the Professor.

"He is sympathetic to all the major faiths," said Germanus. "You will see what I mean when we go to see the Temple of Religious Truth."

"You don't mind if I ask you a few more questions about Christianity?" said the Professor cautiously.

"Fire away. But just remember that I have renounced the Christian faith. What is it you would like to know?"

"Is it true that the Pope was elected because of his universal sympathies? And has the heir to the papal throne got the same qualities?"

"So long as you don't ask more than two questions at a time we shall be OK," said Germanus ironically. "The answer to both questions is yes, I suppose. But then nowadays nearly everybody is free of religious prejudice. Many people think Pope Hadrian is an opportunist, that he planned his moves politically before it all happened."

"Do you think that?" said the Professor.

"No, but I don't agree with those who say God planned it all. I think natural powers were at work. You see, I believe there is a natural force for unity in all human endeavours. The world is a huge beehive, if you like."

"But the Christian view of God is a of a very personal and loving God," said the Professor. "Your view sounds very mechanistic."

"It wasn't meant to be. I'm really quoting a famous Christian thinker who said that planetary unity and religious unity were inevitable. I happen to agree with him and I think Hinduism is the religion which will unite all the faiths eventually."

The Professor fell silent for a while as if he wanted to ponder on what he had learnt. So I said, "You'll be coming with us to see the Pope, won't you, Germanus?"

"Of course. It is my duty to do so. In any case, I admire the man. What I cannot accept is the prison of Christian dogma."

The Professor gurgled with amusement. "You sound just like one of my students, Germanus. You have missed the logic and beauty of the Christian system. It explains all of life's puzzles."

"I'm sure the student you have in mind would now say, 'Nonsense!'" said Germanus.

"Quite right," said the Professor. "That's exactly what he would say. But let's not get into an argument over religion."

"You're just frightened you lose," said Germanus sarcastically. "You can't prove a single one of your silly dogmas."

From that point on I had to listen for the rest of the journey to a boring argument about the Christian creeds.

However, the argument subsided as we arrived at Jerusalem without there being a clear winner, at least as far as I could tell.

....

I had never been to Jerusalem in Transworld so I found it impossible to compare the Jerusalem we were visiting with the other one. However, the Professor said there were a lot of general similarities. For example, both places had an old city and a new city. I think the old city had survived because it had never been out of use, but had been replaced stone by stone over the centuries. The suburbs were just like the modern parts of any other city.

Naturally it was the old city we were particularly interested in. I suppose to some extent this was due to the historical connections with three major religious faiths - or so the Professor informed me. What seemed to fascinate the Professor most was the so called temple area. Apparently several Jewish temples had stood there and more recently a huge mosque. However, the Temple of Religious Truth stood there now, together with the Pope's Palace and the offices of various other religious representatives. All the major religious faiths were permitted to use the Temple, providing certain criteria were met. There were two main criteria, in fact. One was to believe in a supreme being. The other was the association of ideals like truth and goodness with the faiths in question.

The Professor and I looked round the temple on the first day. Germanus handed us over to an official guide who was familiar with all the historical and architectural details of the building. Her name was Esther and she happened to be Jewish. Apparently Jew and Arab had coexisted happily for one hundred and fifty years and there were two countries covering the traditional Holy Land. One was called Israel and the other was called Palestine. At first I made the assumption that Israel was composed entirely of Jews and Palestine of Arabs, but later I discovered that Jews and Arabs lived happily together in either country.

I suppose the tour was really a dialogue between Esther and the Professor. Yet, I found the visit of interest because of the beauty of the buildings and also because of the remarkable unity of purpose of people belonging to so many diverse faiths. This unity was symbolised through the design of the temple. Esther, by the way, was dark and attractive. I could imagine her in a desert tent without any difficulty, though actually she was a graduate of an American university. I think the Professor developed a soft spot for her and I believe he saw quite a lot of her in the remaining time of our stay on the planet.

Esther explained when she first met us that it would be a good idea to go to the top of one of the towers first so that we could get an overall view of the buildings. The central building was a round hall, topped by a cone shaped roof. From this centre twelve roofed archways radiated at equal intervals to the first outer circle which consisted of twelve domed buildings. The circle was completed by raised passageways which joined the twelve domed buildings together. Each domed building on the circle was quite large and each was used by a particular group of religious faiths for special acts of worship. The central building, on the other hand, which contained the Eternal Flame of Truth, was used for meditation and was open to all faiths. The idea behind the design was to show that all true religious faiths lead to the same centre of truth, that is, to the Supreme Being, symbolised by the flame. The whole of the temple was enclosed by a high curtain wall on which stood tall towers, at intervals. These towers were inhabited by monks and nuns, or holy men and women, of the various faiths. The complex of buildings often echoed to the chanting of these dedicated people. I understand Father

Christophoros had spent a few years in residence in the Christian monastery tower.

When we went into the main temple I was surprised to find that there was neither furniture nor adornment. Esther explained that this simplicity was the only way to satisfy all the theologies of the religions involved. Muslims and Jews, she explained, would not accept statues or pictures.

At that point the Professor said, "I can understand that, my dear. The arrangement actually has a positive theological point. It expresses the idea of God in his transcendence and mystery. Ultimately, all human attempts to explain or describe God must fall short, so it is more appropriate to go for the spacious emptiness of this hall."

It was, indeed, very empty. In the centre was a plain bowl of granite in which a bluish flame flickered gently. Round the edge of the room were some cushions for those who wished to meditate. The windows contained plain glass. The only concession to overt piety was a large plaque on which were inscribed texts from the sacred writings of the contributing faiths.

We also looked round the domed Christian building which was part of the inner ring of buildings round the main hall. To reach this we walked through one of the covered archways. The contrast with the meditation hall was striking. The circular church was full of Christian images portrayed in a variety of media. The altar was in the middle of the room and was in the form of a ring with an open centre. Esther explained that the priest took some of the services while standing in the middle of the altar, as it were.

I asked jokingly if the priest vaulted over the altar during the service to reach the middle space. However, she walked across and pressed a button which opened a way through without interfering with the beautiful arrangements of flowers.

The windows in the church were all of genuine, mediaeval stained glass which had been donated by various European churches and cathedrals. By contrast, the chairs were carved in a modern design from mahogany. The murals had been painted by some of the most famous artists of the age in which the Temple had been built. Apparently this had been a hundred years previously. The paintings showed the scenes from the lives of Christian martyrs, starting with Stephen.

There were many sculptures placed round the circumference of the hall. These were from different periods of history. One was a pieta by Michelangelo.

I have to say that what impressed me most about this church was the atmosphere. We sat down for a few minutes and while I was letting my thoughts freewheel I felt a strange peacefulness taking over my whole being. It is the first time I have ever had that sort of religious experience. I can't say it was a conversion - but it was something that penetrated my very soul and never afterwards left me. When I later explained this to Fiona she gave a very mysterious smile and said I had been given a special grace.

The day after our tour we went for an audience with the Pope. We also met his wife, Queen Christiana. I learned that she was only ninety years old, but that the Pope himself was about a hundred and thirty. When we arrived we were shown into a simply furnished room where some chairs were placed in a semi- circle for us. On the walls were paintings of several previous popes. In front of us was a dais on which two chairs were placed ready for the Pope and his Queen. When they came in there was an absolute hush. Without anyone saying anything we all stood. When the royal pair were seated Germanus motioned us to sit down.

The Pope certainly didn't look as old as he was. He was a tallish, scholarly man with thin, greying hair. His face was fresh coloured and he walked with an easy grace. Queen

Christiana, however, though she was much younger, did look her age, that is in This World terms. Her kindly face was wrinkled and her hair was white.

The Pope welcomed us simply in English. Apparently he had been born in the U.S.A. but had lived in Europe during most of his adult life, until he was made Pope, that is. His official title was, in fact, Petros, while his wife was properly referred to as the Petra.

The Petros and Petra customarily wore white cassocks for public audiences. This was to indicate that they had both been ordained to the vocation by the churches. I had learnt from my reading that the main churches had taken part in consecrating the two of them as joint leaders of the all Christian Churches. Apparently the ceremony had taken a lot of sorting out because the idea was that either of them could minister in any of the churches. This meant, for example, that both were Methodist ministers and at the same time Catholic priests.

After the Pope's speech of welcome, conversation was supposed to take place. By common consent the Professor had been nominated our spokesman for the occasion. The only trouble with that arrangement was that the chat became almost entirely theological. Consequently I shall draw a veil over what was said except for two titbits of information which I picked up. One was that the Pope had done a degree in Theology in 1950, that is one hundred and ten years previously. I did find that rather mind boggling. The other piece of information was that Princess Anne who, was married to the heir to the secular throne, was the Pope's granddaughter.

....

When we returned to the hotel after the audience with the Pope, a fax was waiting for me. It contained both good news and bad news. The good news was that Fiona was arriving in Jerusalem the following day. The bad news was that she was bringing her fiancé with her. A wave of dislike for Nicholas surged through me. At all costs I was determined to hate the man. However, I was completely disarmed when I met him and he did become a good friend despite what happened between us.

The three of us had lunch together the day of their arrival. I found that Nicholas was fairly nondescript on first sight. He had mousy hair cut short, was of medium build and had the sort of face you could see in a crowd anywhere. It was when he smiled that his charm became more obvious. It became even more obvious when he told one of his huge repertoire of jokes.

After we had eaten we went onto the terrace overlooking the city to have some coffee. After a while, Nicholas made his excuses and left. He said he had a few old friends to look up. He kissed Fiona affectionately on the cheek. His air of ownership was very galling. I had no alternative but to smile and shake hands. I must admit that it was a relief when he left. I had felt very constrained in his presence and I seemed to have lost the intimacy of my friendship with Fiona.

After a few banalities I said, "You two seem to be getting along well. How are the plans for the wedding progressing?"

Fiona looked at me with her big blue eyes wide open. She said, "It's been postponed for a while, Bill."

"Do you really love him?"

"He makes me laugh and I'm happy when I'm with him."

"Fiona...".

"Don't say it, Bill. Let me say it instead. If I wasn't already engaged to Nicholas I feel I could have a serious relationship with you."

We looked at each other steadily for a while. I could read in her eyes that she was in love with me. I was just about to challenge her when she said, "I shall never let Nicholas down. I can't let my feelings for you alter what is already planned."

She put her hand on mine. I was afraid to speak in case I broke the spell. She said, "If God wills it for us to come together it will happen. That is all I can say."

My recent experience of some powerful presence in the church prevented me from arguing. Instead I said a silent prayer asking the Almighty. whoever he was, to make it possible for me to marry Fiona.

Chapter Seven

Since shortly after our arrival into This World a team of scientists had been working on the problem of how we managed to pass from one world to another, parallel world. They had also been trying to see whether the process could be reversed. A meeting with two of the scientists had been arranged for us in London to coincide with our return to Britain.

All of us were at the meeting. Personally I didn't have much hope of getting back to Transworld. However, I tried to bring an open mind to the meeting. Even by This World standards the two scientists were ancient and venerable. Both were over a hundred and twenty years old. Professor Standish was bald and stooped and had a quavering voice. Professor Burns was grey bearded and had wispy grey hair, but he was as straight as a ramrod.

Several representatives from the media had been invited and a number of distinguished guests were also present. These were mainly from the scientific world, but I noticed at least two well known politicians among the guests. The meeting was also recorded on video for posterity.

Professor Standish started by putting forward a theory. Part of what he said was as follows: "It seems to me to be probable that the weft and warp of time and space as we experience them are only one version of many possibilities. I suggest that there is a stack of such time-space patterns, each rather like a tapestry. Probably there is an infinite number of them so I can't say precisely how they are stacked in terms that you would understand but I could express it as an equation. But as nobody would be able to interpret it except my colleague there is no point in giving it to you. Those worlds that are adjacent or nearly adjacent to each other in the stack are quite similar, though not absolutely identical. The big question is, how did our visitors slip out of one time space warp into an adjacent one? My theory suggests that it was to do with the position of the planets and the sun in relation to each other. The relative speeds and gravities somehow matched each other exactly in both worlds at the same time. At such a time, to use layman's language, it would be possible to slip accidentally through a gap in the time-space pattern. This, however, could only happen if somebody was in the direct line of the conjunction of forces. It's a bit like air blowing through a pipe. The space ship just happened to be in the pipe at the time. I'm sorry if that is a bit confusing. It's the best I can do in layman's terms."

One of the guests who was obviously a scientist said, "Professor, if the x equivalent to y part of the equation could be recreated, could our visitors go back to their own world?"

"Theoretically yes, if they were in the right place at the right time. The only thing is they might go to another adjacent world and not back to their own. Another difficulty would be to know when the clocks in the two continua were synchronised. My own belief is that the two solar systems are matched several times a year because they are really only wobbling out of line. In other words, the two solar systems work together but with minor variations."

Professor Burns said, "Personally I think it depends on whether the stack of possible worlds is relative to other stars in the galaxy. The influence of other suns on the equation is infinitesimal, but it could make all the difference as to which way the space-time travellers would go. We know exactly where the planets were in relation to each other when they arrived, but not exactly where the sun was in relation to other stars. Not that we would need exactly the same pattern in the solar system. The equation works with a number of variables. This means that if a space ship was in the right place in relation to one set of pliable variables, then it would go through the pipe, as it were."

I decided to ask a more practical question: "Can you please tell us, either of you, what the chances are of our return to Transworld?"

The two learned men looked at each other. Professor Burns nodded to give Professor Standish right of way. The latter said, "Frankly, I think we would need at least two more years of study before we could answer that question properly. With our present knowledge, which is only theoretical, there is absolutely no possibility of a planned return, though you could return by chance. I have to say though, that it is a million to one against this happening without a deliberate time-space bearing being used. My advice to our visitors is to accept that they are now in This World and to leave it at that. As I understand it you will have a much longer and happier life here than you would have done in your own world. Perhaps you have been very fortunate to come here."

Our Professor Cherrington piped up: "Speaking metaphysically, is it possible that the stack of possibilities as you describe them is a way of making progress to heaven? What I mean is, when a person dies does he go to the adjacent world to learn some more, and then to the next one, and so on, perhaps ad infinitum."

The two scientific Professors looked at each other in some puzzlement. Then Professor Burns said, "That is an inappropriate question. We deal in facts. If a poet or a theologian wishes to interpret those facts in a certain way, I suppose he is entitled to do so."

By the end of the meeting I had resigned myself to a long life in This World with a good possibility of living until I reached an age well over a hundred. Whether it would prove to be a happy experience really depended on whether I could persuade Fiona to marry me.

....

Each of the people who had come from Transworld was given a further opportunity to decide on a life style and avocation. I had originally decided I wished to be a teacher. I was given to understand that it wasn't difficult to find a suitable slot. One's statistics were fed into a computer and matched with the needs of various schools and the most suitable placing came up on the computer. However, something happened which made me change my mind about what I wanted to do.

We were all staying in London while the counselling sessions took place. One afternoon I decided to look round Saint Peter's Cathedral in Westminster. Towards the end of the afternoon I climbed the tower so that I could look around London from a good vantage point. I had found the church quite impressive, but the architectural marvels of This World were becoming familiar, so I didn't go into raptures over the admitted beauties of the interior. However, my breath was rather taken away when I took in the view from the tower. This London that was stretched out before me was truly a marvel of planning. Some of the individual buildings were beautiful, but the harmony of the whole was wonderful to behold. Most of the buildings were apparently of pink stone. I say apparently because I had learned to mistrust first impressions in relation to architecture. The sun was at a low angle and the pinkish colours of the buildings seemed to glow. A sea of glass roofs glittered like huge diamonds as far as the eye could see. The River Thames became a deep, deep blue as the light began to fade and its sinuous curves merged with the distant, misty blue of the suburbs. I thought of Wordsworth's sonnet about Westminster Bridge. I wondered what the poet would have made of this scene.

As I stood there, way above the network of streets, the waylights, as they were called, were switched on and the city seemed as if it were on another plane. Then I remembered that I was on another plane and a tear came into my eye. I thought of times past and friends I would never see again. A great sadness overcame me. After a while this emotion passed and I was filled with a sense of mysterious tranquillity. I was gripped by a feeling of awe at the strangeness of my experience and I looked up at the sky where the first stars were appearing. I then felt a deep inner urge to know God. I said aloud, "If you are there, God, tell me what to do." Then the world became ordinary again and I was just a man standing looking into the twilight above an all too human city.

When I later pondered on this experience and put it together with the previous mystical experience I had had, I decided that I wished to find out more about religion and philosophy. I had hitherto believed myself to be a very practical man who, moreover, was immersed in his profession. Apart from what was then a conventional Sunday School childhood, I had never thought too seriously about God. It is true that my travels in space had given me a sense of the infinity of the universe, but that had been at a factual level. Infinity was simply a multiplication of miles. I now conceived that infinity might have a spiritual counterpart.

I shared my experiences with Professor Cherrington and he suggested that we both go together to Edinburgh to pursue our studies. He had already made arrangements to live in a College there so I quickly changed my plans and applied to the same College. Fortunately there was a spare place for me.

Whittle fulfilled his already stated plan to train as a Ranger or Warden. He took along with him Joseph Blenkinsop, our youngest officer; Kirkbride the hot tempered Irishman; and Stevenson the Cornishman. I was surprised that Ernest Clamp the assistant engineer hadn't gone with them. Instead he went with Bernard Rawlins, the Chief Engineer, on a course in technical science. I learned later that Whittle had deliberately planned for the two engineers to follow a course that would enable them to understand the workings of This World computers and machines.

The six remaining members of the crew went in different directions and as far as I knew at the time they were not colluding with Whittle. However, I found out by accident when I met one of this other group, that Whittle kept in regular touch with all of them.

When I arrived in Edinburgh I had an interview with the head of the Faculty of Theology and Philosophy. In fact, Professor Cherrington had a similar interview, but as our needs were very different there was no point in us having a joint interview. I found Professor Gandhi a fascinating character. He was a descendant of Mahatma Gandhi and like his forefather was a Hindu with a universal perspective. He looked about forty, but was in fact seventy five. He was handsome, with even features. His face was shaven and he had perfect teeth. (Tooth decay was not a problem in This World.) His hair was a distinguished grey. He was over six feet tall and made an impressive figure when he stood to welcome me. He was dressed in a white robe which stretched to his ankles.

"Welcome," he said. He managed to convey warmth and love without effort. It simply radiated around him. "Shall I call you Captain Stewart?"

I was a bit nonplussed at this simple question. If I suggested he call me Bill he might think me incredibly stupid. However, he said, "Call me Addie. It's short for Adyar."

So I said, "My name is Bill."

He smiled his quiet smile and said, "What brings a space voyager into philosophical enquiry, Bill?"

He waited patiently while I tried to gather my thoughts together. Finally I said, "I've had one or two strange experiences and I'm curious."

"So you don't belong to a particular faith?"

"I was brought up a Christian, but I try to have an open mind."

"Good. By the way, this is going to be very informal. Later you can matriculate. That means you go through a series of processes which enable us to assess your present position and your potential as a religious philosopher."

That felt very threatening. My feelings must have shown in my face because Addie said, "It isn't painful, Bill. Like all of us you have hidden depths and we just want to know where to start, that's all."

"What's worrying me is my inadequate background," I said. "I have no experience at all in this field."

"I think that's very unlikely," said Addie. "You have just told me you have had some strange experiences which make you want to explore meanings. Whatever happened must have made a great impression on you. But tell me, where do you think you want to begin?"

"From the beginning," I said rather lamely. Then, recovering slightly I added, "Perhaps I could survey the field of enquiry first to see what most interests me."

"A very sensible suggestion," he said. "And I know just the mentor for you."

I probably looked slightly blank at that point. He continued, "The mentor system allows you to have an experienced companion in your studies. She will show you the ropes. Of course, she will have all sorts of teaching aids to help you in your search."

I didn't comment on the word, "She." I had learned enough about This World life to know that parity of esteem between the sexes had long been practised. I said, "That sounds fine."

"Good," said Addie. "That's about it really. Why don't we sit in silence for a minute or so? Just let your thoughts free wheel around in space and time."

Actually I thought I'd wandered around in space and time a bit too much. However, I did as he suggested and found the experience less disappointing than I had anticipated.

Perhaps the reason for this was the incense candle he lit. The candle stood on a small table in front of a picture of a lake surrounded by mountains. A text was written above the picture. It read: "Find the reflection of the waters of eternal life within yourself."

As we sat in silence a beautiful perfume wafted across to me and my eyes were drawn almost into the picture. For a moment an image of Fiona came into my mind. Then she quietly faded and my mind seemed to empty itself. I felt very peaceful inside. It was the sort of inner peace which I wished I could find permanently. But it faded after a minute or so.

Addie said, "I don't want to know what you saw or felt just now, but theoretically you should know whether you are doing the right thing by coming here by the nature of the short experience you have just had."

"Did you hypnotise me?" I said.

He smiled. "Of course not. All I did was to provide a stimulus. Only you know whether it was an appropriate one."

"I think it was," I said.

....

My mentor turned out to be a Buddhist monk. She appeared to be sexless almost, when I first met her. Perhaps it was the shaven head and the saffron robe. Her face was very beautiful, but unearthly; a bit like the face of an angel. As I came to know her better her femininity did come through to me. In fact, I eventually found her to be extremely attractive sexually. Perhaps it was the old story of forbidden fruit because Jhana had taken a vow of celibacy and I knew she would never break it. She was sixty two years old but looked about twenty five. It was quite extraordinary.

When we first met it was over a cup of coffee. At least I had coffee and she had water. We had just been introduced and it was Jhana's suggestion that we go to the refectory. This large room was at the top of a mushroomlike building and from the windows there was a commanding 360 degree view. Looking north there was a spectacular view of the firth glistening blue under a rare cloudless sky.

At first we chatted about trivialities. Before long, however, she came to the main point of our meeting. She said, "I have looked at your computer scan, Captain Stewart, and I think we should make good progress. I think our starting point ought to be to make some visits to various religious houses and schools of philosophy and to have conversations with people of differing viewpoints. Books won't be so interesting at this stage."

That sounded a sensible idea to me. I said, "How long will that take us?"

"Time is free," she said cryptically.

I thought it was time I brought out a few aphorisms so I said, "But time also has its limits."

She gave the faintest of smiles and said, "When you have remembered all your previous incarnations you may wish to revise that judgment."

I said, "My previous life in Transworld was real enough and it now seems like an eternity away."

"You have just taken an unusual route," she said. "I can remember my last incarnation clearly also, but I was another person then. But come, I will show you the library where you can browse while I make arrangements for our visits."

The library was divided into numerous sections and divisions. Before we descended in the lift Jhana showed me the plan of the stack rooms. There were forty rooms at different levels and each room was devoted to an area of knowledge. When we got down to Theology I found that there were no bound books, only micro films, videos and Internet entry points. She explained to me how the various machines worked and then left me to it. I decided to start with something simple so I found a video called "Introduction to meditation" and watched that first. I found the technique that Addie had used with me was in the third lesson. I was disappointed because I thought he had simply filched the idea. However, at the end of the video his name was on the credits, so I supposed that he must have invented some of the ideas himself, and I felt ashamed of my premature judgment. I also noticed that Father Christophoros had contributed to the film.

After I had browsed for an hour or so I had had enough and went back to my College. That evening Professor Cherrington eagerly told me what he had been up to and I managed to rustle up a bit of enthusiasm myself to tell him all about techniques of meditation.

I was quite flattered when he said, "Do you know, Bill, I think you have a natural capacity for prayer and meditation. Why don't you become a monk."

I must say I found that idea very amusing, though as time went on I began to see the attractions of the contemplative life. However, while there was any chance of marrying Fiona I knew that celibacy was not an option.

....

After several months of study with my mentor I really began to feel that I had some reference points in my mind so that I could decide the direction of my future studies. One day, indeed, Jhana said to me, "Bill, I think it is time you studied in more depth. You now have a good general knowledge of religion and philosophy. But you will not make further progress without specialising. Of course, you will need another mentor, unless of course you choose Buddhism as your field, in which case I could stay with you."

We were sitting in the park just off Princes Street. On the mound above us stood the Parliament Building of Scotland. At one time there had been a castle there, but when nations were covenanting with each other Scotland had decided to go it alone and had replaced the castle with a parliament building. It was a pleasant enough day and warm enough to sit without discomfort. Some grey squirrels were playing around among the trees just beside where we were sitting.

In response to Jhana's question I said, "The trouble is I find it all so fascinating. If I had several lifetimes I could study many different systems one after the other."

"That's good," she said. "It shows you are an apt pupil. And possibly that you have a calling. But tell me, what do you conclude from your general studies? Can you see any particular pattern in human development, for example?"

"I can see the problem of the One and the Many Ways," I said. "It's not so much a pattern as a dispersal. Why are there so many different faiths if there is only one ultimate goal."

"Your Christian Bible contains the answer to that one, Bill. 'In my Father's house there are many rooms.' That's what Jesus said, I think. And then Hinduism, surely, is capable of binding many faiths together."

"What really troubles me," I said, "is the religions which claim to have had a special revelation. Sometimes they contradict each other. They can't all be entirely true. Now if Christianity is the only true faith as I was brought up to believe, where does that leave your Buddhism? I'm not making judgments about your faith, Jhana, but I think the whole area bristles with problems."

Jhana laughed. I hadn't heard her laugh very often and I felt slightly piqued at being the subject of her amusement. She said quickly, "I'm not laughing at you, Bill. I just remembered the Buddha's parable about the elephant and the six blind men."

"You mean the story about each one getting hold of a different part of the elephant and getting a different picture of what it might be like?"

"That's the one. What he meant, of course, was that all the different religious viewpoints lead ultimately to the one truth. Now I agree that the contradictions you mentioned aren't solved by the parable, but what we're talking about is partial truth. When the elephant is ultimately revealed all the contradictions will be explained."

I was a bit sceptical about that. However, I wanted to broach the subject of my future so, after a pause, I said, "Jhana, I think I want to train as a Christian minister."

She looked at me quizzically. Then she said quietly, "I'm not surprised, Bill, but isn't it amazing how you have gone back to your roots. I know enough about Christianity to know that in Scotland the word "minister" is used by some churches rather than the word "priest" - and you were brought up in Scotland."

"Hardly," I said. "I was brought up in Carlisle."

"Which has been in Scotland for three hundred years."

That rather shook me, but then I remembered that the border areas had often changed hands in past centuries. However, I said, "Not in Transworld. Anyhow, it's immaterial. And I was using the word 'minister' loosely."

"Fine, but what I meant is you are wanting to operate within the group of symbols you can understand."

That made me feel as if she thought I was a bit thick. I said huffily, "Is there something wrong with that?"

The illumination of her smile calmed my irritation as she said, "Of course not. I just hope you won't throw all you've learned out of the window. Try to keep the universal perspective."

"Don't worry," I said. "You have been too good a teacher for me to fall into that trap. But it does seem to me, after my exploration, that Christ had a lot of the answers. What I am a bit uncertain about is the dogma. What is the Trinity, for example?"

She paused for a moment and I thought I had stumped her. Then she said quietly, "I think that will sort itself out, Bill. Just remember that God may be even more complicated than the word Trinity implies."

"So what happens next?" I said.

"We feed your statistics back into the computer and find the right mentor. It shouldn't take too long. I believe you might be able to stay in Edinburgh, by the way. I should think you will have a few months of individual learning; then you will go to a school of Theology."

"Six months ago I would have found the idea inconceivable," I said.

She laughed lightly and said, "Who knows, Bill, you may become a great religious thinker!"

It was my turn to laugh. "Just leave out the great and leave out the thinker. I might just become religious, in a small way at any rate. But surely I need to find if I have a vocation."

Jhana looked at me very steadily. Then she said, "The whisper of the breeze in the lotus tree will come to you while you sleep."

If other events hadn't intervened she might have been proved right.

Chapter Eight

While I was immersed in my studies in Edinburgh, the birth of a royal prince took place in Rome in the year 2061, This World time. This was the year of Halley's Comet and the media made a great deal of the coincidence of the birth with this heavenly phenomenon. I was growing in knowledge of the Holy Scriptures and I knew that the prophecies of the Second Coming of Christ were more frequent and more precise in the Third Testament I was now studying than I remembered in the Transworld Bible. The Christian Bible in This World had three sections, the Old Testament, the New Testament and the Third Testament.

Several religious leaders of note and many of less note proclaimed that Christ had been born again and quoted the Scriptures liberally to prove their statements. I shall quote two of the most cited texts. One such quotation was from the Tenth Book of Enoch. It read:

"From the branch of the royal tree shall grow the royal bud. A light shall flash across the heavens and the world will sound to the clarion of war. So it will be that Christ will come again to bring peace, supreme and universal. Righteousness and justice shall be in his hand and he will bear a sceptre of equity."

When the various self appointed prophets were arguing about the validity of this text none of them was able to explain the reference to war, though all could see the relevance of the flashing light in the appearance of the comet. What none of us knew was that within the year the whole planet would be engulfed in conflict.

Another text that was frequently quoted was from the Testimony of Isaiah's Son. It read:

"The Spirit of God will shine in the world and it's light will shoot like a star from one horizon to another. The young king will be silent in his cradle and he will bring an era of prosperity and peace. The royal house will flourish for the generations of the anointed One."

Of course, this text was also disputed, because the new royal baby, far from being silent in his cradle was giving Prince Edward and Princess Anne many sleepless nights. To do them justice they only employed a nurse during the working day. They really did try to do their duty as parents and this duty included walking up and down the bedroom at two o'clock in the morning rocking the baby.

Strangely, however, this restlessness on the part of the baby passed away when he was about six months old, shortly after the comet had made its first appearance. From then on the baby was as good as gold and the latter day prophets had a field day. Many people were convinced that the child was some one very special.

Even non-Christians came to believe that the baby must have a special mission. I talked to Jhana about it one day in the refectory. She said, "The eastern faiths accept that there have been special signs. Some of my Hindu friends are convinced that the baby Charles is an avatar who will bring to the world three special graces, that is, love, peace and fertility. My Buddhist friends are examining the prophecies about the coming of the next Buddha. The trouble is this is not the right time for him to appear. Some argue that the ancient sages got the times wrong and that Charles is the Buddha reincarnated. Others argue that he is a saint of great holiness, but that he is not the Buddha."

"What do you think, Jhana?" I said. "I know you believe in reincarnation."

She said, "The boy has had a very good rebirth. He must have done many good deeds in his previous existences. I like to keep an open mind, though, and all I am prepared to say at this stage is that he will be very special."

"Surely that's dodging the issue," I said. "Any heir to a royal heritage like theirs is bound to be special. Some people would call it the privilege of noble birth. It's a privilege that will stay with him for life, surely."

"I wasn't meaning that kind of specialness. I meant that he might have great spiritual gifts which have nothing to do with being rich or of noble birth."

"I'm not sure what to make of it myself," I admitted. "Only time will tell, I suppose. I think I can expect another sixty years of life, or so I am told, so no doubt I shall be able to find out what he's like in due course. At least I can say that I've met his parents."

She smiled mischievously and said, "I can see you're going to be a name dropper, Bill."

I blushed slightly and laughed. "I asked for that, I suppose, Jhana - but I don't think I'm normally a name dropper."

"Just teasing," she said.

A few months later the baby was baptised by the Pope. Of course, Pope Hadrian was the child's great grandfather. The baptism was shown on worldwide television in 3D. The event took place in Jerusalem, not in the main hall of the Temple of Religious Truth, but in the Christian building that was part of the same complex of buildings.

Of course, the media had yet another field day. It was certainly a glittering occasion with many members of the two royal families present and a limited number of world leaders. No doubt many other people would have wished to have been there, but the limits of space were inexorable.

I watched the event myself on television. The main commentator had a beautifully modulated voice. He spoke as if he were overcome with the holiness of the occasion and as if he were overcome by his own insufficiency to describe the almost incredible array of the noble and the great. I thought he overdid it a bit myself, but even during my time in This World, the programme did become virtually a classic.

I remember one part of his commentary very well. I shall try to paraphrase some of it. He said, "What a strange and wonderful event this is. Here, in this city where the founder of the Christian faith was crucified, the present Christian leader, the successor of Saint Peter, is bringing into the faith a new baby. Can it be, I ask myself, that this child is the very same Christ who died here over two thousand years ago? Can it be that this child is really the Son of God come again? Can it be that the star of ancient times is shining again in the form of a spectacular comet which we have all observed?

"And, of course, this child is heir to the kingship of the world. Oddly enough, he is not heir to the papacy, because the Princess Anne does not have precedence over her older brother. But if this child really is Christ come again, who can doubt that he will rule over the church as well as over the World Federation of States? It is true, nevertheless, that the two royal families are now related by marriage, so perhaps the heir to the papacy will rule simultaneously with this child who will undoubtedly inherit the throne of the world. Who can tell what mysterious events are afoot here, in Jerusalem, on this spectacular occasion. Have you ever seen so many of the great men and women of our world gathered in one place? Ah, I see the Pope has now taken the baby to the font...".

At that point there was a close up of the baby's face. The child was apparently asleep and blissfully unaware of what was going on around him. As far as I could see the baby's face was no different from any other baby's face. There was no saintly glow that I could discern.

I often wish I had been able to stay in This World to see what happened later to the baby. I can't help wondering whether something similar is going to happen in Transworld. Will there be a special birth in the year of Halley's Comet?

When I first conceived the thought, I realised only too well that if I were in Transworld I should never live long enough to find out.

....

One afternoon I was doing some serious reading in my College room. I was immersed in Anselm's and Aquinas's arguments about the existence of God and was thinking I had mastered the intricacies of the ontological argument when the 'phone rang. When I picked up the receiver and looked at the screen my heart leapt to see Fiona framed there. I assumed initially that she was in Derby, but to my utter astonishment and delight she was downstairs in the College and was speaking from a booth near the reception desk.

"Great heavens!" I said, my heart beating rapidly. "Are you trying to kill off a middle aged man by giving him a heart attack."

Was it my imagination, or was there more than friendliness in her voice as she spoke? "Sorry, Bill, I came on impulse. I just wanted to see you."

"I'll come straight down," I said, as my spirits leapt upwards. "Don't run away."

She laughed and said, "Will you try to catch me if I do?"

"Just try me. I'm on my way."

With light hearted abandon I left Aquinas and Anselm and bounded down the stairs. When I saw Fiona in the flesh my heart overflowed with love for her. I took hold of both her hands and kissed her on the cheek, saying, "How marvellous to see you! You look more beautiful than ever."

She laughed her delightful tinkling laugh again. "That sort of smooth talk won't get you anywhere, kind sir."

"Where are you staying?" I said. "Or are you going back to Derby today?"

"I'm staying at a hotel on Princes Street. Just for one night."

I was disappointed at the 'one night', but I said cheerfully, "Why have you come, Fiona?"

"Never you mind," she said, smiling her Madonna smile.

I was never the one to miss a ready made opportunity. I said, almost purring, "Have you got an hour or so? Shall we go for a walk and then have some tea?"

"Right, dear Captain. Where shall we go?" Her smile was a knock out.

"Have you ever climbed Arthur's Seat?" I said.

She shook her head. "I'm only wearing light shoes."

"There's an easy path right up to the top," I said. "And it looks as if it will stay fine. You'll enjoy the view."

"Was I interrupting something important, Bill?"

"Eternal questions, my dear" I said airily. "They're so eternal they can wait till tomorrow."

So off we set. We went on the conveyor path to the Queen Mary's Park, and then we started the climb up Arthur's Seat under our own steam. In the meantime we shared our news at a fairly superficial level. However, as we wound our way up the pathway Fiona took hold of my hand and said, "I have some news for you, Bill."

As soon as she spoke some intuition told me that it was something to do with Nicholas. I was unbelievably right. She said, "I'm no longer engaged to Nicholas."

We stopped walking and I turned towards her. Her long fair hair was blowing in the breeze. Her face was serious, but her blue eyes were inviting. I didn't need any further invitation. I put my arms round her and gave her a long, exploratory kiss. We drew apart slightly. Then we clinched again, at her initiative, and kissed so passionately that we were slightly breathless when we parted.

Her face was flushed as she said, "I feel as if I've thrown myself at you, Bill."

"Thank goodness for that," I said. "I was half expecting to have my face slapped after what happened last time."

She seemed a bit stuck for words so I kissed her again and said afterwards, "I love you, Fiona. Why don't you marry me?"

"When?" she said.

"Is that supposed to signify agreement?" I said humorously. "How about this afternoon?"

She relaxed and giggled, her blue eyes twinkling with happiness. My own heart was brimming with love for her. She said, "Tomorrow afternoon might be more convenient. A girl needs time to think about what she should wear."

"I knew it," I said. "It's going to take weeks for you to decide what sort of dress would look best on the photographs."

"Let's walk on," she said, putting her arm through mine. She added, "That is, if we can manage to stop kissing long enough to reach the top of this hill."

The rest of the afternoon was rapturous, apart from one moment when I thought I should ask what had happened to Nicholas. She went very serious and seemed reluctant to discuss the matter. At last, however, she confessed, "I'm afraid I've committed the cardinal sin of breaking my promise. I just told him the engagement was off. He was very upset."

"I'm sorry," I said.

She continued, "I felt I was living a lie. The trouble is he was so nice about it. He said he understood, but I could tell he was upset."

I said, "Did you tell him...?"

"I didn't need to," she said, a note of sadness in her voice. "He knew right away that it was you I wanted to marry.

But let's not talk about that now. I still have to come to terms with it all myself. I've never broken a promise before."

I said encouragingly, "There is such a thing as *force majeure*. It's quite legitimate to break a promise under some circumstances."

"Thank you, darling." She squeezed my hand. "But it still hurts and I need time to allow the mental forces to simmer down. What makes it so abominable is that I'm so happy."

"In that case," I said, "let's talk about the future. How are we going to be able to see each other regularly. Till we get married, I mean."

"I shall come to live in Edinburgh. There is a monastery here where I can continue my spiritual development."

I had rather mixed feelings about that part of the plan. I wondered if she would fall under monastic influence and decide to become a nun. However, I said cautiously, "Wonderful, but won't a passionate relationship disturb the spiritual development?"

"Will it disturb yours?"

I laughed heartily and she smiled at my amusement. I stammered between giggles, "No. But then my theology is rooted in reality. God gave us our bodies to enjoy. Or to quote an eastern mystic, 'Love is many splendoured at many levels and true agape does not exclude eros.'"

"My goodness," she said, her eyes twinkling, "you have been fishing in some fascinating theological waters."

"I know," I said. "And all the time I have been doing it I have been thinking of you."

"That's impossible," she said, turning to look me in the eyes. "You can't have thought about me all the time."

"My love for you is like the air I breathe," I said, and I meant it. "It's always there."

"That's a beautiful thought, Bill. It's exactly the way I feel about you."

"Checkmate," I said. "That is the answer to your conscience. How could you do anything else but break off your engagement?"

"You are right, of course, but it's awful to have to hurt someone deeply."

Later that week, after a journey back to Mount Zion, Fiona moved into an associated monastery in Edinburgh.

....

As the months passed, Fiona and I moved into a sort of routine. I suppose it would have been too much to hope that the rapture would continue unabated. However, the routine never became boring because we were so fascinated with each other that our companionship was endlessly interesting.

One evening we were watching television together in my room. As a film about Henry VIII finished I was just about to switch off the TV when Fiona said, "Can we just watch the first part of the news, Bill? I think there might be something on about the new religious movement in India."

However, the first item on the news put out of our minds any thought about new Indian religions. The announcer said, "Good evening and welcome to our summary of today's news. This broadcast will be extended to allow coverage of a special news item. It seems that several of the aliens who came to our world almost two years ago have been making trouble in Rome. Over to our correspondent there for the latest news. Are you there, Jeremy? Good. Can you tell us, please, what is happening? All we know at this end is that the aliens are causing trouble of some kind."

"Dear God," I said, "what on earth has Whittle been up to? The man is an absolute menace."

Fiona didn't say anything but she held on to my hand tightly. The commentator in Rome appeared on the screen with the World Federation Parliament Building behind him. He said, "The picture is a little unclear as yet, Chris. However, it seems that five of the aliens have taken control of the Parliament building during a parliamentary session. Most of the world representatives are in there and they are being held against their will."

"Why don't they just walk out, Jeremy?"

"It seems, Chris, that the aliens are armed with old fashioned hand guns and they are threatening to shoot anybody who walks out. What makes things worse is that three of the aliens are ranger-wardens. In fact, the chief Warden in Rome is speaking to the leader of the aliens now."

"That would be the captain of their space ship, would it, Jeremy?"

I burst out, "Bloody hell, I'm in Edinburgh you stupid bastard."

I had never sworn in front of Fiona before. She didn't say anything but held onto my hand even more tightly. I relaxed slightly when the man in Rome said, "No, Chris. Apparently it's the second in command, a man called Whittle, who is masterminding the operation. He and two of the other aliens are fully qualified as wardens, but where they got the weapons from I don't know. Anyway, I hope to speak to the chief warden in a minute or so. Fortunately, I happened to come out of the assembly for a breather - otherwise I would have been trapped in there as well."

"We'll come back to you in a moment, Jeremy. Let us know when you are going to interview the chief warden and we'll switch back to you. Well, viewers, there you are. A strange and unusual situation in Rome which seems to take us back a hundred years and more. Are the prophets of doom going to be proved right. There were those, you may remember who said that nothing but trouble would come from the intrusion of the aliens into our world."

It was most peculiar hearing myself spoken of as if I were a dangerous animal or a primitive human being with an infectious disease. I had known that there had been some adverse comment about our arrival, but I hadn't realised that it had been so pointed. Fiona and I waited with bated breath for the interview that was about to follow. We were to discover that the situation was much worse than I could have imagined. We didn't have to wait for long.

After a few comments about general world news the commentator called Jeremy appeared in the frame again with a tall, dark haired swarthy man in a green uniform. Jeremy said, "Here we are then, viewers. I have with me, Anatole Bernatti, the Chief Warden of Rome. Tell me General Bernatti, what is actually happening in the Parliament building?"

"Things are very grave indeed," said the general, speaking almost perfect English with just the faintest of Italian accents. "This man Whittle is holding several hundred parliamentarians as hostages. I have spoken to this criminal over the tele-visual and he tells me that the aliens have shot three members of the assembly dead because they tried to walk out."

"This is sensational news, General," said the interviewer. "It must be over one hundred years since a murder took place on this planet, and now we have three people dying at the hands of alien assassins in one day. What do you think is going to happen next?"

"I have to say that there is little we can do at the moment but accede to the demands of these rebels. Otherwise there will be more bloodshed. However, my forces are keeping the situation under surveillance and we shall intercede if we get an opportunity."

"But your wardens have no weapons, general. How can they interfere?"

"I cannot discuss the details of our strategy. The aliens have asked for food to be taken into the assembly room. Their plans are unclear to us at the moment. The man Whittle says he will let me know what his further requirements are when he is ready. So there is little we can do."

"Thank you, general. Over to you, Chris. That seems to be all the news at the moment but I shall let your station know as soon as there are any new developments."

The home commentator continued: "I now have with me the Training Warden from the establishment where Whittle and his friends were trained. Tell me, sir, what do we know about this man Whittle?"

"He has an excellent record with us in most respects."

"You seem to be sounding a note of caution, sir?"

"I suppose so. It's partly to do with the present situation and partly to do with rumours I have heard about his views on different races of people."

"Surely, sir, that's not an issue in today's world. We all know that we share the basic human factors, whatever our racial characteristics."

"I would have thought so, yes. But some of his comrades on the training course...".

"You mean other aliens?"

"No, I mean people of This World. Some of our men were beginning to accept his political views before the course was finished. I understand he wishes to introduce an ancient system called apartheid. The white races will stay in Europe and parts of North America. The black races will stay in Africa - and so on. He believes the white races are superior and that they will be a master race. That's the story I'm receiving second hand anyhow. Of course, preaching such stupid doctrines isn't the same as having the power to put them into practice. The man will be stopped by the wardens, I'm sure of that."

"Thank you, sir. There you are, viewers. This man Andrew Whittle is of primitive character, and he is a possible danger. But we have the view of somebody who trained him that the disease of racism will be cured easily. At the same time, we have to remember that Andrew Whittle and his associates are holding members of the World Federation

Parliament as hostages. We return now to our scheduled programmes, but if we have any more news we shall give a special news update. Goodbye."

I looked at Fiona miserably. She said, "Don't worry. They'll soon control things. And they won't classify you and the Professor as primitives, I'm sure."

I wished to believe her, but I had a deep sense of foreboding.

Chapter Nine

The outcome of the hostage crisis was not good for anybody except Whittle and his supporters. Whittle promised he would release all the hostages except five in exchange for the King. There was great debate by those world leaders who were not in Whittle's hands as to whether it would be proper to let King William give himself into the hands of the rebels. However, the King himself insisted that the exchange should take place. At a stroke Whittle had strengthened his position and at the same time made it more manageable. After all, it is much easier to look after six hostages than several hundred.

Whittle set up his headquarters at the main communication centre in Rome. He was joined there by a number of wardens whom he had converted to his views. They decided to call themselves the White Supremacy Army, but on the "free" media they became known as the White Slavery Party which was shortened to the Slavers. This name was given to them because of the policy outlined in Whittle's book, which was for a master race of white people who would make slaves of other races.

Somehow Whittle had discovered a means of making rifles and hand guns. I assumed that it was Ernest Clamp, my ex-assistant engineer, who was the master mind behind this operation. It was amazing how quickly Whittle gained control of Rome and large parts of Italy, together with all the resources in the area. It was even more amazing how many people wanted to join his party. The recruits were mainly young men and women looking for adventure. Power makes people drunk, I have found, and I think it was this factor which enabled Whittle to disturb the political balance. It seemed obvious to some that Whittle was unstoppable and therefore many decided to join the side that would win. Once people had the feeling of power and command they wanted to keep it. I talked this over later with Father Christophoros and he said that sin was always latent in the human soul and that, despite centuries of social training, people were only too ready to follow the temptations of Satan. At the time I thought this was rather fanciful, but later I came to see that there was a lot in his theory.

Shortly after Whittle's political and military exploits began, I had some unexpected visitors. I was just walking into the College building when two men in wardens' uniforms stopped me. One said, "Are you William Stewart, formerly captain of the spaceship Leviathan?"

"Yes," I said, not suspecting that I was about to be arrested.

"You must come with us to our HQ. We need to question you about the rebellion in Italy."

I said quickly, "May I pick up some things and make a 'phone call?"

The two wardens looked at each other, suspicion in their eyes. Then one said, "We'll have to come with you."

I went up to my room and 'phoned Fiona to tell her what was happening. She said she would join me at the Wardens' HQ, the men having given me the address. Then I put a few things in a bag in case of an overnight stay. I had been around a bit in my own world, so I thought this was a wise precaution. They might not let me visit a manufacturing outlet if they wanted to question me for long about the Whittle affair.

When we reached the HQ building, a structure I can best compare to an octopus with a box at the end of each tentacle, I was shown into a small lounge where, to my surprise, I found Professor Cherrington. I said, "Hello, Professor, they seem to have arrested us."

"If that's what you wish to call it," he said. "I am hoping myself that we are simply helping them to deal with

Whittle. I must say I'm disappointed in that man. He seemed so charming."

"He can have considerable charm when he feels that way inclined," I said, "but I've worked closely with him and he can be a bit unpredictable."

At that moment Fiona was shown into the room. Apparently she had dropped everything when I 'phoned and had rushed round to join me at the HQ. She gave the Professor a peck on the cheek. He said, "Congratulations on your engagement, my dear. I'm sure you'll both be very happy."

I said viciously, "If Whittle was dead and buried we might stand a chance of being happy. I could strangle that man with my own hands."

Fiona took hold of my hand and sat beside me. She said, "I wonder why you've been brought here like this?"

"I think they want to pump us about Whittle," I said. "The trouble is, what I know about him is not especially relevant now - except that I can vouch for his efficiency - which is probably something they don't want to know about."

"Has he any weaknesses?" said the Professor. "Only you know him well enough to know that and it might be important."

"He's very vain," I said, and it was an honest opinion. "He hates losing. But I don't think he would be tempted by sexual favours, for example, if that was the kind of thing you were getting at."

Fiona said, her face quite serious, "Do you mean there are still women who would sell their bodies for profit?"

The Professor and I looked at each other. I said gently, "In Transworld there are, but I haven't met any here."

"There used to be women like that some centuries ago," she said reflectively. "But they were cured."

The Professor and I looked at each other again. I suppose we wanted to laugh, but fortunately neither of us did. Fiona was so wise in some ways, but so childlike in others.

She reminded me a bit of Eve in the Garden of Eden, except that she would need a very good reason for touching the forbidden apple. Our courting was passionate but I knew it had its limits. I assumed the apple wouldn't be mine until we were joined in holy wedlock. However, I discovered later from some of my comrades that there were parts of This World where the women were less innocent.

After about fifteen minutes the Chief Warden of Edinburgh came into the room. He looked about my age, so I suppose he was at least twenty years older than I. He was of a tall, Nordic type with an intelligent and handsome face and fair hair, cropped short. He looked very efficient in his green uniform.

"I'm sorry to have inconvenienced you," he said affably. "May I introduce myself. I'm Colonel Browning. You must be Professor Cherrington - and Captain Stewart, I presume. And you are...?"

"I'm Captain Stewart's fiancée," she said clearly and firmly. "And I wish to know what is happening."

"I can tell you that immediately," said the Colonel. "Captain Stewart and Professor Cherrington are to be interned as enemy aliens."

Fiona was speechless and so was I. The Professor, however, said angrily, "Don't be such a fathead. We're both in Edinburgh to study Theology. I'm a clergyman and Captain Stewart is likewise training to be a minister in the Christian Church. I've never heard anything so ridiculous in my all my born days."

"I'm sorry," said the Colonel. "The matter is beyond my control. But I shall pass on your comments to my superior."

Fiona had recovered sufficiently to say, "Where are they to be kept?"

The Colonel replied, "My instructions are to take them under escort to a monastery near Derby. They have to stay there until further notice. It's called Mount Zion."

"That's all right then," said Fiona. "I'm coming too."

....

The course of the Apartheid War, as it came to be called, was swift and decisive. A surprising number of eminent people sided with Whittle. His influence, as well as his army, spread far and wide. In every continent sides were taken and old, forgotten antagonisms, buried for centuries, surfaced again. Another name by which Whittle's party became known was Whiteniks which was a pun on his name in relation to his belief in a white master race. Opposing groups rallied under the name of the Polyglots to signify their view that racialism was evil and that every human being, regardless of race, colour or creed, was entitled to basic human rights.

It was soon apparent that an arms race was inevitable. At first the Polyglots took a pacifist view in the hope that war could be avoided, but events took over and the survival of civilised life on the planet became the real issue. The moralists, even Father Christophoros, concluded that war was the least of possible evils in the circumstances. The old arguments about the just war were brought out for public consumption.

Oddly enough, Britain did not succumb to Whittle's evil influence in the way that many other countries did. The vast majority of people became Polyglots and the country became a haven for leading politicians and others who were fleeing from Whittleism - another label coined by the media.

At first the weapons used in the war were fairly primitive. Rifles and handguns were manufactured by the million. However, technicians and scientists on both sides of the conflict soon began to reconstruct more sophisticated weapons from museum models and from plans in museum archives. Artillery pieces were made, and then tanks. Planes were converted into bombers and space ships were used to spy on the enemy. Fortunately, both sides seemed reluctant to introduce atomic warfare. I guessed that Whittle knew he could only gain his ends if the real weapons of mass destruction were kept under wraps, at least until he had won the war. However, the media were awash with rumours about possible germ warfare or about the use of poisonous gases.

Within six months of Whittle's coup the global picture was one of violence and destruction. In each continent huge armies faced each other across hastily constructed barriers. People other than whites who happened to be in Whitenik areas were hounded, tortured and raped until the survivors were forced to flee to a Polyglot area. Whittle was in direct control of the whole of southern Europe. Northern Europe remained Polyglot to a large extent, though pockets of Whittleism grew at an alarming rate. The strongest area of Whittleism outside Europe was in the southern states of the United States of America. Another stronghold was in southern Africa.

Throughout all this, Whittle kept King William as a prisoner. The rest of the royal family, including the baby "Messiah", came to live in London. Those religious leaders who had prophesied that doom and gloom would accompany the arrival of Christ in a new incarnation claimed that their words had come true. They also claimed that the spiritual powers of righteousness would ensure that the Polyglots would win in the end. However, there were times when it seemed likely that Whittle would take over the whole planet. There was even an unconfirmed report that he had threatened to execute the whole of the royal family, including the new baby. Whittle himself, it was reported, had ambitions to be king. He was nicknamed Satan's King by his enemies. The thought of Whittle as a self appointed king of the world didn't exactly cheer me up.

As far as my life at Mount Zion was concerned I settled easily into the routine of life there. There were two reasons for this. One was that I was in familiar surroundings with the woman I loved. Another was that my theological explorations had given me new attitudes towards religious institutions and I was ready to take a full part in the worship of the community. Having said that, it was rather galling to have to sit on the sidelines while the war was mounting in intensity. It was like watching a war story on television. It was difficult to realise that people were being killed all over the world. It was little wonder that the aliens were so unpopular in Britain, even those innocent ones who were interned.

As well as the Professor and myself, there were six aliens at Mount Zion. To my great disappointment Bernard Rawlins, my ex-chief engineer, had joined the Whitenik forces. The remaining six were good men who simply wanted to lead a quiet life and to settle in This World. Their efforts in this direction had been as rudely interrupted as mine had. It was not that we were physically restrained or anything like that, but nevertheless, there was this constant feeling that one was being watched with suspicion by everyone at the monastery, except perhaps Father Christophoros and, of course, Fiona. She and I became formally engaged but initially decided to postpone the wedding until we saw what was going to happen in the political sphere.

One afternoon, about six months after our internment, Professor Cherrington and I were out walking with Father Christophoros. As we were walking through a nearby village an old man walked right up to us and spat in the Professor's face. The man then said, in a voice trembling with fury, "You've killed my two sons, you primitive ape. Why don't you go back to your own world before you are exterminated like the vermin that you are."

The man then walked away shaking his fist in the air and shouting, "God in heaven, smite these evil aliens."

Father Chris said, "I'm sorry Anselm. It's obvious the man has had a tragedy in his family. And no doubt it has been caused by the war. Do not feel in any way that it is your fault."

After the Professor had wiped his face he said, "The man wasn't responsible for his actions. But it just illustrates the far reaching consequences of the evil that people do. Evil is like a gigantic beast with tentacles that stretch into every corner of the universe. The only weapon against it is love."

I said with some feeling, "I'm afraid I don't feel very loving towards Whittle and his men. They surely deserve to go to hell for the pain and upheaval they have caused in what was a peaceful world."

Father Chris said calmly, "They cannot ultimately avoid the consequences of their actions."

I was still worked up and I said rudely, "Just when is God going to act then? He seems to be lying very low at the moment."

The Professor said, "Come, come, Bill, don't get so worked up about it. God is giving the human race freedom to choose. He always has done. Those who choose evil will suffer evil and those who choose good will experience good. I know it doesn't always seem like that, but the moral law of the universe is quite clear. All the great religious leaders agree upon that."

I said more quietly, but yet firmly, "I've decided to postpone any idea of becoming a priest. I'm sorry to have to say this, but I think the only way to deal with evil is to fight it in practical ways. We can't just sit back and wait for divine intervention. I've decided to apply to join the Polyglot army. I don't know what my men wish to do, but I shall invite them to join me. I'm determined to show that not all the aliens have evil intentions. The thing is Father Chris, will you help me to

120

bring this about. What I mean is, will you speak to the powers that be so that those of us who want to do our bit can be accepted for service?"

Father Christophoros smiled warmly. "Of course, Bill, if that is what you wish. As a clergyman, and an elderly one at that, I cannot do the same, but I sympathise with your position."

The Professor said firmly, "I'm not going to be left out, Bill. To be sure, the army must need chaplains and that's what I am. In fact, I did have a spell as an army chaplain when I was younger."

That same evening I gathered together the six comrades who were interned with me. We borrowed one of the smaller meditation rooms for our meeting. I looked round at the six, trying to weigh what their reaction might be to the suggestion that they join the Polyglot forces to fight against their own ship mates. Kevin Oakley was a tall man with a dark beard and luxuriant black hair. He had been a technician with us. Jack Gratton was broad and of medium height and he had untidy brown hair and an equally untidy brown beard. He had been an assistant navigator on my ship. Daren Quigley was slim and cleanshaven, just above middle height. He had been a mineralogist. Dryden Jenkins was the oldest of the group, being about fifty. He was stocky and plumpish with dark, receding hair. He had been a navigator. Tom Adsworth was of medium height, clean shaven with mousy mop of hair, though he was a good looking man. He had been our cook. Finally, there was Jim Catchpole, a tallish man, slim, but wiry and strong. He had brown wavy hair and was clean shaven. He had been our general repair man, though that implied that he had a wide technical knowledge of everything to do with space ships. In fact, all of these men were intelligent and well educated. They were a good lot. The question was, would they wish to defend the cause of right and the reputation of Transworld by enlisting as soldiers?

I started off by making it absolutely clear that they were no longer beholden to me personally in any way. I then explained what my intentions were. Then I said, "I'm not a recruiting officer. However, if you feel as I do and you wish to enlist, then all of our names can go forward together. There will be formalities to see to. For a start, we have to be released from this internment. Then presumably it has to be decided where we can best serve. You needn't necessarily make the decision now, but on the other hand while we are together you might find it helpful to talk about things."

Daren Quigley said in his usual quiet voice, "Skipper, have you given up any hope of going back to our own world?"

"Yes," I said, in as firm a voice as I could muster. "As far as I'm concerned my life is in This World. I expect you all know I'm engaged to be married. I wouldn't have got engaged unless I believed absolutely that there is no way back for us."

"In that case," said Quigley, "I'm with you. This was a good world when we arrived. And now it's all gone wrong and it's really because we arrived. I know those of us here haven't done anything wrong, but I still feel responsible. I think we ought to try to help to put things right. Then we can get on with our lives."

There was a murmur round the group, some seeming to support Quigley, others seeming more doubtful. Dryden Jenkins said, "What's worrying me skipper is the prejudice we're likely to meet. It doesn't matter what we do or say, people will regard us as being responsible. But here in Mount Zion, at least we're safe. I just feel that we could get a bullet in the back from somebody on our own side."

Everybody turned rather quiet. I thought for a moment. Then I said, "That's a risk I'm prepared to take. After all, the reason I want to fight is to show I disagree with Whittle's lot. I'm sure most people will understand that. Anything else?"

Tom Adsworth said cheerfully, "I expect they want catering officers. What is it they say - an army marches on its stomach. I'm for joining."

"Me too," said Jim Catchpole. "I can mend tanks or whatever. And I don't mind being in the firing line. I'd like to get a pot shot at Whittle. He's ruined my plans. I was just getting on with a nice girl, too, and now she's told me to get lost."

In the end they all agreed to join the services with me, even Dryden Jenkins. However, I thought I'd give them a night to sleep on it so I said I wouldn't take any action till the following day. In the event they all stood firm, so Father Chris set the ball rolling.

Within a fortnight our offer had been accepted. We were all to report to a new army camp on Salisbury Plain. The old connections between that area and the army had been recently renewed. I hadn't told Fiona about my plans, so I was feeling a bit apprehensive when the news came through. I decided the best thing to do was to take her for a walk along the river, away from the monastery. We had had many romantic walks in that direction and I felt that I could tell her about the coming separation more easily in a place where I could then comfort her with my kisses. I had some sort of idea in my mind that I would play the scene of the soldier going to war and I saw myself as a prospective hero bidding a fond farewell to his lover.

As things turned out Fiona had a different script in mind. We hadn't gone very far on our walk when she said, "I hear you're leaving the monastery."

"I was just going to tell you," I said lamely.

"I'm leaving too," she said. "I'm going to join the army."

I was lost for words. She said, "As soon as I heard you were joining I knew I had to join too."

I found my tongue: "Why didn't you discuss it with me, darling?"

That was the only occasion that I ever heard Fiona use strong language. She said angrily, "I'm not a bloody dummy you stupid man. Why didn't you tell me what you were going to do?"

I was flabbergasted. She had never lost her temper before. It seemed as if Whittle really had opened a Pandora's Box. The ramifications of his ambitious plots were affecting our lives, his evil penetrating every crevasse of our being. I said, "I'm sorry, darling. I didn't wish to alarm you and it seemed silly to get you all worked up if they wouldn't let us join up."

She was somewhat mollified and took hold of my hand again. She said, "I have to leave the day after tomorrow. I'm going to work in a hospital in Germany. Wounded men and women are being transported there at an alarming rate and they need all the help they can get."

I said, "But you haven't got any medical experience."

She laughed. "I'm sorry, Bill, we still have a lot to find out about each other. I did do a medical course when I was young. I'm a bit rusty, I suppose, but the basics are unchanged. Anyway, the sort of wounds people are receiving are straightforward enough from the medical point of view. It's a matter of mending torn flesh and removing foreign bodies, things like bullets and shrapnel. I've been doing some reading. It's all coming back to me."

"But there hasn't been a war in your lifetime," I said. "How did you get practical experience?"

"People do have accidents, you know, especially in Switzerland and other places where people do adventurous things. I'm quite excited about the prospect. It will be wonderful to do something to help people."

"What about me?" I said, feeling rather woebegone.

She laughed. "You look just like a little boy who's lost his mother."

That was just how I felt. I had had this picture of Fiona waiting patiently at Mount Zion for her conquering hero to return. "Sorry," I said, "I suppose I asked for that. When will we see each other again, that's what's in my mind."

She put her arms round me and gave me a whacking kiss. Then she said, "Come to my bedroom tonight, darling. We can get father Chris to marry us before I leave, but we'd better start the honeymoon as soon as possible. We have so little time."

I immediately cheered up. In fact, I changed from being a woebegone and lost little boy to being a youth mad with passion for his girl. We kissed again. When we parted just for a moment I whispered, "Darling, I can't wait."

"Neither can I," she said, and she fiercely pressed her body to mine.

Chapter Ten

General Anatole Bernatti, formerly Chief Warden of Rome, was chairing the meeting. I had met the General on my visit to Rome and I had been quite impressed with his demeanour and intelligent grasp of affairs. Now he was head of special operations in the royalist army. The object of the meeting was to plan a rescue operation to bring King William out of Rome. We were in a Polyglot enclave near Naples. Present at the meeting were about twenty people including my six faithful comrades and myself. We had been invited to take part because of our knowledge of Whittle and the other "aliens".

The General was saying, "I'm going to lead this operation myself. We shall parachute into the enemy HQ area which is now in the royal palace. Intelligence reports suggest that the King is a prisoner there. We know that Whittle has commandeered the best rooms for his own use, but remember that the main purpose of the operation is to rescue the King. If we can capture other prisoners, well and good. Any of the aliens is to be shot on sight - sorry Captain Stewart, but that seems to be the safest policy."

I nodded my agreement. My comrades murmured their approval. The General continued, "There will be air support to keep the enemies' heads down and bombs will be dropped just before we land. Hopefully, that will mean that the enemy will be thrown into confusion. If our attack comes as a surprise - and it should, if nobody talks about the operation - then we stand the best chance of achieving our objective. We shall split into two groups. Captain Stewart will command one group and I shall command the other. The idea of dividing the party and the command is to give us two chances of success."

One of the soldiers said, "Provided we don't get in each other's way, sir."

"Good point, Tremayne. We shall wear red armbands. So whatever you do, don't shoot anybody with a red armband. Anybody else is fair game - except the King, of course. And I assume everybody can recognise the King on sight. I have an album of pictures of him taken in various poses if anybody wants to examine it. Now let's take a look at a plan of the palace. My group will gather here after the drop. Captain Stewart's group will assemble here. My group will go in this way and your lot, Bill, should go in by this door. Remember the tactics for storming buildings. I'm sure your training will not be wasted."

"What about our getaway?" said Daren Quigley, one of my men.

"Helicopters will land on the forecourt of the palace at 13.00 hours sharp. If you are not there we shall have to leave you."

"Sir, that doesn't give us long to find the King," I said.

"True," said the General, "But if we stay longer, there will be time for the enemy to bring up reinforcements. It has to be a slick operation. We shall have to leave behind any of our wounded and, of course, if you are captured, we shall have to leave you to your fate. Any man who wishes to withdraw from the operation should do so now."

Every man jack was a volunteer, so the General wasn't expecting anybody to leave. He was right. The men's faces were rather tense, but very determined. They were all dressed in khaki battle dress. It was rather odd, really. Handbooks of tactics and weapon training had been rescued from museums and the war was a fair imitation of the Second World War in Transworld as I remembered it from films.

Our Dryden Jenkins spoke up. I noticed that he had become much less plump and that he looked ten years younger. He said, "When will the operation take place, sir?"

The General smiled. "It will be better if you don't know. There are several dates under consideration. Captain Stewart and I will decide which day in due course. In the meantime your training will be intensified."

There were groans all round. The General said quickly, "But we're having a party tonight. The drinks are on me."

It was a couple of days after that planning session that I had some very bad news indeed. A town in a Polyglot area was raided by the Whitenik forces and a number of hostages were taken. These included some staff from a hospital. Fiona was among those captured. I heard this from a friend of Fiona's who had managed to escape. Whittle made an announcement about the new hostages through the media. The gist of his message was that any attempt to rescue the King would result in the execution of the hostages. I prayed that Whittle wouldn't find out that Fiona was my wife. As is customary in This World, she had the choice of keeping her own name and she had elected to do so. Consequently, there was a good chance that our marriage would remain secret from the Whittle faction.

When Anatole heard the news he offered to call off the rescue attempt or to free me from any involvement in it. However, I argued that Whittle's evil tactics had to be faced squarely, otherwise he would ultimately triumph. "If the man gets away with it this time he knows he has us beaten," I said. "In any case, I'm sure Fiona or any of the other hostages would not wish us to change our plans. And Whittle may be bluffing."

I certainly hoped he was bluffing, Life without Fiona would be unbearable.

....

I wasn't surprised when I had a serious attack of butterflies in the stomach on the morning when our 'planes took off for Rome. I tried not to show my nervousness. I guessed that everybody else was feeling a little apprehensive. However, nobody showed it, except that I thought our laughter sounded rather forced and our voices were pitched just a shade high. When the 'plane got going the chatter stopped and we all sat silently examining our navels.

I was more worried about the parachute drop than about the attack. When the fateful moment arrived I felt virtually paralysed. Somehow I managed to jump without being pushed. When the parachute opened I heaved a sigh of relief and all my butterflies miraculously disappeared. Before we hit the ground we were spotted and there was sporadic gunfire, which was not very effective. All the men in my group were OK and arrived at the rendezvous in one piece. We lay in a tight circle facing outwards, firing at anybody in sight. I was watching the other group. After they had stormed through the main entrance I waited for a full minute before giving the signal for my group to go. This had been agreed, the idea being that the defenders would all rush to the main entrance, thus allowing us reasonably easy entry.

When the moment came I shouted, "Go! Go! Go!" Five men remained where they were to give covering fire. The other five, including myself, ran for the side door. When we reached it safely I waved for the others to join us. We then made our way through the building, moving in a leapfrog sort of tactic, five moving at a time while the others covered them. We had memorised a plan of the palace and we went from room to room. We certainly found our training useful. In the time honoured manner we burst through the door of each room, guns at the ready. I was carrying a very handy machine pistol with loads of ammunition. A lot of the rooms were empty. Some were not. In the latter case we had to be ruthless, because we found that everybody in the palace was armed and prepared to shoot.

Events moved very quickly. The deafening sound of the gunfire, the whine of ricocheting bullets and the screams of the dying and the wounded made the place into a good imitation of hell. My blood was up and I was half crazed with battle lust. I noticed first one of my men fall, and then another. This made me even more crazy and I was yelling at the top of my voice.

After a while, when we had covered all the floors and rooms we were supposed to cover, the opposition seemed to have stopped. I glanced at my watch. The helicopters were due to pick us up in eight minutes. I knew we had to go. I just hoped that the other group had managed to find the King. I called my men together and we re-divided into two groups. We had no time to find out whether our fallen comrades were dead or just wounded. We returned cautiously to the ground floor, but we met no opposition. There were dead bodies lying around everywhere. When we reached the side entrance we had used earlier we waited under cover for the helicopters.

We were only there a couple of minutes when we heard the roar of engines from beyond the trees. Two helicopters swooped down. I waved the first group away and they ran to the forecourt. There was a hail of gunfire from somewhere up above. I edged out and saw that some of the enemy were on the roof firing down at the helicopters and our men. The first group got into one helicopter. I saw that Anatole's group, or what was left of it, was heading out to the other machine. I yelled, "Right, off we go!"

I gave my men a few yards start. Then I stepped out and aimed my gun upwards at the roof towards the place where the enemy were firing . I gave them a savage burst and then ran like blazes. When I was halfway across the forecourt I felt a stabbing pain in my back. I stumbled and fell. Then I blacked out.

....

When I came to consciousness again I felt as if I had a hundred hammers ringing in head and a red hot poker shoved into my back. Cautiously I opened my eyes. I could see what looked like the sky, a blue blur above. But round the blue blur was a circle of white blobs. I closed my eyes again. Then I heard a voice speaking from a great distance. It said, "What have we here, then? The great Captain Stewart, I believe."

My head was whirling, but I grasped that the voice was Whittle's. I opened my eyes again. I saw that the circle of white blobs had become a circle of faces. Nobody was smiling. I couldn't make out which was Whittle till he spoke again. He said silkily, "Very good of you to drop by, Bill." Then I felt somebody give me a vicious kick in the ribs. I passed out again.

When I next came to I found myself lying in bed. My head was still throbbing and my throat was parched. I tried to move but grunted with the pain and changed my mind. I found that the upper half of my body was swathed in bandages. I looked around the room. It was sumptuously decorated and the curtains hung like rich swathes of gold. Then I remembered. Yes, I must be in the palace. But Whittle had spoken to me. Where was he? Had I dreamed that bit?

I lay puzzling for a while. When I thought about it I was sure it had been Whittle who had spoken to me. But why had he allowed somebody to tend my wound and make me reasonably comfortable in bed? I could only conclude that he must have some ulterior motive in mind.

Experimentally I moved my legs. They seemed to be OK. I tried to sit up. Again I felt an excruciating pain and decided I had better lie still. After a while I dozed off.

When I awoke a nurse was bending over me. She had a syringe in her hand. When she saw I was awake she smiled. I panicked when I saw the syringe and said, "No!" My voice was very hoarse.

"Don't worry, Captain Stewart," she said. "This will help to relieve the pain."

She seemed genuine enough so I allowed her to give me an injection. Then I said, "Where's Whittle?"

"The President is in a meeting," she said sweetly.

"President?" I said stupidly.

"Yes, President Whittle has given instructions that you are to be well looked after. He'll come to see you in a couple of days."

I decided not to ask when Whittle had made himself President. I wondered what he was President of. I concluded that he must have declared himself President of all the countries under his control. The nurse said, "Have a drink, Captain. I'm sorry, it would be unwise for you to eat anything just yet. What you need most is sleep. To help you to recover."

With difficulty I took two or three sips from the glass she held out to me. I said hoarsely, "Thank you."

She smiled again. "Now don't worry about a thing. Just try to sleep."

She then went away. It was all right for her to tell me not to worry. For several minutes I pondered my situation. I wondered where Fiona was. I wondered if any of the hostages had been shot. Then gradually I began to drift away. I felt warm and free from pain. Sleep swirled over me like an enveloping mist. I could see Fiona waving to me in the distance. She beckoned to me and I felt myself trying to walk towards her, but I couldn't. Then merciful oblivion took over.

....

As I was recuperating Whittle did drop in to see me now and again. Those with him treated him with great deference and he was obviously annoyed when I addressed him as Andy. I didn't want to extend my stay in hospital so I stopped calling him Andy and simply addressed him as you.

One day he sent his minions away, saying he wished to have a private conversation with me. When we were alone he said, "You know Bill, we could be a great team together. Surely you can now see that I was right. The whole planet is ripe for picking."

"I don't know why you need me," I said evasively.

"It's not that I need you. I want to share it with you."

I knew that Whittle's character was complicated but I found this need to have me in on his empire building difficult to understand. Perhaps he was seeking my cooperation for moral reasons. If I supported him he could then be convinced that he was acting legitimately. That was the only theory I could think of to explain his behaviour. He never stopped trying to get me onto his side.

He went on, "You could be in charge of a whole continent. Just think about that for a moment. Viceroy of Africa."

I said, "I was training to be a clergyman before this lot started."

That seemed to take him aback. He said, "But you're now a soldier and you have killed people. Surely that doesn't match your so called vocation. You must have got it wrong, Bill. You're a man of action, not a priest."

I decided it was wiser to stay quiet until he said something else. I might have known that such a cunning operator would have something more up his sleeve. He smiled pleasantly and said, "Fiona is my guest, you know."

My heart thumped down to my stomach. I was caught completely off guard. I had assumed that Fiona would be just another anonymous hostage.

"She's very well, Bill. I haven't told her yet that you are my prisoner. But I must say I admire your taste. She's a very attractive woman."

I wasn't sure how to react to this piece of information. If I showed eagerness to see Fiona he would probably either torment me or blackmail me. If I told a lie and said I didn't care what happened to her then she might be killed or worse. So I simply said, "I hope she is well."

"You know, Bill," said Whittle, "you're a cold blooded devil. Is that all you have to say? You can talk to her if you like. Mind you, there is a condition."

"What's the condition?" I said.

"Join our side. That's all you have to do. Now that's not difficult, is it?"

"I'm sorry," I said. "I can't do that."

"In that case," he said, "you can join the other prisoners and rough it for a while. We'll see how you like that."

He stalked out of the room and left me in a state of despair. I said a prayer and asked God to watch over Fiona.

I had always guessed that Whittle had a sadistic streak in his nature. This tendency had shown itself in small incidents in the space service. It was the way he treated subordinates. Also, I had heard rumours that he was vicious in his dealings with women. This was partly why I was so worried about Fiona.

A couple of days later no less than six armed men came to my room. I was told to dress. All I had was a shirt, a pair of trousers and a pair of sandals. I donned these hurriedly and was then dragged out of the room and escorted into the courtyard. In the middle of the courtyard there were two posts concreted into the ground. They were about twenty yards apart. I was unceremoniously tied to one of the posts and the six men lined up a few yards away. I heard a voice behind me. It was Whittle's. He said, "Now is the time to pray, Bill. Perhaps your God will rescue you."

I heard Whittle walk away.

The men raised their rifles and aimed them at me. One of them gave the command to fire. I did say a quick prayer. They all pulled their triggers and there was an explosion of sound. However, I was unharmed. I knew that there had been real bullets in the rifles because I had heard them whistling past my head. The men fired again with the same result. When they fired the third time I was sure I was a dead man. However, they deliberately missed again. I heard Whittle chuckling somewhere not too far away. Then I heard him say, "Bring the woman out."

My blood froze. He could only mean Fiona. I turned my head to look at the other post. My tormentors gathered round it. Shortly afterwards Fiona came out escorted by two women who were built like Sumo wrestlers. My mouth went dry and I couldn't have shouted even if I had wanted to. Fiona was dressed in a blouse and a pair of jeans. Her blonde hair had been rather untidily cut. Her head was bowed and I was sure she didn't know I was there.

I watched fearfully as the men tied her to the post. The firing squad lined up in front of Fiona. I managed to find my voice. I shouted, though with difficulty, "I love you, Fiona."

She looked round as the guns fired. I saw her jump, but was relieved to see that it was from fright and not because she was hit. As they had done with me, they went through this horrible charade three times. Each time the guns fired Fiona jumped involuntarily.

Finally, on Whittle's order the men marched away. Fiona turned her head and gave me a piteous look. It would have moved the heart of Adolf Hitler, but apparently had no effect on Whittle. He walked over to stand beside me and said, "What a touching scene. I wish I'd recorded it on video, but never mind, there will be other occasions. I'll tell you what I'll do, Bill. I'll leave you two love birds to contemplate each other for a while. And then I'll come back to see how things are going."

Whittle waved two men over and they gagged both Fiona and me tightly so that we would not be able to speak to each other. Whittle was cunning enough not to blindfold us. He knew very well that it would be sheer torture for us to look at each other without being able to move or speak.

I guess it must have been three or four hours before Whittle returned. He had my gag removed. Then he said, "How about it, Bill? Are you going to join me?"

I didn't trust myself to speak in case he arranged something painful for Fiona by way of retaliation. I shook my head.

"Right, then," he said. "You can have a spell with the other hostages and prisoners. And I shall keep the delightful Fiona all to myself. I wonder if she's a virgin?"

His lip curled with a mixture of amusement and contempt.

However, it was obvious that he didn't know that Fiona and I were married. That was something. If he found out the truth he might treat Fiona with even greater cruelty just to spite me.

....

The prison regime wasn't too bad. There were a dozen men, including myself, in one large room which contained a table for our meals, a wash basin and a single lavatory. Perhaps the most irritating aspect of the imprisonment was the constant flushing of the loo. There was one compensation, though. One of the prisoners was Jim Catchpole, our former general repair man. He looked even leaner than before, but he hadn't lost his cheerful grin. I suppose he was the most useful man I could have been cooped up with because of his practical skills. If there was any way to escape he would be the one to work it out.

He was very glad to see me when I was literally thrown into the room, though his pleasure was mixed with concern at the state I was in.

He clasped my hand warmly and said, "Great to see you, skipper. I thought you had got yourself killed."

"Did the other group get the King out?" I asked, when I had managed to pull myself together. Whittle had been canny enough not to tell me the outcome of our raid.

Jim shook his head. "I don't think so, skipper. I was hit in the leg and couldn't make it, but I only saw our own guys get into the helicopters. We must have lost one or two men though, and as they're not here with us I guess they must be dead."

"Unless there's another prison," I said.

Jim shook his head. "The guards say not. At least not in the palace. Except for three women. Some of the hostages have been exchanged for Whitenik prisoners, I believe. Mind you, I guess there are prison camps all over the place by now, so some men could have been moved from here."

"Do you know where the women are kept, Jim?"

"No. The guards don't know either. They're quite chatty at times. And they keep us up to date with the news."

Over the next few days Jim and I discussed possible ways of escape. He reckoned it wouldn't be difficult to get out of the prison itself. The main difficulty, he thought, would be to get out of the palace area.

I made a deliberate policy of chatting to the guards who brought in our food. But however much I pumped them I couldn't find out where the women prisoners were kept. I decided reluctantly that any escape would have to be without Fiona. Staying there wasn't going to help her. At least if I managed to escape I could try to negotiate with Whittle to give him something he wanted in exchange for Fiona, perhaps. At any rate, that seemed to be the only possible way to help her.

A week after I had been placed with the other prisoners Jim Catchpole came up with a plan of escape. The plan meant taking the other prisoners into our confidence, but all of them were trustworthy, so Jim assured me. The plan involved overpowering the guards and stealing their uniforms and weapons. Normally three guards came at any one time. Their last visit in the day was fairly late at night when they came with some coffee. If they went missing then there was a chance that their non appearance would not be noticed till morning. This would give three of us a reasonable opportunity of getting away from Rome. It was our intention to steal whatever form of transport came to hand.

There was, of course, the question of deciding which of our fellow prisoners should come with Jim and myself. It went without question that Jim and I should go because we had come up with the idea. Finally, it was agreed that the others should draw lots. The lot fell on Caspar, a stocky Armenian who looked as if he would be useful in a fight. The others agreed not to escape at the same time so that we three would have the best chance of getting away.

There was no point in waiting so we decided to make our escape that evening if we could. The guards had become careless in their familiarity and they thought that as they had three machine pistols they were invulnerable. Of course, in a sense they were, unless we could disarm all three simultaneously. Our ploy was simple. Each guard was to be engaged in conversation by two men. In fact this was not unusual. At my signal, everybody would act simultaneously to overpower the guards.

All went as planned. The coffees were poured out. The guards agreed to join us in having coffee and to tell us the day's news. I was to say, "Would anyone like another cup of coffee? Speak now or forever hold your peace."

This I did, and on the word "peace" the designated men threw coffee (deliberately cooled with milk) into the faces of the guards. Their weapons were easily taken. Their khaki uniforms were stripped off them and they cowered in their underclothes, expecting to be killed. The only snag was the uniforms were anything but a good fit and it took us far too long to dress. At last, however, we were ready. Each of us grasped a gun and away we went, locking the door behind us and leaving the keys on a nearby table.

We crossed the courtyard without seeing anyone. When we came to the main gate there was a sticky moment. There were two armed guards there blocking the way. Fortunately they felt it was their main duty to keep people out and it apparently never occurred to them that three armed and uniformed men leaving the palace could represent any threat. I warned Jim and Caspar not to speak. I simply waved and said, "Ciao," and off we went up the street.

We found a fast looking car in a car park. It took Jim two minutes to break into it and another two minutes to get it started. Without further ado we roared off through the night towards Naples, passing guard posts with great aplomb. We simply slowed down, waved our weapons about and said, "Emergenza!"

I thought it was better to stick to Italian, even though I knew English was universally understood.

The following day we arrived in Naples and found our way to our HQ. There we found General Bernatti without any difficulty. His face was a picture when he saw me.

He grasped my shoulders and then kissed me on both cheeks. "Bill," he said warmly, "I thought your were a goner. And here you are large as life. Come and have a drink and tell me all about it."

Chapter Eleven

Over the next few weeks countries fell like dominoes into Whittle's hands. He controlled most of southern Europe, except for a few Polyglot enclaves. The whole of Africa was his. The whole of South America was also under his dominion. Much of North America stayed in Polyglot hands, though areas of Whitenik influence were growing. However, great efforts were made by the royalist forces and many Whitenik areas in North America were conquered. Asia and Australasia were about equally divided between Whitenik and Polyglot supporters. Vicious civil wars were going on in both of these continents.

Whittle began to put his unsavoury theories into practice. All people who were not classified as white were placed in special areas and many of them were made to work for the white races. Often enough, menial work was invented for them so that they would be humiliated. It was morally indefensible to take a fully automated system of production and de-activate large parts of it. But this became necessary for Whittle's theories to work. His crazy political blueprint included the idea that the inferior races should be made to work for their food. The whites, on the other hand, were to become a leisured aristocracy waited on hand and foot by other races. I agreed with the Professor that the whole thing was a work of Satan.

While all this was going on I was worried sick about Fiona, of course. I decided to talk to Anatole about ways of rescuing the hostages, including the King. He was due to go to Australia with one of his special units within a fortnight, so I asked him if I could try another rescue operation.

"I don't rate your chances of success very highly," he said. We were walking round the grounds of the mansion that served as our HQ and training depot.

"I've been think things over," I said. "Perhaps we need a very tiny force of four men to sneak in at dead of night. Whittle's guards will be watching for another air operation probably. But I could be dropped with three of my colleagues somewhere well out of sight. Then we could penetrate the perimeter wall and find the King without raising the alarm. Remember that we have had word from our mole that the King is in a particular wing of the palace. If he's still there that would narrow down the search."

"It might," said Anatole. "It's a pity we hadn't had that intelligence report before the previous attempt. I suppose you want to get Fiona out as well?"

"Of course," I said, "but I wouldn't jeopardise the main operation. When the King was safely out I would go back alone to try to find Fiona."

"Let me sleep on it, Bill. I'm happy in principle to let you go ahead, but I'd like to consider possible snags or even other options."

We left it at that. However, that same evening some news came through which could possibly make my idea redundant. I was in the mess after dinner. Somebody switched on the 3D television to watch the latest news. We caught the beginning of the bulletin.

"Good evening," the announcer said. "First of all, news about the war situation. The self appointed President Whittle, leader of the Whitenik block, has announced that he wishes to have a meeting with President Schmidt about the exchange of prisoners or hostages."

Schmidt was the newly elected President of the United Polyglot Nations. Previously there had been no such office because the Round Table system under the monarch hadn't required one. However, in order to keep up with Whittle's machinations the Polyglot countries had thought it wise to give the people a President as well as a King, especially when the King was in enemy hands. There were some, indeed, who wished to move away from the royalist position altogether to have a universal presidential office instead.

The announcer continued, "President Whittle has little to lose over such an exchange and a lot to gain. It is thought by some commentators that he might even be prepared to release the King. Which other people are involved is difficult to say at this stage...".

Of course, it struck me immediately that Whittle might release Fiona. If both Fiona and the King were released, then my proposed operation would be unnecessary and I could perhaps go with Anatole to the Australian front. However, when I thought about the possibility, I just had a gut feeling that Whittle would never let Fiona go. No doubt he would feel that while he still had Fiona he wielded power over me. And when I thought about the King I knew in my heart that Whittle would only release King William when the monarchy was completely devalued. The election of a rival President had already weakened the monarchy as an institution, though great sympathy was felt by royalists for King William. At the same time I had noticed a tendency for people to talk about President Schmidt, rather than the royal family, as representing the future of free nations.

The news reader was saying, "Representatives of the two Presidents will meet on Wednesday with lists of people they wish to exchange. If agreement can be reached then the two Presidents will meet to discuss the arrangements for exchange. At the same time, it is thought by some political observers, that President Whittle may suggest a carve up of the world into permanent zones, one set for Whiteniks and their dominions and the other set for the Polyglot nations. If such an agreement can be reached, then it is possible that a peace treaty could be signed. And now to other news items...".

I suspected that Whittle was wanting time to reorganise his resources. I knew that he would never give up his ambition to control the whole world, so if any peace treaty was agreed it wouldn't last for long. When Whittle was strong enough he would attack again. I hoped that President Schmidt was astute enough to see through his opponent.

The following day I met Anatole in his office to discuss my plan. To my relief he agreed with my assessment of the political situation. However, he insisted that we wait until the exchange had been agreed before we made any move. In due course an agreement was reached between the two sides and the presidents fixed a date for their meeting. It was clear that the King was not to be released, but I was still anxious to know whether Fiona would be on the list. Anatole said he had a friend who was part of the Polyglot delegation and promised to 'phone to find out if Fiona was one of those to be freed. Anatole's friend refused to release any precise information, but he did admit that there were no women on the list.

When Anatole told me this he added, "That seems to settle it, then Bill. Your operation might as well go ahead."

"I've got it all planned and my men are briefed," I said. It was a relief to be able to do something which might result in Fiona's release.

....

All of my six comrades wished to go with me on the second rescue operation. However, I insisted on keeping the numbers down to four people altogether. Eventually I chose the three men I judged would make the best team. One was Jim Catchpole. By now he was a close friend and I trusted him absolutely. Moreover, his practical skills were going to be very useful, I was certain. Kevin Oakley, an ex-technician, was also chosen. Not only was he useful because of his technical background, but he was tall and muscular and very determined. To be honest, I wouldn't like to take him on in single combat. The third of my companions was to be Daren

Quigley. Like the others he had been on the first operation. He was a useful man to have around and he was extremely reliable.

We had practised climbing walls and jumping from heights. We had improved our skills in unarmed combat, as well as our weapon training. We had all four of us memorised a plan of the palace and its surroundings so that we could find our way around even in the dark. The wing where the King was supposed to be had been studied with extra special care. However, our source was by no means infallible. While we didn't know precisely which room he would be in we felt that after the last attempt his room would be guarded. This might possibly have the advantage of allowing us to find his exact whereabouts without difficulty.

When we set out I felt we had a good chance of rescuing the King. As to my chances of rescuing Fiona, I was less hopeful because I couldn't pinpoint her whereabouts at all. I would simply have to rely on providence to lead me to her. Jim Catchpole had volunteered to help me to find Fiona after we had seen the King safely onto the escape helicopter, but I refused his help, not wishing him to risk his life twice in one night.

We were dropped off with folding bicycles about half a mile from the palace. We were wearing Whitenik uniforms, though we intended to discard these when we reached the palace. Underneath the outer layer of clothing we were wearing black sweaters and black trousers. We also had Balaclava type helmets to pull over our heads. We agreed a time for the helicopter to pick us up again behind the palace at our planned point of exit, which was also our planned point of entry. Our uniforms would be concealed there so that we could pick them up again later if we needed to. I had been fairly modest and wore the uniform of a major. The others were disguised as non-commissioned officers.

....

It was one o'clock in the morning when Jim Catchpole broke into the palace via a downstairs window. The rest of us followed him silently. We found ourselves in a dimly lit corridor. I knew there was a staircase at the end of the corridor. There was a lift at the other end but we had decided not to use it in case our approach was signalled to any guards who might be around. We needed to be on the second floor. We crept up the stairs, pausing every time the boards creaked. This part of the building was quite old.

When we got to the second floor I peeped round the corner into a corridor of the same pattern as the one downstairs. Outside one of the doors a man sat in a chair. He had a rifle across his lap underneath a book he was reading. He was obviously awake, but he was alone. The question was, how could we silence him before he could raise the alarm. There was no way we could cover the twenty yards that separated us from him without being seen. If I tried to shoot him I might only wound him. Even if I borrowed Kevin's pistol which had a silencer fitted there was still the risk of only wounding the man.

Kevin whispered, "It'll have to be the rabbit's tail trick, sir."

I knew precisely what he meant. We needed something to distract the guard and, if possible, to bring him along the corridor. Something on a piece of string might do the trick, even if it wasn't a rabbit's tail. I thought quickly. Any string or cord we had was too visible to play the rabbit's tail trick successfully, but we could adapt the idea. Another game we had played as children was to tap on house doors and then hide not too far away, so that we could watch the unfortunate householder get exasperated. I whispered to the others that I was going to tap with my pistol butt on the stair. "Be ready to overpower him if he evades my blow," I said.

"I'll shove my rifle into his groin and then club him with the butt."

I started to tap on the wooden stair. I tapped for a full minute, but nothing happened. I didn't dare look round the corner. I started again, this time a bit louder. I heard the man's chair scrape and I knew his curiosity was aroused. I stopped tapping and waited. The man didn't appear. I assumed he was looking and listening. I started tapping again with a slow rhythm. I heard footsteps coming our way. When I saw the man's shadow I jumped out and shoved the business end of my rifle towards his groin. I saw that he was simultaneously pushing his rifle forward and he managed to parry my thrust. I knew that he was going to yell for help. I aimed a kick at the same area of his anatomy. He jumped back, his mouth opening to shout. Then I heard a phutting sound. A hole miraculously appeared in the middle of the man's forehead. He emitted a sort of strangled gasp. Thick blood oozed from the bullet hole. He flopped heavily to the ground with a very loud thud. We waited to see if anyone had heard. All was silent.

I turned round. Kevin had his revolver in his hand. It was he who had reinvented the silencer. I thanked God for this fortunate intervention. We pulled the dead guard into a cupboard and tiptoed along the corridor to the room he had been guarding.

I said, "The King will be frightened. If necessary we may have to knock him unconscious. But I'll put my hand over his mouth if I can, while we explain who we are.

I turned the handle slowly. The door opened with only a slight creak. I flashed my torch into the room. I saw a four poster bed in one corner. A gentle snoring cam from its occupant. I walked over silently and shone my torch into the face of the sleeping person. It was an elderly man. I couldn't be certain it was the King. There was only one way to find out. I put my hand over his mouth and waved for Daren to hold him down. The man awoke and a pair of terrified eyes rolled around as the man weighed up his situation. He obviously thought his last hour had come.

I said quietly but urgently, "Don't worry. We are here to rescue you."

"Switch the light on, Jim. It's OK, I think. The curtains are drawn."

The man in the bed blinked as the light flashed on. He began to tremble. I knew he would scream hysterically if I removed my hand. I said, "Hit him, Kevin."

Kevin Oakley hit the side of the man's head with his pistol butt. The man passed out. I took my hand from his mouth and pulled the bed clothes back. There was no doubt about it. The man in the bed was King William. He was haggard and almost looked like a corpse. Just to make sure he was alive I felt his pulse - which was quite strong.

"We'll have to carry him," said Jim.

"Suppose we meet somebody," said Kevin.

"I wish now we'd kept the uniforms on," I said, "but never mind, we'll shoot our way out if necessary."

We were dead lucky. We didn't meet anyone and we managed to get to the rendezvous a few minutes before the helicopter was due. We had time to put on the uniforms again. Before I had fastened my battle dress jacket the King began to stir. I stooped over him and held my hand over his mouth again. When his eyes opened I said quietly but firmly, "Sir, don't be frightened. You are safely out of the palace and a helicopter is coming to pick us up."

His eyes widened. I took my hand away from his mouth. He gasped and said, "Who are you?"

I said, "I'm Bill Stewart. We met. Remember. I'm the captain of the alien space ship."

He started to tremble violently. "Don't kill me. Please don't kill me."

I said gently, "I'm not on Whittle's side. He is my enemy. That is why we have come to rescue you."

147

It was then that I heard the distant burr of an engine. "I think that's our helicopter," I said. "Sir, tell me quickly, where are the women prisoners kept? I have to go back to rescue my wife."

He looked at me in a sort of daze as if he didn't know what I meant. "Sir," I said, pleadingly, "did you see any women prisoners?"

His eyes showed he had understood. "Only one," he whispered. "I heard her but I didn't see her. There was a woman prisoner in the next room to me. I could hear her talking when the guard took her meals in."

I was furious with myself when I realised how close I might have been to Fiona.

The helicopter was now swooping down. I said frantically, "What is her name? Who is she?"

He said something but I couldn't make out what it was because of the noise of the helicopter. I cursed under my breath. The helicopter landed twenty five yards away. We carried the King over to it and bundled him in. My comrades climbed in also and I stood waiting for the take off. However, as the helicopter rose, Jim Catchpole jumped to the ground and crouched down to avoid the undercurrent of the blades. In a moment the machine was away over the trees.

"Are you stupid, or what?" I said. "You know we stand a good chance of getting killed, don't you."

"I'm not leaving you alone, skipper. And Kevin has given me the gun with the silencer."

He brandished it triumphantly.

"Did you hear what the King said, Jim?"

"Sure. Let's go and get her. It's bound to be her, isn't it."

"I'm very hopeful," I said.

Then a thought struck me. I hadn't thought to ascertain which room the woman prisoner was in. Was it the one on the left of the King's old room, or was it the one on the right. And then I said to Jim, "Can we identify again the room the King was in?"

"Of course. We left the guard's chair outside the door."

We made our way back to the wing of the palace which we had entered previously. With extreme caution we went back to the corridor where the King had been imprisoned. Yes, the empty chair was still standing outside the door. The body of the guard was still lying as we had left it.

We tiptoed along the corridor. I listened first at one adjacent door and then at the other. There was no clue as to whether there were any occupants. I whispered, "Jim, you cover while I open this one."

With great care I twisted the handle. The door opened without a sound. I swept the beam of my torch round the room. It was completely empty. There wasn't even a stick of furniture.

I motioned to Jim to go to the other room. He led the way and before I could stop him he was opening the door. All seemed to be quiet. We both tiptoed into the room. The torch revealed that there was somebody in a bed. I gasped with surprise. There were two people in the bed.

Before I could decide what to do the light was switched on. A gunshot shattered the quietness. Jim staggered, his hand to his shoulder. A man was sitting up in bed. It was Whittle. His torso was covered with black hair and it was glistening with sweat. When he saw me he grinned and grasped the woman by the hair, holding his gun to her head.

"One move from you, Stewart, and she's dead."

I couldn't see the woman's face, but she was a blonde with long hair just like Fiona's. I heard the sound of people running in the corridor. I knew the game was up. Four hefty guards came into the room and two of them grasped me by the arms. Whittle released the woman. She sat up, holding a sheet to cover her breasts. Her face was twisted with fear. I saw immediately it was not Fiona. Later, of course, when I had had time to think about it, I knew that Fiona would rather die than sleep with Whittle. However, at the time I had had a fright, because I wondered if he had blackmailed her into bed, or something like that.

"Throw them into a cell," shouted Whittle, losing control now that the emergency was over.

"This one's dead, sir," said one of the men.

"Get rid of the body, then. And find out what's happened to that bloody guard. I'll deal with you tomorrow, Stewart. You won't get away again you slippery bastard."

....

"How do you like the new flag of the White Federation?" said Whittle, pointing out of the window.

There, on a nearby flagpole, hung a white flag bearing a green swastika. I offered no comment.

"I think it's very evocative, don't you?

I still made no comment. Whittle was sitting at a huge mahogany desk. I was on the other side of the desk. Two uglies with white arm bands bearing green swastikas stood by the door. They were both carrying guns. Whittle said, "This may be your last opportunity to join us, Bill."

"I don't know why you're so keen to have me on your side," I said. "I don't agree with many of your ideas."

"I'm sure I could convince you," he said, his swarthy face breaking into a smile. "My system has a certain moral purity about it. It's perfectly obvious that evolutionary processes have brought the white race to their present supremacy. We should follow our destiny."

"What about loving God and loving your neighbour?" I said, unsmiling and not hoping for a very constructive response.

"The first idea is a meaningless concept," he said. "Show me God and I might change my mind. You can't, can

150

you? The fact is there's nobody there. This life is all there is. I believe in morality of course. But ultimately it's based on mutual interest. You scratch my back and I'll scratch yours."

"So concepts like love and service to the community don't come into your system?" I said.

"Of course they do. Service to the flag and the lawful authority are at the centre of my system. Love comes in as well. I believe in family life. That's where the love should be. But I also believe that mixed marriages are evil. The races have developed separately and they should remain separate. We should also love our neighbour by defending him from harmful influences."

"What about justice and the law?" I said.

"Law is important. It's in nature, and if you contradict nature then trouble follows. That's why God ideas are harmful. They do not relate to anything in nature - or to any reality. As for justice, that is related to keeping the laws promulgated by the lawful authority. Those who break the law will be brought to justice."

"There are such things as beauty and truth," I said. "Where do they fit into your godless system?"

"Beauty is in the mind. It's a development of nature to teach us to protect nature, to protect the environment if you like. Truth is simply fact. If I don't state the facts as they are then I am not speaking the truth. It's common sense. We must live with reality, not with invented fables."

"Your philosophy is very arid," I said. "You seem to think there is no power beyond yourself, and no power beyond this world."

"Of course there's a power beyond myself," he said persuasively. "It's the power of nature. But beyond that there is nothing. You are simply a cell in the body of nature. Cells die and are replaced, by the nature of things."

"What about creation?" I said, determined to defeat his arguments.

He laughed derisively. "There was no beginning and there won't be any end. The force of nature is the constant. We have to be true to that."

"Why did you have to go and destroy an ideal world?" I said bitterly.

"Don't you see?" he said, his eyes burning fervently. "It was a false world, It was guided by false ideas, god ideas and the like. We must be true to nature and true to what we are. The man who said, 'Be true to yourself,' was dead right."

I realised then how dangerous Whittle was. He had thought out his position very carefully. I could see how he had managed to convert so many people to his viewpoint.

It's no good," I said. "I believe in God and I believe in the presence of Christ in the universe."

"Tell him to show himself," sneered Whittle. "The man Jesus was a fool. He had the power to be great, but he threw it away. I'm not going to make that mistake. I'm going to take over the world."

"You are also going to roast in hell," I said.

He chuckled. "Old wives tales like that don't frighten me. I'll tell you what I'll do, Bill. I'll give you a week to think things over. I'll let you have a copy of my latest book. That may help you to clarify your ideas. If you still refuse to join us, then you must take your chances with the losers."

Chapter Twelve

Whittle and I had many conversations at this time. I tried my hardest to show him the error of his ways, but he had a kind of messianic zeal which was impermeable. He really believed he was the saviour of This World and that he would found a new civilisation which would last for at least ten thousand years. Part of my difficulty, of course, was that I was a prisoner and therefore vulnerable. It is difficult to win an argument with your gaoler. Even Saint Paul had needed God's help to do that. Not that I didn't ask for God's help. I prayed many times about the perils that faced the whole planet. At the time I wondered whether or not God was listening, though later I had to conclude that God must have intervened, but in his own mysterious way. Even then, I wondered why he had allowed us to come to This World when he could easily have stopped us. In such a case Whittle would never have had to face the temptations to grasp power which were obviously dormant in him.

One day Whittle offered to let me talk to Fiona. I was very suspicious and I asked him what the price was to be for such a concession. However, he insisted that it was an act of free compassion on his part. I realised, of course, that it was undoubtedly a ploy to get me onto his side. Nevertheless, it was an offer I could not refuse and I accepted it, but with some attempt to conceal my joy.

The result was that Fiona and I were allowed an hour together. To my surprise this meeting took place in a comfortable sitting room in the palace. I had become used to the rigours of imprisonment and it almost made me weep to move into a civilised environment again, especially to meet the woman who had seized my heart and made it her own,

I was shown into the room first. I just couldn't sit down while I was waiting. I stalked up and down like a tiger in a cage. After the first sweeping glance I hardly took in the rich furnishings. Ten minutes after I had entered the room the door opened and Fiona was ushered in. She was wearing a plain navy blue dress. Her luxuriant blonde hair was as well groomed as in better times. But she looked uncertain and lost. I realised immediately that she hadn't known I was going to be there. I said, "Don't worry, my love."

She gasped. Then we threw ourselves into a melting embrace. It was like having an orgasm without the sex. An absolute delight filled my whole body and mind. We kissed and embraced again and again without speaking. At last she said, "Darling, what's happening?"

I lowered my voice in case the room was bugged: "Whittle is allowing us an hour together. We may be on video or something, so be careful."

At last we sat down together on a sofa. We held hands and talked. She told me all that had happened to her. I was relieved to learn that she had not been seriously molested. I then told her all that had happened to me. When we had thus updated each other we began to speculate about the future. We spoke in whispers.

I said, "Have you told anybody we're married, by the way?"

She shook her head. "I haven't had any reason to mention it. Why do you ask, darling?"

"I hate falsehood," I said, "but if Whittle knows we're married he might try to make capital out of it. So it might be better to keep it dark."

"This hour is so frustrating," she said. "It's not long enough or private enough to...".

"I know," I said, "but it's just wonderful to be together."

"What are Whittle's plans?" she said.

"Eventually to take over the whole planet," I said. "But I assume the Polyglots are working on ways to stop him.

Surely they won't let him just walk away with absolute power over everybody and everything."

"The man is diabolical," Fiona said feelingly. "It's like the Fall in Eden all over again. But how can we win? Is it now a matter of victory in war? Is that what the world has come to?"

"I guess so," I said. "Who can drop the first atomic bomb? That may be the decider."

"I've read about such bombs in the history books," she said. "Surely, nothing is worth that amount of pain and suffering!"

"It's a question of the greater good," I said. "If you drop a single bomb on one city and kill everybody, you may save the whole of the civilised world."

"But suppose Whittle drops the first atomic bomb?" she said.

The thought pierced my heart and soul. I said earnestly, "If he does, that will be the end of all you care for. It must not happen."

She lost her eager smile and began to look despondent again, as when she had first entered the room.. "Can't you stop him, darling? After all, you were his superior officer."

"The emphasis is on the word 'were'", I said, wishing with all my heart that my command could stop the process Whittle had begun. "Now that he has made himself President, his lust for power will never be stopped, except by an assassin's bullet. Even that wouldn't stop his evil ideas from spreading. Another leader would arise. He has converted so many sincere and formerly good people to his views. I've tried all the arguments I know, but to no avail."

She held even more tightly onto my hand as she said, "Suppose he ultimately wins. What would happen to us then?"

"I suppose there are several alternatives, though none of them is very appealing. One would be to accept life as it would then be. We could be reasonably comfortable. The only trouble is more than half of the world's population would be no better than slaves. I doubt whether we could live with that. Another possibility would be to go underground."

"How do you mean?" she asked, looking puzzled.

"I mean continue to resist, but secretly, and hope for a miracle to change things. Or we could die fighting, I suppose. I could never bring myself to commit suicide, could you?"

She shuddered. "Never! But my darling, how long have we got left? Now I mean."

"Not long," I said sorrowfully. I wondered if this was part of an exquisite torture devised by Whittle, to allow us to come together and then to part again.

"Let's just hold each other then? Let's not talk any more about how horrible things are."

"Before we do that," I said, "can you describe to me where you are held? It's possible that I could escape again and take you with me."

She described where her prison was. After that we said little, except to reassure each other of our undying love.

At length the door opened. To my surprise Whittle walked into the room. He said, "I'm afraid I have to interrupt. Don't bother to stand. I wish to talk to both of you together."

I felt as if a magic spell had been broken. As a space ship man I had often been subject to jokes about coming down to earth with a bump. Now I knew what it meant in a desperate, metaphorical sense. Neither Fiona nor I said anything. However, we automatically sat further apart.

Whittle said, "I need an envoy, Bill, to talk to the enemy. I want to make a deal."

I said, "What exactly is involved?"

As if I hadn't spoken he continued, "I need somebody I can trust and you are the ideal man."

For a moment I thought he was going to suggest that Fiona and I should be joint envoys. However, he then said, "I shall keep this lady as security, of course. But if your mission is successful you will both be freed immediately. So there will be a reward for your labours."

I said again, "What is involved?"

He still ignored me and I began to feel very frustrated and angry. Fiona must have sensed this. She put her hand onto mine reassuringly. Whittle continued, "My scientists have produced an atomic bomb. I shall be ready to drop the first prototype in a fortnight. I want you to tell that to the opposition, especially to your friend Bernatti. He's making quite a name for himself as a general. But I shall make sure the first bomb is dropped on him. Tell him that it will be to encourage the others - to adapt a famous saying by Voltaire."

He laughed heartily at his own wit. He continued, "What I want to suggest is a division of power throughout the planet. You can tell them it will be permanent."

"They won't believe you," I said angrily, "and neither do I."

It's true," he said. "I'm really a peaceable man. I don't want the war to continue. Of course, I shall still try to convert them to my way of thinking. But I shall use peaceful means. One day there will be a united planet and I shall be in complete charge." His eyes shone as he visualised himself as the universal ruler.

Fiona said quietly, "There was a united planet before you came."

He said, his voice rising, "Of course there wasn't. Revolution was seething in people's minds all the time. All I did was to give one little twist and the truth came to the surface. I wish I could get you two to face the facts. We whites are a superior race. It will always be that way."

Fiona was about to speak again but I stopped her with a pressure of my hand. Instead I said, "Listen Andrew, Mr President if you like - we're in the wrong world. We don't belong here. Why don't you get all the scientists to find a way of getting us home again. That way, we can leave This World to sort itself out, and we can get on with our lives where we really belong."

He looked at me scornfully and said scathingly, "I have been sent to save the people of This World. Why don't you accept that, Bill? Come on, join me, and I'll give you all the power you can handle. But first I want you to go on this mission for me. Will you?"

I looked at Fiona. She nodded almost imperceptibly. "Very well," I said, "but I shall need a detailed brief."

He beamed ecstatically. "You shall have one, Bill. And you will take a team of experts with you. I can't trust them on their own yet. They may become contaminated by the old ideas. It will be different in five years time. There will be no thought of turning back then - because everybody will see my ideas working. The brave new world will be in existence by then. But in the meantime I shall put them in your care, Bill."

"Isn't that risky?" I said.

"Not when I've got your wife, Bill. There's no risk at all. You'll toe the line all right."

I gasped when he revealed that he knew we were married. He smiled sardonically. "I'm sorry I can't give you more time together. It will make you try harder. When you come back I'll let you sleep together. I can't be fairer than that now, can I?"

....

The team that went with me to Geneva included Bernard Rawlins, formerly my chief engineer. I gathered from this that Whittle was making doubly sure that none of the "natives" would turn against him when they were back in something resembling their normal environment. I was quite cool with Rawlins and he was uncomfortably aware of it, I noticed. I determined to stick to business while the discussions lasted.

I managed to buttonhole Anatole shortly after my arrival in Geneva and I explained my personal position to him, under an oath of secrecy. I also explained that I had tried to persuade Whittle in various ways to give up his empire building. Anatole was very understanding and wanted to know if a rescue attempt to bring out Fiona would avoid the need for me to go back.

In response I said hastily, "It would be too risky. Whittle would kill her without compunction. Mind you, I haven't given my word that I shall go back - but I have to because Whittle now knows that Fiona and I are married."

While we were having this conversation we were walking by the lakeside. Anatole was in mufti. He looked just as handsome whether he was in uniform or not, and I noticed that a lot of women looked in his direction as we were walking along.

The bright sunshine and the deep blue of the water made me feel light headed after my spell in prison. At one point, when I said that Whittle had made an atomic bomb, Anatole looked very grave. His swarthy face showed lines that had not been visible before. He said, "We are not quite as far ahead as that. Will he really bomb one of our cities?"

"I am in no doubt that he will," I said. "He also threatened you personally."

Anatole laughed, though not with any real humour. "I take that as a compliment. He must think I'm dangerous."

"Can't you hurry your boffins?" I said. "Once this man has total power he will be almost impossible to shift."

"We are three months away from producing a bomb, or so I'm told. I wonder if we could sabotage the Whitenik operation?"

"We could if we knew where it was," I said. "It's a great idea. And I know just the man to talk to. One of my former officers is part of the delegation. I know the man. I don't think he would want an atomic war, even though he has gone over to Whittle."

"So he might know where the bombs are made?"

"He was my chief engineer. I feel he would have taken sufficient interest in this kind of development to know where it's happening. Could we drop conventional bombs on the site?"

"It might be safer to make a commando raid," said Anatole. "I would go myself. How about you?"

"No, Anatole. Not that I don't want to. It's just that I'm very worried about what might happen to Fiona. Anyway, let me talk to Bernard Rawlins first."

....

Very unwillingly I became the centre of media interest at the Geneva negotiations. Unfortunately, my appearance on behalf of the Whiteniks, even though it was done under duress, was interpreted so as to place me in Whittle's camp. In vain I protested that I was a neutral trying to create harmony out of discord. I was not able, of course, to say that my wife was being held by Whittle because I knew he would mistreat her in some way if I divulged that information.

My trouble as negotiator was that my hands were tied. Whittle had dictated minimum terms from his viewpoint and I couldn't move from these. The Polyglot group wouldn't agree to the amount of territory that Whittle was wanting to claim permanently. Meanwhile the war continued and the casualty rate was rising daily.

I did manage a conversation with Father Christophoros while I was in Geneva. Under a symbolic seal of the confessional I explained to him what the true position was. It was wonderfully refreshing to speak with this tall, ascetic man who was now a close friend. He was unchanged either in attitude or appearance by recent events, except perhaps for several extra crow's feet around his eyes. I went to his local monastery to have a meal with him. It was while we were chatting afterwards that I confided in him. He gave me this advice: "Never give in to evil, Bill. The fight, even if it is physical, must go on. In fact, the true war is one of the spirit. The powers of darkness will prevail if they can, but the powers of light will always win through prayer and perseverance. I can tell you that all my monastic colleagues are engaged in a ceaseless chain of prayer for the victory of the righteous cause in this conflict."

My heart was warmed by this revelation. I said, "I can't understand how so many people have been gullible enough to accept Whittle's ideas. The trouble is, everything he says has a sort of logic about it. But any discerning person should be able to perceive the evil results of his actions."

"It's an old story," said Father Chris, his voice calm, despite the urgency of the situation. "Evil appears in many fair disguises. But tell me, Bill, how is your spiritual life? Don't you wish to be a priest any longer?"

"I can't answer that," I said, and truly I was now very uncertain about my previous calling. "At least, not until all this is over. But I guess if Whittle gains complete power my faith will be seriously dented. If God is listening to your monks then something awful must happen to Whittle, surely."

"Either in this life or the next. God moves in mysterious ways. Also, God's sense of time is different from ours. Our prayers may be answered a long time hence." Peace and love, as always, emanated from Christophoros as he was speaking.

"I find that very depressing," I said bitterly.

"You have to remember, Bill, that God's perspective is different from ours. To him there is no difference between this mortal life and what we would call post-mortal existence. Souls are on an endless pilgrimage towards God. Sometimes they slide back a little, but eventually they are called to resume their climb."

161

"It sounds a bit like salmon trying to go up river," I said, not at that moment too convinced of the truth of his theory.

"Not a bad analogy. But why don't you join us in chapel for a short service."

"I don't think so, Father Chris," I said. "My mood is out of tune with any form of worship at the moment."

He took hold of my hand and said, "I'll hold you in my prayers constantly, Bill. And so will my brothers."

I went away feeling somewhat comforted. The long perspective of the truly religious can be helpful at times."

....

I had to return to Whittle without an agreement. His reaction was predictable. "They're asking for it and they're going to get it," he said.

We weren't alone at the time. The whole delegation was reporting back. I knew that he would never retract his decision to drop an atomic bomb. The only question was where he would drop it. Unfortunately I hadn't had an opportunity to talk with Bernard Rawlins about the matter. I had promised somehow to let Anatole know if I found out where the atomic bombs were manufactured and stored.

After the meeting Whittle asked Bernard and myself to stay behind. "You'd better read this," he said.

He held out a newspaper and pointed to a headline which read, "Aliens to be banished from the planet."

I quickly scanned through the article. Apparently the Polyglot Parliament had passed a decree to place all the aliens in their space ship and send them off into space without a return ticket, and this regardless of whether we would have any hope of returning to our own world. Moreover, all aliens captured were to be put into solitary confinement until the arrangements for banishment had been made.

"Well?" said Whittle, raising his eyebrows sarcastically.

I remained silent, wondering what was coming next. He said, "Does that change your mind about which side you're on? It's now a matter of survival. I hereby give you freedom to return to the Polyglots. Alternatively, you can stay here with us."

"What about Fiona?" I said, inwardly fearful.

He laughed raucously. "I've arranged for you both to have a private flat in the palace. She's already in it. Why don't you go and try the bed for bounce?"

I thought quickly. The best plan seemed to be to go along with Whittle's offer until Fiona and I could escape. Meanwhile I could tackle Bernard and try to get him to help me to foil Whittle's plans. I said, "I'll join you, Andy. It's the only sensible thing to do."

He smiled broadly and said, "I knew you were too intelligent not to see where your best interests lie."

Bernard said, "When does the balloon go up?"

"I shall issue an ultimatum. One week from now a bomb will be dropped on New York. That should serve as a serious warning of things to come."

I must say I admired Bernard for what he said next.

"I'm a bit worried about this, Andy. Wouldn't it be better to keep the atomic bomb in reserve. the trouble is they may also have it and they could drop one on us."

"Don't be so faint hearted, Bernard" said Whittle scornfully. "Anyway, if they already had the bomb they would have dropped it by now. I must go. I have things to do."

He stalked out and left us. I said, "Why don't we take a walk in the gardens, Bernard? I could do with some fresh air."

Bernard seemed surprised, probably because I wasn't dashing off to the flat to see Fiona. However, he agreed to my proposal readily enough.

When we were well away from the main building I said cautiously, "How do you feel about an atomic war, Bernard?"

"I'm frightened," he said. "We could destroy ourselves and even life on this planet."

"I agree," I said. "But how can we stop it?"

He looked puzzled. "I'm not sure what you're getting at, skipper."

I decided to put my cards on the table. "Listen Bernard, I know Whittle has done brilliantly in some ways, but I really don't agree with the way things are going. He must be stopped. What do you think?"

I looked him straight in the eye and he turned red. I waited, not wishing to let him off the hook. I thought I knew my man. Finally he said, "OK I agree with you. I think Andy's gone too far. I didn't realise what I was getting myself into when I joined him."

"Where are the bombs?" I said bluntly.

"Honestly I don't know," he said. "Andy follows a policy of deliberately not letting the right hand know what the left is doing."

During the next week Bernard and I did everything we could to stop Whittle pressing the bomb button, but it was of no use. Exactly as Whittle had promised, an atomic bomb was dropped on New York. The results were predictably devastating. However, Whittle had underestimated the resolve of the Polyglots. They swore to fight on. I expected Whittle to drop another bomb, but he didn't. He didn't explain to anyone why he didn't follow up the first attack with another. I could only guess that his scientists had not yet produced enough bombs to be able to expend another one just yet.

Chapter Thirteen

Fiona and I had an early night. We made love with great passion and tenderness. Afterwards I got up to make some coffee. Then I sat on the edge of the bed sipping mine while Fiona sat up in bed to drink hers. Her full breasts showed through the veil of blonde hair which fell across her body like a golden cascade. It was an enchanting sight. My love was very physical, but the spiritual quality of her beauty also gave my love an unearthly quality. It was as if I were aware of her simultaneously in two dimensions which, however, did not contradict each other. Her beauty was enhanced by the goodness which always radiated from the centre of her being.

"What are you thinking about?" she said.

"You, of course," I said truthfully.

"What are we going to do, Bill?"

I was rather stumped at her question because I was wondering the same thing myself. I said, "At the moment, I'm just so glad to be with you again that I don't particularly care. I have become an existentialist. Only now is important."

"I know you don't really mean that," she said. "Of course, I feel just as happy as you. But deep down there is this feeling that we are still prisoners."

I lowered my voice to a whisper, just in case there were any bugging devices around. "I mean to escape as soon as possible, sweetheart. I hope I will be able to persuade Bernard to come with us."

"When?" she said, just as quietly.

"I shall speak to Bernard tomorrow and if he agrees we'll go at the first possible opportunity."

"Suppose he doesn't agree," she said, her voice trembling slightly, despite her great self control. "Won't he tell Whittle?"

I tried to speak with a confidence I did not feel. "I don't think so, darling. I'm sure he's seen the error of Whittle's ways. Mind you, I'm not looking forward to walking straight into a prison and solitary confinement. But I hope to get support from Father Chris and Anatole."

She shook her head doubtfully. "But the idea of going to prison might be sufficient to stop Bernard Rawlins from coming with us. After all, he's an important man here, and he has his freedom."

"I shall try to negotiate his freedom on the other side as well, so that he can work with us for a Polyglot victory." If we managed to escape, I was very hopeful that we could retain our freedom so that we could fight.

"I'm torn in two," she said. "I want the end of the war, but when victory comes and Whittle is captured you will all be banished. I want to come with you, wherever the space ship takes you, but I suspect they won't let me. In any case, how long would we be able to survive in space?"

"They might let me stay here because of you," I said. "Fortunately, I have good friends. We can only put ourselves in God's hands."

She looked so sad I felt like weeping myself. "If they separate us, Bill, I shall be miserable for the rest of my life. I'm not even sure that I could face life without you."

"Me too," I said. I leaned over to kiss her.

"I shall pray that we can stay together," she said, a tear falling down her cheek. "I did so want to have children with you."

We remained silent for a few moments, holding on to each other for comfort. Then I said, "I wonder if they would let us stay here together, in This World I mean, if we did have a family. That's a thought. But if they still decided to send me off into space without you, that would leave you on your own to bring up a family."

Her eyes were moist with tears as she said, "At least I would have a bit of you to look after, my darling. But let's see what happens if we can get back to our own side."

"You do realise I'm tarred with Whittle's brush," I warned. "The mass media made a meal of it. I'm a real villain according to them."

I was really beginning to feel something like a leper. I suppose, if someone keeps telling you that you are bad, then you start to accept it.

"I shall soon put the record straight," she said. "And surely Anatole will make sure the true story is spread around."

She then smiled invitingly and said, "I'm not really sleepy yet. Aren't you coming back to bed?"

I didn't need a second invitation.

....

I managed to get Bernard on his own during the following day. He was crossing the courtyard of the palace and I caught sight of him through the window, so I hurried down and invited him to come up for coffee, which he did. He looked more than a little embarrassed when he greeted Fiona. However, we soon settled down to chat, mainly about generalities like the war situation. After coffee the three of us went for a stroll. At length, I said, "Bernard, Fiona and I want to get away from here. Back to the Polyglot side, I mean. Would you like to come with us?"

He paused for a moment, his brow furrowing. Nervously he swept back his unruly dark hair with one hand. "I'm not too sure about that," he said. "I have a good life here and if a treaty is eventually signed life will settle down. But what happens if I come with you? I'll walk straight into gaol. And by all accounts it will be in solitary confinement. That could be forever, because I don't think they will ever capture Andy. Even if they did, they would then shoot us off into space where we would die shortly afterwards. Honestly, skipper, it doesn't sound like a very brilliant prospect to me. Perhaps I should take my chances with the Whiteniks, even though I don't agree with what is going on."

There was logic in his argument. However, I said, "The same could apply to me, Bernard. But I have friends in high places. So has Fiona. We hope to persuade the powers that be that we are on their side. In fact, I hope to spend the rest of a very happy life in This World."

"There was something else," he said, turning slightly pink. "I have a friend. Well, more of a fiancée, I suppose. Shirley and I hope to get married when things settle down a bit. I can't leave her."

Fiona said quickly, "She can come too, of course."

"I can't speak for her" he said cautiously. "It means I shall have to tell her everything and she will have to make up her own mind."

Fiona and I looked at each other. I was worried about this new factor, but I said, "If you can guarantee that she won't talk about what Fiona and I want to do, that's OK The thing is, if she doesn't object to coming, will you both join us?"

"I can't make any promises," he said evasively. "But neither of us will give you away. That's all I can guarantee. I need a bit of time to think out my position."

I said, as persuasively as I could, "Sometimes, Bernard, principle has to be strong enough to stand against the crowd. Anyway, your talents are wasted on Whittle. He would drop you any time, if he thought you weren't of use to him. It's a question of what's right. Good against evil, if you like. I know it sounds a little pompous - but what we're talking about is the survival of civilisation on this planet. You have to vote with your feet and every vote counts."

He gnawed at his lower lip, obviously in a quandary. Then he said, "I think she'll come. She hates Whittle. If she will agree, then that's it. We're with you."

My spirits rose slightly and I said, "Let's assume we are going to go ahead with the plan, Bernard. What is the best way to make our move? We need a reason to get out of the palace, don't we. And then we have to cross the border, which will be guarded."

He thought for a moment. "Shirley lives half a mile away. Why don't you invite us to dinner here. I'll mention it to Whittle. Then we can invite you back - which I will also mention to him. I have the use of an electric car. It's a pity, of course, that the intercity underground has been sabotaged. I think I'm right, though, in saying that only the main roads across the border are strongly guarded. On one of the minor roads there will be a small guard, but we could probably bluff our way through. People are allowed to cross for funerals and things like that."

"I see," I said, hopeful ideas beginning to form in my mind. "Fiona could have an imaginary dead aunt. The trouble is she can't fib convincingly."

Fiona laughed. "Don't you believe it. A lie in a good cause is justifiable. If my conscience is clear I can lie if necessary. I'm sure I can."

Bernard smiled for the first time. "It could be Shirley's aunt, if you like."

We all laughed and relaxed. I now felt fairly confident that at least we could have a go.

....

Whittle said, smiling broadly, "I'm pleased you and Bernard are on social terms, Bill. He told me he was coming to dinner with you. Actually, my own social life needs broadening."

I could see he wanted me to invite him as well. I was searching my mind for a way to put him off, but he continued, "I could bring my girl friend, if you like. You've already met her, remember?"

I did remember. The first time I had met her she had been in bed with Whittle. I couldn't do anything else but agree, otherwise he would have been suspicious. Consequently, Fiona found herself (with a little help from me) cooking for six instead of for four. I could see that this unforeseen event could complicate our plans. Suppose Whittle insisted on coming to Shirley's house when we accepted the planned return invitation?

The dinner party in our flat was an uncomfortable affair. This was not only because Whittle was in the way. The discomfort was caused mainly by the immediate, mutual dislike between Fiona and Whittle's girl friend, who was called Trish. There were some superficial similarities between the two women. Both had long, fair hair. Both had good figures and were about the same height. However, Trish was an inveterate giggler and she particularly giggled when Whittle cracked one of his awful jokes. Power had not improved my former second in command. He had become overbearing and quite crude. Bernard's girl friend was different again. She was a quiet, shy brunette who said very little during the whole evening. She seemed to be a sensible woman and Fiona took to her readily. Shirley had, in fact, agreed to escape with us.

It was a great relief when it was time for the guests to depart. Just before they went Bernard said, "We'll expect you next Thursday then, Bill. You and Fiona, of course. How about you and Trish, chief? Would you like to come?"

I was thunderstruck at this invitation. What on earth was Bernard playing at? However, Whittle said immediately, "Sorry, Bernie. I shall be away for a couple of days and I shan't be able to come. But everybody must come to my place. I have a first class chef and he'll do us proud. We'll fix up a date when I return."

Bernard and Shirley stayed behind for a few minutes. It was then I learned that Bernard had known all along that

Whittle would be away the following Thursday. By his clever stratagem he had removed any possible suspicion that Whittle might have had.

When we were alone Fiona said, "I'm not surprised Whittle has to use a chef. I can't imagine that woman being able to boil an egg."

I smiled secretly. It was not often Fiona was catty about another woman. In a sense it was a relief to know that she shared the weaknesses of other people. Sometimes she seemed so perfect I felt I couldn't live up to her standards.

....

We decided beforehand that the pseudo dinner party at Shirley's house would actually take place, even though we planned to leave for good just after midnight. During the meal Bernard noticed that his fiancée was looking rather sad. Indeed, I had noticed this myself and I was worried about her. However, Bernard said, his deep concern showing, "What's wrong, my sweet petal?"

Fiona and I looked at each other, hardly daring to smile at this affectionate form of address. Shirley said, though with trembling voice, "Nothing, my love. Nothing at all."

Fiona said, "Really, men haven't any idea. I know what's wrong. She's upset at leaving this beautiful little house, and this lovely city where she's lived for the whole of her life. That's it, isn't it, Shirley?"

She nodded and strove to hold back the tears. Bernard said, ""We'll build a new one, just like this, in Napoli, my darling sweetheart."

We were going to head for Naples where there was a strong Polyglot enclave. At this promise Shirley managed a watery smile, but conversation wasn't exactly sparkling.

When we had finished eating Shirley said, "I'll clear the table and tidy up."

"What's the point, darling?" said Bernard. "We shall be leaving in an hour and we shan't be coming back."

Shirley said, "I want to leave the house tidy. I want to think of it as a tidy little house."

I said quickly, before she burst into tears, "What an excellent idea. We'll give you a hand."

....

To convince any guards we might meet we wore black armbands when we set off in Bernard's electric car. We headed south on a route planned by Bernard himself, keeping away from important trunk roads. It was a moonlit night and very warm. The hills and woodland were bathed in a silvery glow that was almost unearthly.

There was some desultory talk, but we were all slightly nervous, and idle chatter was difficult. At one point, where the scenery was exceptionally beautiful, I said, "This sort of night reminds me of Walter de la Mare's poem. I remember learning it at school. What's it called again? I remember. It's 'Silver'. How does it go? 'Slowly, silently, now the moon, Walks the night in her silver shoon...'."

"What a lovely poem," said Fiona. "I can't say I've heard of the poet, though."

"In Transworld he was early twentieth century, I think," I said. "A bit before your time. You've heard of him, haven't you Bernard?"

"Can't say I have. I'm not keen on poetry. I don't see the point of it really."

I was disappointed at this reaction and we all lapsed into silence for a while. Then Bernard said, "We pass through a village along this valley shortly. We'd better be ready in case we're stopped. Remember, let Shirley do the talking."

Strangely, it had turned out that Shirley did have an aunt in what was now categorised as a Polyglot area. This meant that she would be able to tell the absolute truth in every respect except for the one detail that her aunt was presumably alive and kicking and not lying in a coffin.

We came to the village Bernard had mentioned. It was called Monte Bianco. It was like a ghost town. The roofs were shining white under the moon and the buildings seemed to be in a mediaeval style, though I assumed this was a convention used by some architect. We sped through the village without incident. Bernard said, "I don't think there are any other towns or villages on our route. There is only the border to contend with."

"Have you any idea how it might be policed?" I said.

"Not really," said Bernard. "I couldn't ask questions about it in case I aroused anybody's suspicions. But the usual thing is a Whitenik post on our side. And probably about half a mile further on a Polyglot post."

"Blind bats and blundering buffaloes," I muttered. "It hadn't occurred to me that we would have two posts to pass. We might have more trouble with the Polyglot side. After all, they are the ones who will feel they are having to admit enemies into their territory."

Fiona took hold of my hand and squeezed it. "If they don't accept Shirley's story leave it to me," she said.

I must admit I wondered what she had in mind. I was soon to find out. It was just breaking dawn when we reached the border. A Whitenik soldier waved us down. He seemed to have several comrades in the small house that marked the crossing point. Shirley told her story in a few well chosen words.

The soldier said, "Which town did you say?"

"Alife," she said.

"I come from there," he said. "Where does your aunt live?"

"In the Piazza del Duomo," said Shirley, at the same time beginning to sob.

"Off you go then," said the soldier, waving us off.

173

When we came to the Polyglot border post we were again stopped. Four guards were outside and others were in the neighbouring house. One of the guards was an officer. There was a metal gate across the road and we had no choice but to stop. The officer walked over. He had a slightly pompous air about him. He was a dark, handsome man, aged about thirty five, I should have guessed.

"Where are you going?" he said officiously.

Shirley went through her story again. The officer said, "Kindly get out all of you."

We did as he said. I felt quite scruffy, partly because of my unshaven cheeks. The officer said, "You do not look smart enough to be going to a funeral."

Shirley explained we had been travelling a long way and that we would clean up when we reached our destination. He looked us up and down suspiciously. After a couple of minutes he said, "Right, you can go."

Just as he said this one of his men shouted, "Just a minute, sir, I think I recognise one of them."

He pointed to me. "I'm sure that man is one of the aliens."

I remained silent. The officer looked at me carefully. Then he said, "I don't recognise him. Are you sure?"

The man came over to take a closer look. He stroked his chin. "Now I'm not so sure," he said.

The officer said to me, "What's your name?"

Before I could answer Fiona said, "He is one of the aliens and he is also my husband. He wishes to place himself in the hands of the authorities. This man wishes to do the same."

She pointed to Bernard who, at Fiona's words, looked as if he were ready for his own funeral. "But," Fiona continued, "I want you to 'phone this number. Ask for General Bernatti and tell him to send some men to pick us up."

The officer looked very doubtful. "If you don't, you will be in serious trouble," said Fiona. "All you have to say is that Bill and Fiona need his help."

"I think I'd rather hand you all over to my immediate superior," said the officer.

Fiona spoke more sharply than I have ever heard her speak before. She said imperiously, "If you don't do as I say I'll see that you are demoted. General Bernatti is our oldest friend. In fact, I'm sure he'll come himself when he knows we're here."

That seemed to convince the man. "Come inside," he said. "I'll put you under guard until I check your story."

Fiona was right. Within the hour a helicopter arrived and Anatole came into the house. The officer looked quite crestfallen. Anatole greeted us ecstatically. Bernard Rawlins began to look more cheerful. Fiona whispered something to Anatole. I couldn't catch what she said, but she was pointing towards the officer who had stopped us. Anatole went over to him and said in a voice everyone could hear, "Well done. You will receive a promotion for this."

The officer beamed his thanks at Fiona. She smiled graciously. Then, within minutes we were flying away in the helicopter.

....

On the way back to Napoli, Anatole told us several pieces of news. One was that a team of scientists claimed to have cracked the problem of how to send the aliens back to their own world. However, the exact details were not to be confided to anyone outside the research team who had come up with the results. Moreover, in due course, when the banishment was to be put into effect, all the aliens would be put onto their spaceship at the appropriate astronomical moment, in the hope that they would be transported back to Transworld. When we had disappeared from the universe known in This World, it would be assumed we had reached home safely and the secret formula would be destroyed to prevent any further contact between the two worlds. As the research leader had said, "We don't wish to be contaminated again by these amoral, intrusive, primitive life forms."

Another piece of news he gave us, which was particularly pleasing to Fiona, was that a vast prayer chain had been initiated by the group to which Father Christophoros belonged. This extended way beyond his own group and even beyond Christianity. All the main religions were taking part, the idea being that an irresistible spiritual force would enable good to triumph over the evil spread by the satanic alien forces. I'm not sure that I was very pleased to be classified as a satanic alien, but nevertheless I hoped that the prayers would be answered.

A third piece of very good news Anatole gave us was that Professor Cherrington and myself would be exempt from the sentence to solitary imprisonment which had been imposed on all the aliens. I immediately pointed out that Bernard had sacrificed his comfortable life with the Whiteniks to help the Polyglot cause. Anatole promised that he would do his best to obtain exemption for Bernard as well. In due course, this exemption was achieved and Bernard and I together were able to devote our energies to helping the Polyglots to victory.

Three days after our escape Whittle announced to the world that he was going to use another weapon of destruction against what he called the Sodom and Gommorah of Polyglot power. He did not specify which two cities he intended to attack. It was assumed by everybody that he was going to drop some more atomic bombs. In the event he dropped bombs containing poisonous gas on London and Toronto. By the grace of God, gales of some force arose around both cities at approximately the same time as the bombs were dropped. The gas was largely dispersed into the atmosphere and nobody was killed, though many suffered burns. This event was presented as a saving act of God by those who were taking part in the chain of prayer. Certainly, it was a very strange coincidence. When I discussed it with Fiona she was sure it was an example of divine intervention. Personally, I decided to keep an open mind in case Whittle acted again, but more successfully.

Chapter Fourteen

Fiona and I went to stay at the Mount Zion monastery in Derbyshire for a while. It was Father Chris who had invited us. Bernard Rawlins and Shirley were allowed to come along as well. Professor Cherrington was also invited along and he, too, had been exempted from solitary confinement in prison. Regrettably, all the other "aliens", except of course for those with Whittle, were put in gaol. The best that Anatole was able to do for them was too see that once a week they were allowed to come out of their solitary state to spend an hour with their friends.

At this time, back in a religious context, I was able to resume some sort of prayer life. One of the things I did was to compile two prayer lists. One was of those in solitary confinement. When I prayed for them I tried to picture their faces. Jim Catchpole was unfortunately dead, as was Daren Quigley. However, I thought constantly about Kevin Oakley, Jack Gratton, Dryden Jenkins and Tom Adsworth. They were all good men. The second list included Whittle and those comrades who had gone onto his side. I still believed there was a lot of good in them, except for Whittle. I really thought he had brought so much evil into This World that the Almighty would take a very dim view of him. Still, I thought it was right that he should be included on the prayer list. The others, for whom I still had hopes of a conversion to the side of right, were Joseph Blenkinsop, Ernest Clamp, Kirkbride and Stevenson.

Professor Cherrington took a very gloomy view of events and so did Father Christophoros. They were both convinced that in the short term Whittle would take control of the whole planet. I think they were deliberately taking the most pessimistic view in public, but that they were actually hoping privately that the Polyglots would win. Of course, they both believed that ultimately God would see that justice was done, but that would only be after the disaster to the planet had run its full course. Anatole and I had discussed the possibility of Whitenik victory and we had agreed that the only policy would be to organise a resistance movement.

It was at this time that a very strange phenomenon occurred. In my experience, when great disasters come about, there is always somebody who puts on the mantle of a prophet. This was what happened during the time we were at Mount Zion. The would be prophet who appeared could be described as a dispensationalist, or so Professor Cherrington informed me. This means that a person believes that God's master plan is divided into stages, each of which is revealed in turn. During each stage human beings are tested and, at the end of the day, are found wanting. Then they must face God's wrathful judgment. Various groups have defined the stages in different ways, but essentially they all agree that the last stage will include the return of Christ in majesty to rule the world.

The man who set himself up to be a prophet was an American evangelist. His name was Noah Smith. I saw him on television several times. He was a tall, dark, good looking man with a heavy black beard. He was normally dressed in a robe made of skins and he wore a girdle round his waist and leather sandals, presumably in imitation of John the Baptist.

One day Father Chris announced to the monks and guests that there was to be a television broadcast by Noah Smith throughout what was now called the free world. We were all invited to gather in the largest room the monastery possessed in order to watch this programme. During that day the monks were all agog in anticipation of a wonderful evangelical experience. Father Chris himself was more moderate in his expectations. However, The Professor was just as excited as the monks. Fiona and I tried to remain calm, but despite ourselves we were infected by the air of excitement in the monastery.

The programme was introduced by an American Archbishop of the Episcopalian Church tradition, though of course, in This World, denominational boundaries existed only as traditional ways of doing things and these imaginary barriers were crossed frequently for true intercommunion. Nevertheless, the various traditions persisted in all their glory. The Archbishop was in the commentators' box in a huge stadium which was absolutely packed out for the occasion. Noah Smith had apparently created quite a stir in North America. On the platform was a women's choir, each member wearing crimson robes. There must have been a hundred of them and they started off the proceedings with a traditional hymn about God's love. It seems the idea was to build up the tension during the service with Noah Smith's sermon as the climax.

The hymns became hotter and hotter and a series of readers and speakers made incidental contributions. The emphasis began to change and the themes developed into a catalogue of human sins interspersed with threats of coming judgment. Just before Noah Smith appeared there was a great fanfare of trumpets. Then the great man strode on, flanked by six acolytes whose job was to orchestrate the applause and to shout Amen or Alleluia at frequent intervals. There was thunderous applause when Smith walked onto the middle of the platform. When the applause subsided Smith held up both hands and then stood with his head bowed while the choir sang a beautiful version of the Lord's Prayer. When the music stopped Smith stood up, still silent, and held out his arms as if to embrace everybody. After a pause he said emotionally, "Bless you my brothers and sisters," in his deep booming voice.

The camera swept across the congregation, pausing here and there to take in an enraptured face. As soon as Smith began to speak the camera again focussed on him. He began almost in a whisper and every ear was straining to hear his words: "My friends, my dear friends, my companions in the Lord, I have been sent here today by the Spirit. I did not choose to come. The Lord chose me to come."

He paused dramatically. The acolytes clapped enthusiastically and everybody cheered. Noah Smith smiled beatifically as if he stood on a cloud and was looking down from heaven. He continued, his voice rising a shade, "My dear friends, I have some terrible news for the world. God's awful judgment is impending. It is hanging over us like a sword that will pierce the heart of every person breathing God's good air which has been fouled by a horrible pestilence. It is the pestilence of sin, my friends, an infectious pestilence which will take over the world unless we all pray simultaneously for God to act."

He paused once more. The wait seemed interminable before he spoke again. "Brothers and sisters, pray with me for the world as it reaches its final revelation. Pray that we shall be ready. Indeed, the time is ripe now and the Holy One is with us. He has been born again. As Scripture says, 'He is a prince in the line of David.'"

He then went on at some length to explain that the new Prince who had been born in the royal family was the Messiah. Whittle was cast in the role of King Herod and the Emperor Nero all rolled into one. The aliens were castigated as the emissaries of Satan who should be exterminated. Fiona held my hand tightly at that point. This dramatic introduction was followed by a rather boring review of the history of the world according to Noah Smith and his dispensationalist sect. Beginning with humanity before the Fall in the Garden of Eden, which he called the Age of Innocence, he proceeded through six stages. At last he came to the final and seventh stage and he became very dramatic again. He spoke now with great power and volume. "This is a war, not of the world, but of the cosmic powers. The forces of Satan are lined up against us; but the angels are on our side. The angels' chariots are greater in number than the chariots of the devilish powers. Stand up and fight, brothers and sisters. Stand up in the Lord and fight the good fight. What matter if you die in God's cause? He will raise you again like a seed in the ground and you will wear a crown in heaven. March onwards, Christian soldiers. March on to victory. Who is on the Lord's side?"

There was a great cheer at this point. The sermon concluded on a more sober note. To me, this part of what he said sounded much more sincere than his previous rhetoric. He made an appeal for the Whiteniks to lay down their arms so that peace could reign as the Messiah grew to manhood. Finally, to another fanfare of trumpets, he left the platform, after speaking for an hour and a half.

....

Somehow or another the mass media found that Professor Cherrington was staying at Mount Zion. He was asked to appear on television in order to answer the accusations of Noah Smith. However, the Professor refused to do so unless he could meet face to face with the prophet himself. It was several weeks before Smith agreed to a confrontation. Meanwhile the world war was increasing in intensity and this added urgency to Smith's message. The mass media were portraying Whittle as the epitome of Satan and even as Satan himself. Yet again, all the monks gathered in the big hall to watch the self acclaimed prophet. Yet again, the atmosphere in Mount Zion was electric. All the monks liked and respected Professor Cherrington. At the same time many of them agreed with the views expressed by Noah Smith, in general terms anyway.

The programme was arranged as an armchair discussion. Because of the three dimensional nature of This World television it almost seemed as if the protagonists were sitting in the room with us. Professor Cherrington looked nervous at the beginning of the programme, whereas Smith looked confident and calm. However, the prophet was taken aback when the Professor suggested that the programme should begin with a prayer. The chair person, a woman Professor of Theology in the States, agreed to this immediately and Smith had no choice but to accept the idea, each man having agreed to say a prayer. Noah Smith said his prayer first. I must say it was impressive, though somewhat extravagant in its language. Mainly he appealed to God's help in defeating the powers of Satan. Professor Cherrington's prayer was more restrained. He asked for the Holy Spirit's guidance in the discussion "that the light of truth should dwell among us."

Smith looked slightly less confident after the prayers and the Professor looked much more relaxed. The chair person asked the Professor to speak first on behalf of "the visitors to our planet." I must say I was proud of Anselm Cherrington that day. He started off by agreeing that some of the aliens had created the war situation because of their ambitions for power. He then argued that only some of the aliens had succumbed to this temptation and that the others were not to be placed in the same category. He went on to argue that while Satan had certainly been at work it had been in his capacity as tempter and that Whittle was simply a human being who had taken the wrong turning, but who certainly deserved punishment for his wrongdoings. Finally the Professor explained that some of us wished to stay in This World to help to reconstruct society after the misguided powers led by Whittle had been defeated.

By contrast, Smith's introductory statement rambled in all directions and added very little to what he had already said many times in public. Nevertheless, there was a hypnotic quality in his voice which was hard to resist. Will power was needed to separate the content of his speech from the overpowering personality of the speaker. I knew that discerning people would be able to achieve this, but that many others would accept his words because of the astonishing capacity he had to convince people of his sincerity. He had the ability to utter almost meaningless banalities as if they were the Ten Commandments newly carved in stone.

These two introductory statements were followed by a series of questions from the chair. Again, the Professor came across as a simple but good man who stood for justice and peace. Smith, on the other hand, now seemed to me to be a religious bigot of the worst kind who was also a warmonger. Unfortunately, not everyone agreed with my assessment of the two men. Certainly the vast majority of the monks agreed that the Professor had done well, but most of them still believed in Noah Smith as the man divinely inspired for the times. The mass media were equally committed to adulate Smith. Professor Cherrington was virtually damned by faint praise. Others apart from myself found this infuriating. Father Chris was fuming at what he called the "prejudices of the uninformed." Some commentators still argued that in due course all the aliens would have to be deported as had been agreed earlier. Headlines like "The scum must be skimmed", were common enough.

....

During ensuing weeks it became clear that the war was going Whittle's way. Above all he was winning the armaments race. Heavy bombing raids took place all over Polyglot territory, though no further atomic bombs were dropped at that time. The Polyglot side was unable to match this onslaught and morale fell very low. We listened to several more speeches by Noah Smith. His message changed as the Polyglots lost ground. He began to preach of defeat at the hands of Satan and put forward the idea that evil powers would rule the world for a thousand years. He seemed to have forgotten his earlier message about the Messiah and, indeed, he didn't mention the royal prince at all in his later preaching. In one respect his message was unchanged. He insisted that the aliens were possessed by Satanic powers. A few monks at Mount Zion remained faithful to Smith's strange gospel, but most of them became very sceptical about the man. I was relieved at this, because I thought that if other people felt the same way then attacks on the aliens might cease. However, this did not prove to be the case. Even though sensible media people recognised that not all the aliens were tarred with Whittle's brush, nevertheless they argued that it would be better if all the aliens were banished for ever from the planet.

One day about this time Anatole Bernatti arrived unexpectedly at the monastery. He was alone. After a meal with the monks and ourselves he was closeted with Father Christophoros for some time. This all seemed very mysterious and I couldn't help speculating about the purpose of Anatole's visit. Two hours after the two men had started their meeting a monk came to me where I was working in the garden. He said, "Bill, the prior would like to see you, if you have time."

The monks were always very polite and normally I complied with their wishes without demur, as I did on this occasion. However, the extra ingredient was my curiosity as to what was going on and I wasted no time in going to Father Chris's office. When I went in the two were sitting looking at each other in silence and their faces were very grave. A ghost of a smile flitted across the Prior's face as he said, "Thank you for coming, Bill. We feel you might be able to help us."

"What's the problem?" I said.

Father Chris nodded to Anatole who said, "The political situation is looking grim, Bill. In fact, I think the Polyglot armed forces are going to have to surrender."

I was shattered by this news, but I managed to stammer, "How terrible. What are we going to do about it?"

"We're worried about the royal family," said Anatole. "I mean the members of the family close to the King. The Queen, of course, and Prince Edward and Princess Anne - but above all the baby prince Charles. As you know, they have now moved to Munich which is the Queen's home town."

"How do you mean? " I said. "What particular issue is worrying you?"

"Whittle will almost certainly execute them, according to our intelligence. He intends to give himself the title of Emperor and he won't stand for any rivals."

"Where can they go?" I said. "And why are you telling me?"

"Father Christophoros and I have been talking about the situation. That's why I came - but I had you in mind as well. I want you to bring the royal family to Britain. They must go into hiding."

"Are you sure I'm the best person to do this, Anatole? After all, I am something of a marked man."

Father Christophoros smiled broadly and said, "You can become a novice monk for the occasion. That should be a good disguise."

I stared at him, wondering if he was serious. Then Anatole said, "We talked it over before you came in, Bill. We need a man of action, but he needs a good cover story. You know enough about the monastery to pass yourself off as a monk, I'm sure."

I must admit I felt slightly confused. Father Chris said gently, "Moral decisions are often difficult. And perhaps it will be even more difficult if we ask you to let Fiona come as well. But she would be able to cover up for any deficiencies in your knowledge of our ways."

"I'm not too sure about that," I said. "Fiona will have to decide for herself, and in any case, I need to know more about your plan. How on earth am I going to get four adults and a baby from Munich to Britain, especially when they are as well known as the royal family?"

"You'll get some advice from experts," said Anatole. "The thing is we shall contact the King beforehand to apprise him of the situation. That will ensure he is expecting you. At the same time we shall warn him that the family must pose as refugees fleeing from the war zone."

"How shall we travel?" I asked. "The underground connections between Britain and Europe have been disrupted. Presumably we can travel by electric car across to the North Sea, but how do we get across to Britain?"

"That's all taken care of," said Anatole confidently. "A submarine will pick you up off the Dutch coast and will drop you off in the Humber Estuary. Provided Britain isn't occupied by enemy forces by then we can collect you and bring you here."

"What happens after that?" I said, eaten with curiosity.

"The royal family go to live on a farm as tenants of the monastery. It's about eight miles from here. They can stay there till we regain control."

"I have only one condition before I agree to go," I said.

I must say Anatole looked slightly worried when I mentioned a condition. He had assumed that I would undertake the mission at the drop of a hat. "What is it?" he said tersely.

"I want to be with you if we start an underground movement."

Anatole's expression changed to a wide grin. "You're on. Now why don't you go and have a chat with Fiona to see if she will go with you? There are one or two other things I wish to discuss with Christophoros."

....

München or Munich was an interesting city. This was true in my own world and it was certainly true in This World. However, there was little time to look round when Fiona and I arrived at the underground station of Munich after a fretful journey. The communication system had been badly dislocated because of the war. We had crossed the channel by motor launch, after which we had made no less than four separate underground train journeys when one would normally have sufficed. Between these journeys we had done some motoring and some river journeying. In all, it had taken us five days to do what should have been a journey of a few hours. I was in a very irritable state when we arrived, partly because of travel hold ups, but also because I was supposed to be playing the part of a celibate monk. This meant that Fiona and I couldn't show each other any overt affection and it surprised me to learn that this had the effect of upsetting our relationship in a very real sense. I suppose frustration leads to anger.

Anyway, we managed to find the mansion where the royal family was living on the outskirts of the town without any difficulty and we had been able to hire an electric car to get there. Our supposed reason for travelling was to take part in a minor religious assembly which was taking place in Munich at the time - and we did put in a token appearance during the day following our arrival. However, our main objective was very much in mind and we met all five members of the royal family the evening we arrived. They were in a very nervous state because there had been an air raid the night before.

King William looked even more ordinary than I remembered. However, he had lost some weight and wasn't quite so heavy round the waist. The Queen was very quiet and pale. Her hair had turned completely white. Prince Edward, on the other hand, was confident and cheerful and asked me all kinds of questions about the possibility of working with an underground force. Princess Anne was dressed in a green leisure suit. My impression that she had a deep inner tranquillity remained unchanged. She looked very beautiful. When I tried to analyse this beauty I found that her various features were not too different from those of any other attractive woman. I concluded that it was her mysterious inner radiance that made her special. This was particularly the case when she was with the baby Prince Charles. We were allowed to see him in his cot. He was a golden haired boy with chubby, pink cheeks. As he lay there, fast asleep, it was difficult to think of him as a Messiah.

We discussed our plan with the royal family and they readily agreed to our proposal. On the journey they would dress in undistinguished clothes. Fiona and I would supposedly be on our way back from the conference and the tale would be that we had picked up a family of refugees who were trying to get to Britain where they had relatives.

....

We travelled north to Nürnburg and then across to Frankfurt without incident. Here and there we did come across little groups of people who were obviously refugees and this, I thought, lent colour to our cover story. We also passed several groups of soldiers who accepted our reasons for travelling readily enough. We stayed a night in Koblenz and then journeyed on towards Holland. It took us three days to get to the coast. We first saw the North Sea, in fact, at a little place called Scheveningen. This, however, was too far south for our rendezvous.

We drove along the coastal road, taking our time, because we couldn't contact the submarine until noon the following day. The agreement was that the crew of the submarine would surface each day at noon until we turned up. Fiona was showing relief and happiness that we had come so far without mishap. She took the child onto her lap and began to talk to him. Not that Prince Charles could respond to her remarks, of course, though he seemed relaxed enough to be with Fiona. I kept glancing at the two of them as I drove and I must say I thought Fiona looked very much at home with a baby. I wondered if we would ever get round to having any children of our own.

It is a strange fact of life that just when people are beginning to relax after a period of danger, very often they are snapped back to an unpleasant reality by the occurrence of something unexpected. This is precisely what happened to us on that pleasant afternoon. We came to a road block where groups of people were gathered waiting to be let through. To my dismay I saw that the soldiers manning the road block were wearing Whitenik uniforms. I conferred quickly with my companions and we decided to change our story to say that we were going to Amsterdam to stay with friends. We felt we could hardly say we were wanting to go to Britain when it would have made more sense to be travelling southwards. In any case, we were now so close to the rendezvous that we didn't wish to arouse the least suspicion.

When it came to our turn to be inspected we were all told to get out of the car. A young officer said curtly, "We are in charge now. The war is over."

My heart sank. Was it possible that Whittle had actually won the war? Later we discovered that the story was slightly exaggerated, but nevertheless the Whiteniks had by then gained control of most of Europe.

We were asked where we were going and why. Fiona spoke for us. When she had explained, the officer said, pointing to me, "What's a monk doing with you?"

She said, "He's my brother." Then pointing to the King, "This is my uncle and his family. We all belong to Amsterdam and in these troubled times we want to go back there."

I must admit that my heart was in my mouth, but the officer seemed to accept what was said. I suppose many people were travelling for similar reasons. Fortunately he didn't ask any questions about Amsterdam, otherwise we would have been caught out. He looked at the baby in Fiona's arms and smiled.

"A pretty baby," he said. "Is it yours?"

I froze. I wondered what Fiona was going to say. She threw her head back slightly because her long fair hair had come over her eyes. She then said, "Yes, he's mine. His name is Karl."

I thought that was a nice touch. And very wisely she had decided not to draw attention to Princess Anne. If any of the soldiers looked too closely at her they might recognise her. The Princess was wearing a scarf over her hair and she kept her head bowed slightly.

The officer pinched the baby's chubby cheek and said, "He's just like my second child. He's a true Whitenik, isn't he?"

"Isn't he!" said Fiona, smiling with apparent pleasure at this supposed compliment.

"OK," said the officer, waving for us to get back into the car. "Have a good journey."

Chapter Fifteen

By the greatest good fortune we managed to install the royal family on the farm in Derbyshire before the complete collapse of the Polyglot forces. To my horror Whittle, after the defeat of our opposing army, then held undisputed sway over the whole of This World. I pondered deeply as to what my best course of action might be. In the end Fiona and I decided to stay where we were at Mount Zion. There was just a chance that Whittle might forget about us. I hoped, however, to hear from Anatole so that I could help to form a resistance movement.

In some respects life at Mount Zion pursued an uninterrupted course. The work and worship of the monastery kept going as inexorably as the seasons. It was like living in a time capsule. However, everybody watched the television news at every possible opportunity to see what was going on under the new regime. Almost every programme, including the news, poured out a stream of propaganda. Even concerts were preceded by a speech from a Whitenik agent who attempted to portray Whittle as a vehicle of divine providence. So called decadent music was banned and this included all sacred music. How anyone could so twist religious ideas was beyond me - but of course I knew that Whittle was using a kind of negative religion as a tool to promote his political ends.

Some news items were very disturbing. Whole populations were moved from one continent to another in order to complete the ultimate apartheid plan. Slave towns were built and the people were put to work on menial and often unnecessary tasks. The virtues of hard work and paid employment were extolled. Of course, the Whiteniks did not portray these settlements as slave camps. They painted an idyllic picture of people undertaking pioneering projects willingly and with enthusiasm. Information programmes were produced to show how the leisure time of the non-white races was organised. Some so called pioneers were persuaded to praise the apartheid system as a new utopia. Their testimony was obviously forced in some cases and in others I suspected that drugs had been used to brainwash people into believing in the system. All in all, I felt that the new world was not one in which I wished to live.

We were left alone at Mount Zion for about two months. It was then that the inspectors arrived. They were pleasant and charming throughout their stay. They claimed they simply wished to study the way of life of the monastery as part of a stocktaking of cultural life throughout the whole planet. Father Christophoros made them as welcome as he did every other visitor to Mount Zion. They stayed for a fortnight and then they left as suddenly as they had arrived. They took away with them a complete list of people living in the monastery and copies of documents related to the leasing of the premises from the previous government.

A week after the inspectors had left a party of soldiers arrived. There were twenty of them under the command of a man called Captain Duprés. They encamped in their own prefabricated huts just outside the monastery buildings. When they arrived Captain Duprés asked to see Father Chris. They were closeted together for several hours. When they emerged the Prior looked very grave indeed. He straightaway summoned the whole community into the main assembly room, even though it was quite late at night.

Father Chris made an impressive figure as he waited there in front of the community. That is how I shall always remember him. He stood like a statue for some time until we all simmered down. His fine features looked almost as if they had been chiselled in marble and his tall figure was very still. Normally speaking he was a very relaxed person, but that evening he looked unnaturally tense, as though he were waiting to be hung. In truth, the position he was in was not unlike that of a man condemned to die. His whole life was bound up in that community.

At length he began to speak: "My dear brothers and sisters, I am afraid I have some very difficult news to impart to you. All branches of our religious community in all our provinces are to be abolished more or less immediately. The authorities have decided that we are a subversive influence within the new regime. I ought to say that we have not been specially selected for closure. The ban will apply to all religious communities like ours. Each of you must make your own arrangements for the future. However, I have to say that our buildings must be evacuated within seventy two hours from now, or to be more accurate from midnight."

When he mentioned the evacuation of the monastery, his was the saddest expression I have ever seen on a man's face. He paused and looked around. Nobody spoke. He continued, "I am told that the transport system is virtually back to normal. The only difference is that anyone travelling needs a pass. Each of you will be provided with one by Captain Duprés before you leave. There are restrictions on where you will be allowed to travel. There will be no difficulty in Europe, I believe, but the only other continent which is open to you is North America. These have been designated as Whitenik areas."

When I thought of the freedom every single person had possessed when we arrived in This World, I became very depressed. I really began to think that we aliens must have been like a virus which had spread evil throughout the planet. It was almost unbelievable that a handful of people had produced such disastrous effects in so short a time.

Father Christophoros talked on for several minutes. He expressed his sorrow at the separation of the members of the group from each other and he promised that he would pray for them all. I noticed that he did not express the hope that they might be able to restart their community at some time in the future. Moreover, he was so restrained in expressing views about the actions of the authorities that I wondered whether he was under strict orders as to what he could say. In fact, I found out later that Father Chris was aware that Captain Duprés was listening to every word that was said.

An opportunity was given for questions, but we were all too stunned to ask any. Then the Prior said, "I suggest we say the evening office together, but before we do so I have to announce that some of you will be placed in custody by Captain Duprés and his men. He has a list of people who are thought to be too dangerous to be free. I am on this list myself, as a matter of fact. I am not allowed to say who else is listed, but if you are, you will be told when you are interviewed.

When he had finished speaking Father Chris led us in the evening office. As he was repeating the familiar prayers he visibly became more relaxed. Perhaps it was habit which took over. It was as if he automatically assumed the thoughtfulness of serious prayer and that this activity put all else out of his mind.

After the office, people gathered in small groups and whispered their concerns to each other. Fiona and I talked to Father Chris and the Professor. The gentle Prior didn't actually say that we were on Captain Duprés' special list, but he did hint that all four of us would be restricted as to where we might go. I asked Father Chris for the umpteenth time if he had heard anything about the whereabouts of Anatole Bernatti, but he said he had no idea what had happened to him.

....

The next morning I was called in to see Captain Duprés. As soon as I went into the office he had commandeered I asked if Fiona and I could be dealt with together because we were man and wife. The Captain looked at me appraisingly as if he were testing my potential power as a former colleague of Whittle's. Then he said coldly, "I'm afraid that will not be possible."

He wore a grey uniform and he had a grey personality. He was of medium height by This World standards, slim, with blond, wispy hair. He also had a fair, wispy moustache. His voice was high pitched. I took an instant dislike to the man and I believe I should have felt the same way even if I had met him in more propitious circumstances.

He waved me to a seat and said, "I regret to say that you and your wife will be going to separate destinations."

I was flabbergasted by this bald statement. However, I decided to hold my peace until I had learned more. He went on, "You see, Mr Stewart, you are classified as a dangerous agent provocateur - and I have that in writing with the President's signature as authorisation."

He licked his lips as if he were savouring what he was going to say next. "It wouldn't surprise me, Mr Stewart, if you were tried for treason and executed."

He looked hard at my face to judge my reaction, but I think I managed to control my features sufficiently well to disappoint him. He then said, "There is a cut and dried case against you, because you were the one who inspired the defection of one of the President's close associates."

I could see that in any court organised by the present regime I should certainly be found guilty of such a charge.

I said tersely, "Where are you taking me?"

"Rome," he said. "I have strict orders to see that you are taken to Rome."

"What about my wife?"

"She will be re-educated and rehabilitated. Then she will be allowed to lead a normal life."

My blood ran cold as I thought of the various methods that might be used to neutralise Fiona. She could end up like a zombie. I made up my mind there and then that I was going to escape that very night and that I was taking Fiona with me. I decided for the moment to go along with Captain Duprés' version of forthcoming events. I said, "Why can't I be given the same treatment as my wife?"

He grinned. showing a perfect set of teeth. "Believe me, Mr Stewart, nothing would give me greater pleasure than to take your re-education in hand myself. Sadly, that will not be possible. The President wishes to deal with your case personally. I'm proud to say that he interviewed me himself before allowing me to come on this assignment. What a great man he is! He has reversed hundreds of years of history and put the human race back on its proper course."

I was obviously dealing with a fanatic. What puzzled me then and later was why all these tendencies had remained dormant in people like Duprés for so many years. If Whittle hadn't preached his evil message then Duprés would have lived an uneventful and reasonably trouble free life. As soon as that thought occurred to me I realised what it was that Whittle was offering. He had a magic formula for excitement and adventure. The people of This World had become bored with too much civilisation. Perhaps if we hadn't come along something like this would have happened anyway, though perhaps not for hundreds of years.

I decided to frighten Captain Duprés a little. I said, "The President and I used to be very close. I can now see that he was right after all. I shall explain that to him and he will no doubt renew his offer to make me his right hand man."

I could see that my words had hit home. The man's eyes moved rapidly from side to side. He said quickly, "Everything I have said has been under orders. I bear you no personal animosity. But I do have to do my duty and I shall see you reach Rome safely."

....

I very quickly explained to Fiona that we had to leave Mount Zion immediately. She insisted that we ask the Professor and Father Chris to go with us. She said, "I can't bear the thought of those two holy men in the hands of mindless barbarians."

I must have looked hurt. She squeezed my hand and said, "Not you silly. We've got mindless barbarians too."

I didn't wish to cause a great stir in the monastery so I decided to go and see Professor Cherrington first and then Father Chris later. I promised Fiona that I would make them come along with us.

I found the Professor at his prayer desk in his room. He welcomed me sadly. He was very cut up about the break up of the monastic community. I quickly explained what I had in mind.

"Where will you hide?" he said.

"I thought I'd join the royal family initially," I said. "Then I hope to make contact with the resistance movement."

"We don't know that there is one," he said. "Anatole may be in prison, or even dead. Have you thought of that? Perhaps if we go along with the Whiteniks we can change them gradually and peacefully."

I shook my head. "I don't think so, Anselm. Anyway, if there is a resistance movement perhaps the King will know about it. I have a gut feeling that Anatole is alive and kicking somewhere. I want to join him. But I'd like to see Fiona and yourself in a safe place first."

"I'm not coming with you," the Professor said. He sounded very determined.

"Why not?"

His cherubic face opened into a smile. "I'm not going to play gooseberry to you and Fiona."

"Be serious, Anselm. You know that's not the reason."

"No, you are right. I have two very logical reasons for not coming with you. If you honestly convince me that my reasoning is wrong, then I'll change my mind."

"What are your reasons?" I said, hoping I might be able to influence him.

"One - a man of my age and disposition would be a nuisance. I would just hold you back and you would get caught more easily. And also two people can escape detection more easily than three. That's my first reason."

"We want you to come," I insisted, but my voice lacked complete conviction because I suspected he might be right.

"My second reason is more important. I feel I could minister as a priest in captivity, if that's my fate. Also, I may be able to meet up with our former shipmates and I could help them spiritually as well."

I said, "I'm going to see the Prior. I want him to come with us."

The Professor looked thoughtful. He then said, "If Christophoros goes with you I'll come. But I can tell you now that he won't. I'm certain of it."

"I'll come back and tell you his decision," I said.

"No, don't. If somebody is watching you it could cause more suspicion. Christophoros will come for me if he wants me. Let's leave it at that."

"OK, Professor, we'll play it your way."

I found Father Chris in the chapel. He was sitting alone. When I tiptoed up to him he said, "Hello, Bill. Have you come to say a prayer?"

"I'll say one later, Father. I want to speak with you. I'm not sure this is the most appropriate place."

"God is present everywhere, my son, so what difference does it make? You can speak freely in front of Him here or elsewhere. I assume it's important, so shall I just say a little prayer before you start?"

The man's simple faith always confounded me. He was like a child. He asked God to guide and help us and then motioned for me to speak. I explained quietly what was in my mind. When I had finished he said, "You're a man of action, Bill. I suggest you go with Fiona and leave me to my fate. I am very happy to place myself in God's hands."

I said, "Anselm won't come unless you do. Please come with us."

"I'm sure Anselm has his reasons for not wishing to go with you. For my part I feel I have to follow the guidance of my conscience. Like Socrates I will obey the dictates of the lawful authority. If they decide to kill me then I shall go all the earlier to join my Lord."

"I haven't time to argue, Father, but I can't agree that Whittle is a lawful authority. I appeal to you again. Please come with us."

He shook his head. "No, Bill. This is Gethsemane for me. I must drink the cup that is presented to me."

He stood to indicate the conversation was at an end. "You have my blessing. Go, and may God be with you."

I turned round to look at the Prior as I left the chapel. His tall figure was slightly bowed. I could have sworn I saw a halo round his head, but concluded it must be a trick of the light. He raised his hand and smiled faintly. That was the last I saw of Father Christophoros.

An hour later, Fiona and I slipped out of the monastery by a side gate. It was dark and there was no moon. Fortunately we had often walked in that direction so we managed to follow the pathway without a lot of difficulty. In five minutes we were well out of hearing of any guards and we relaxed slightly. I felt it was safe enough to switch on my torch occasionally. We followed the river for two miles and then hit a road that took us in the right direction. I didn't expect to reach the farm where the royal family was until morning.

....

The four adult members of the royal family were delighted to see us and invited us to stay as long as we liked. There wasn't anyone else there except for an elderly farming couple whose family had lived there for generations. The newcomers had been provided with papers which purported to prove that they were relatives of the farming couple. King William, in fact, had always been interested in farming and had settled down to his new way of life very happily. He had lost inches from his waistline and he was quite weather beaten. Prince Edward, on the other hand, was chafing at the bit and wished to start an underground resistance movement. However, the King insisted that the baby was too important to be left without a father for any length of time. The Queen and the Princess had little interest in farming but were pleased enough to help with the chores. Apart from that they spent their time amusing the child, talking and reading. Nobody seemed to be musical, but they were delighted when Fiona offered to play the ancient piano.

It had not been unusual under the old regime for some people to spend their time in agricultural pursuits. One school of philosophy had been very keen on the rural way of life as the ideal form of living. Consequently, a small group of people living in comparative isolation would not necessarily attract any attention. Even if the new authorities decided to inspect rural communities, it might be years before they got round to visiting Two Hill Farm.

I thought it was advisable to lie low for a few weeks. We learned from the television news that Fiona and I were being sought by the army and that a substantial reward had been offered for information leading to our whereabouts. After a while our names dropped out of the news and the bulletins concentrated on the marvellous achievements of President Whittle. After several weeks of this sort of news I almost came to believe that Whittle was a real force for good in This World - such is the power of well planned propaganda. I had to keep reminding myself of the truth.

Fiona and I took to walking in the area, though we never strayed very far. Occasionally we took the baby Prince Charles with us. He was a charming child with a very equable temperament. I never heard him cry once. He made no demur when Fiona or I picked him up. However, he was a grave little fellow and while he didn't cry, he very rarely laughed. Playthings that would have amused most babies of his age seemed to be of no interest to him.

One afternoon I had a long talk with the King. I was helping him to milk the cows and when we had done he took my arm and said, "Let's go for a stroll, Captain Stewart."

It was odd to hear myself addressed as Captain Stewart again. We walked over to the potato field and I thought he had taken me there to show me how well the potatoes were doing. However, he started to talk about the future in a very serious way. He seemed to think that I was the key to ending Whittle's domination. It was certainly an ambition of mine to do just that, but I wasn't at all sure how I might achieve this objective.

"I know you have been threatened with banishment," said the King, "but I feel that decisions made in the past are now outdated and that we must look to the new world of the future. If you can succeed in getting rid of this tyrant Whittle, I shall see that you have an important position in the new scheme of things."

I said quickly, "I don't wish for any position, sir. I merely wish to pursue a vocation as a priest."

"I didn't know you were a clergyman," he said rather huffily. "Why didn't you tell me?"

I explained that I wished to train as a priest, but that in the meantime I wanted to free the world from the evil powers which had taken control if it.

"Whatever you wish, Captain Stewart. But may I share some thoughts with you. It has been a bit limiting to have so few people to talk to here, especially as my son and I don't always see eye to eye. I have been thinking deeply about the sort of world we might build afterwards. After the defeat of the enemy, I mean."

"What was wrong with the world as it was when I arrived?" I said, wondering what he was getting at..

"There must have been something drastically wrong with it for it to have collapsed so easily," he said, his forehead deeply furrowed as he thought. "My present belief is that people had too easy a life. Perhaps we should build farming communities and go back to the golden age of human history when everybody was close to the land."

While I was quite struck with this idea, I knew deep down that it would not work. I said, "Sir, surely that is only one option of many. What about the cultural heritage of This World - all the music and poetry and so on?"

"I still think it would do everybody good to do some regular physical work," he said obstinately. "And moreover, I think I should take a stronger personal line in government. Look at what this man Whittle is doing. Even if I don't agree with what he's done, he has certainly changed things. I have learned a lot from him. Perhaps I can be an equal force in the world, but on the side of goodness and justice."

"I can't quarrel with that," I said diplomatically. "But we can't achieve anything unless we change the political system. It seems we can only do that by the use of force. I've been meaning to talk to you about it, sir. I agree with your son actually. Perhaps we should form an underground movement."

The King laughed aloud. "Excuse me, Captain Stewart. It's the position of my son that amuses me. He doesn't know that there already is a resistance group led by General Bernatti. He contacts me occasionally, using a secret code we have devised for the telephone."

"I'd like your permission to join General Bernatti, sir."

"You must be psychic," said the King, his eyes twinkling. "That's the very reason why I brought you out here - to ask you if you would like to do just that."

<u>Chapter Sixteen</u>

It was good to see Anatole again, and the memories came flooding back.

"I'm pleased you have been able to join me, Bill," he said, his face beaming with friendship. "For a number of reasons. Of course, we're happy to have you on board anyhow, but more to the point at the moment we have a master plan to get rid of Whittle."

"That sounds like a good idea," I said, my enthusiasm rising rapidly.

This conversation was taking place in a disused storage depot in a London suburb which was a regular meeting place for members of Anatole's resistance group.

"As you know Whittle so well," said Anatole, "it will be useful if you are present at the meeting." He looked at me questioningly.

"Who's going to be there?" I asked. I was naturally curious, but I was also worried in case any people who were there might be ill disposed towards me.

"Apart from ourselves, only four of Whittle's officers. They are of quite high rank, but they hate his guts. And they are ready to take drastic action to bring This World back to its former position."

"How drastic?" My voice was sharper than I intended, but Anatole took no notice.

He said calmly, "They have agreed to assassinate Whittle and to take over power. There are difficulties, of course. Catching Whittle unawares won't be easy. That's where your advice will be useful. And even if the attempt succeeds there will be other ambitious people who will want to take power. The four who are prepared to come to our side are not Whittle's closest associates. The coup will need some sort of support. As yet I'm not quite sure how help can be given. We must find out if they have any other people they can rely on."

"I'm not quite sure how I can help." I thought the idea was brilliant, but my own possible part in the coup was not at all clear to me.

"Have you any ideas as to how we can catch our man off guard?"

So that was it, I thought. It was just advice they were seeking. I had hoped to take a more involved part. "Well, Anatole, I have to say that Whittle is normal in his reactions. Or at least he used to be."

"You mean with women?"

I wondered why Anatole had thought of that aspect first. I supposed he thought it was a weak spot for so many men, that Whittle would be vulnerable in that area. I said, "Not especially. What I mean is if there is a serious problem in his domain he will forget everything else to deal with it. In other words a form of threat to his position which is really a feint might work. It's an old trick which I've often used. It's surprising how often people fall for it."

"I see," said Anatole thoughtfully. "So if we carried out a guerrilla attack somewhere not too far away from his HQ he would obviously deal with it."

I began to have hopes of further action. "Yes, he would. One thing he was never good at was delegation. That's why he never got his own ship. And in his present position he will not trust anybody to deal with a real emergency. That's my reading of his character anyhow."

"That's very helpful. The meeting is a week today in Paris, by the way. Travel is virtually back to normal so we can get there without any difficulty. The main danger is that we're both on Whittle's wanted list. We need a cover story and disguises which are unobtrusive. You can't be a monk this time."

"I'm more worried about where I'm going to sleep tonight," I said with a wry smile.

Anatole grinned. "We have a place here. It's a secret bunker. You can stay in it for a week. It's well supplied with food and everything else you are likely to need."

"When shall we meet again?"

"I'll come and see you tomorrow," he said. "We can talk about the details of our trip to France."

The bunker was really a luxurious flat. When I had settled in that evening I could easily imagine that I was in my own world again, snugly at home somewhere in Britain. I felt a great nostalgia for home. And then I thought of Fiona and I knew that life without her would be almost unbearable.

....

The four officers Anatole and I met were, on the face of it, men of genuine character who had been duped by Whittle's ideas. Now that they had had time to see the results of his political actions, they regretted their involvement with him and wanted to put matters right.

One of them was a general and the other three were colonels. All were in their mid-forties or thereabouts. General Karpov was a Russian. He was an impressive man with a thick, black moustache and a head of black, curly hair. He was well over six feet tall, but of course that was not out of the ordinary in This World. The other three were of south European extraction and to be honest I can't remember their names now. None of the officers was in uniform.

Our meeting was fairly informal. Anatole explained that we would arrange for a tactical sideshow to distract Whittle which would give them an opportunity to carry out their plan. The assassination plot was a simple one. All four men would carry handguns and would force their way into Whittle's presence. Each man would shoot simultaneously, aiming to kill.

I was quite surprised at how calmly I talked about the murder of my old shipmate. But I felt that he had done so much damage to the population of This World that any method of getting rid of him was morally justifiable.

After we had discussed our plans for the assassination Anatole said, "It's very important that we decide how to proceed after Whittle is dead. We must move quickly."

General Karpov said, in a conspiratorial voice, "We four have talked this over. We'd like you to take charge, Anatole."

"That would only be temporary," said Anatole, though I could see he was pleased with the suggestion. "We must reconstruct the political system and reinstate the King. But we can only do that when we have complete control. I suspect there may be breakaway groups. They can be dealt with in due course. The main thing is to gain control of the media and all the supply lines. We need good people for particular tasks."

I was very impressed with what General Karpov came out with next. Without hesitation he said, "It's essential that we have Polyglot men and women involved. But we need to be even handed. Some of our best people, ones we know can be trusted, must be involved too."

"That sounds sensible," said Anatole. "But again, these measures can only be temporary. Once proper channels are re-established all the people we appoint must withdraw. Of course, they may be reappointed, but that will not be our responsibility. Anyway, I suggest the two of us get together separately after we have consulted our colleagues. We can then make out provisional lists. Now, what date are we fixing for Operation Maverick?"

So that was the name that had been thought up for the assassination attempt. I supposed it was meant to be a sarcastic comment on Whittle's character.

"As soon as possible," said Karpov briskly.

"Good," said Anatole with equally briskness. "I like short deadlines. They concentrate the mind. Deadline is quite a good word actually, in this instance. But I think it will take at least a fortnight to set everything in place. Shall we say a fortnight today. Our attack will begin at 6 a.m. and you should be able to deal with Whittle before noon. I'll fly in as soon as I get your signal. It's vital we have a good communications system, both before and during. We can sort out those details at our next meeting. Bring a communications expert with you and I'll do the same. Now, has anybody got anything else that needs dealing with now. How about you, Bill?"

"I hope I'm going to be directly involved," I said.

The four Whitenik officers looked slightly uncomfortable. I guessed that they thought I wasn't entirely to be trusted. Anatole said quickly, "You can be my personal aide, Bill. And incidentally, we must sort out what is going to happen to the...".

His voice trailed off. "You mean what is going to happen to the aliens?" I said.

"He looked embarrassed. "Something like that. But now the subject's come up, I think I ought to say the question is for the new government to decide. Not that I'm opting out, Bill. I shall fight like blazes to have you and Fiona remain here together. The trouble is there's a lot of ill will against you all because of Whittle."

"I know," I said. "I just hope the powers that be will recognise that we're not all like Whittle." Inwardly I was resigned to the idea that we should all have to leave the planet as soon as the authorities could manage it. I could scarcely blame them for that.

However, General Karpov and his comrades looked slightly more relaxed when I said so firmly that I was very different from Whittle.

"OK then," said Anatole. "I suggest we get to the drawing board and come up with detailed proposals."

The day for Operation Maverick arrived all too soon. Last minute arrangements had to be made and I was full of foreboding. I liked my arrangements for important events to be made well in advance. As Anatole's aide I was deeply involved in what went on and I could see clearly that there were several weak links in the chain of communication. Fortunately Anatole decided to delegate the actual attack on Rome to a trusted and experienced officer. There was to be a parachute drop of men and weapons about a mile from the presidential palace. This action was planned to be a noisy one and it was expected that every soldier in Rome would come running to take part in the fight. Precisely how Whittle would behave was unknown. I was certain, however, that he would be directly involved one way or another in whatever counter attack took place.

Meanwhile Anatole and I were waiting in a village about twelve miles from Rome. We had a strongly armed group with us and three helicopters at the ready. Once the attack had begun we were on pins as we waited for news. We had established a radio link with General Karpov's office. This was on a wave length not previously used as far as we knew, so communication should be confidential. Nevertheless, we had selected coded sentences to cover various eventualities.

The helicopters were tucked away on a makeshift landing pad we had constructed behind some trees. We had also rented a small house on the outskirts of the village. We had spread the tale around that we were scientists experimenting with satellite communications. As part of our cover we had set up a small radio telescope and some radio beacons.

We heard from our own people that the attack had taken place as planned and that defending forces had been rushed to the scene. We were now waiting impatiently for news from Karpov. It had been agreed that no communication should come from him until there was hard news either way. The radio link had been tested, so there was no worry on that score. Of the coded messages that had been agreed, one of course, was simply to say that the assassination had been successfully carried out. In case the coup failed we had several possible alternative messages to indicate whether there had simply been no opportunity to kill Whittle or whether something more serious, from our point of view, had happened.

Seven o'clock came. Eight o'clock came. Nine o'clock came. Still there was no news. Anatole kept repeating, "Of course, we couldn't realistically expect news before ten."

However, ten o'clock came and went. Anatole was walking up and down like a lion in a cage. The radio man sat calmly at his desk reading a book. For my own part, I was extremely restless, but not quite as worked up as Anatole. He, after all, was the master mind behind the whole affair. Moreover, he was worried about the men in the battle. It had been hoped that they could have withdrawn by now.

It was eleven thirty five precisely when a message arrived. It said simply, "The turkey is alive and the foxes are dead."

Anatole groaned and put his head in his hands. The message was the worst one we could possibly have expected. The turkey represented Whittle and the foxes were the four officers who were supposed to kill him. The message was from another officer who was sympathetic to our cause.

I thought it was wise to wait until Anatole had recovered his composure before I said, "Hadn't we better recall our invading force at once."

"Of course," he said, "they can achieve nothing now."

....

In my opinion, the character of a man can be tested by the way he reacts to failure. In Anatole's case, his reaction to the failed coup was to set afoot another plan immediately. This, I thought, was an indication of his determination to fight for his ideals. His second plan could be described as a chain of grenades lit by a slow burning fuse, rather than a single explosion designed to destroy Whittle's evil political system. He talked this plan over with me to gauge my reaction to it. I must say I thought it stood a much better chance of success than the assassination attempt.

The idea was to recapture Britain for the Polyglot side and to place the King on the throne at Westminster. Anatole argued that this would give a focus to old loyalties and would inspire new ones. This would be followed by similar small takeovers of small countries in different parts of the world. Then, it was hoped, each of the countries so captured would expand its power under the banner of the King and re-conquer each continent. When the King was crowned it would not only be as King of Britain, but it would be openly declared that he was being proclaimed as King of the whole planet.

Whittle had not yet got round to declaring himself King. My own guess was that he was waiting until he was sure of majority support for such a move. What he had done, however, was to get married. His wife was already pregnant and it had been announced that the unborn baby would be the natural successor of his father in due course. In other words, Whittle had proclaimed his hope for a ruling dynasty founded by himself. Somehow I couldn't imagine him as King Andrew and the idea of him having a coronation seemed ludicrous. But then, I suppose it must have seemed ludicrous to some people when the first Roman emperor was appointed. It's all a question of expectation.

The takeover of Britain was unexpectedly easy. I think this was because the coup was a well kept secret and, of course, superbly planned by Anatole. I was keeping a low profile at the time because there was a price on my head, but as soon as the Royalists had control of the country Anatole invited me to organise an SAS type of force which could be used in any part of the world if the need arose.

President Whittle was naturally furious at losing Britain and he lost no time in retaliating. Frequent bombing raids on London took place. Propaganda leaflets were also dropped. Fortunately, neither of these measures had much effect. The bombing was ineffective because huge underground shelters had been created. In addition, buildings which were destroyed above ground could be rebuilt very quickly using This World advanced technology. Such technology had advanced even further in the time I had lived in This World. However, the propaganda was ineffective because not even Whittle's former converts in Britain were impressed by his political philosophy any longer. It was even rumoured that some of Whittle's own staff, that is the people who had benefited most from his conquests in terms of raw power, were disillusioned by their President's "ideal world".

I was talking to Anatole one day about Whittle's failure to hold the moral high ground among his own people. We were walking near the Serpentine, as we had done on several previous occasions. Anatole was explaining to me how far he had advanced his plans for further takeovers and I was reporting on my progress with the new SAS force's training. In the course of this conversation I said, "I wonder if we could take a short cut. Suppose we could capture Whittle. Wouldn't that lead to the collapse of his whole empire?"

Anatole was not impressed by my suggestion at first. He said, "Look what happened to the assassination attempt. I don't think that idea's a runner, Bill."

"I know our chances of success would be small," I said, "but surely it's worth a try. The trouble with the assassination attempt was that we were relying on other people. What I'm suggesting is a well planned SAS raid on his palace. We could be into the palace before anybody knew what was happening. And if we knew precisely where Whittle was we could grab him and be well away before the cooks got up to make breakfast."

"I suppose it's a possibility," he said doubtfully. "Why don't you work out some details and then we can have another chat about it. But I honestly believe our long term plan is safer."

"The long term plan is splendid," I said quickly. "All I'm suggesting is that the removal of Whittle from the centre of the stage might help the various coups you have in mind. Resistance would be lowered and people might be more ready for a return to the old system."

Anatole pursed his lips slightly. "I don't want to make you feel guilty, Bill, but I don't think it will ever be possible to go back to where we were before...".

"You mean, before I lost my way in space and time and brought Whittle here."

"Something like that. I think I agree with the King actually. Much as I hate what has happened it may help us to build a more exciting world for the future. It's obvious that some element was missing from our civilisation."

"Not as far as I'm concerned," I said quickly. "I think your world was perfect. If only Fiona and I could have continued with our plans. If only...".

"The past has gone for ever," said Anatole abruptly. "But I hope it will be possible for you to rebuild a life with Fiona afterwards."

I didn't like the sound of that. There was a note of warning in his voice which worried me. However, I was more concerned at that time to push forward my idea of kidnapping Whittle.

Anatole was insistent that I shouldn't take part personally in the kidnap attempt. I reluctantly accepted this stricture at that stage, but I hoped to persuade him later to let me go. I felt, however, that I couldn't actually disobey what amounted to a military order, mainly because of my growing respect for this unusual man. However, I suppose I knew deep down that my whole future in This World depended upon the goodwill of a few people, and two of these were the King and Anatole Bernatti.

Chapter Seventeen

Fiona and I were together again for a while. Once Britain was in Royalist hands she was able to join me in London and there we managed to live some semblance of married life. The trouble was I had to give more and more time to training my SAS force and I had to spend a lot of time in planning meetings. Fiona decided to do hospital work again and worked as a counsellor in the psychiatry department of the Kingsway Hospital which was near where we lived. In those troubled times many people experienced psychological difficulties. This was a new phenomenon for adults in This World. In the past such difficulties had been cleared up in childhood. With us both being so busy our relationship wasn't able to mature as it might otherwise have done. One advantage though was that our times together were like being on honeymoon. In that respect I have wonderful memories of this period.

Enquiries about the whereabouts of my former shipmates at this time did not prove fruitful. Of course, I was not troubled about those who had remained with Whittle. They would have to take their chances. But of Professor Cherrington I could find no trace. Nor could I trace Bernard Rawlins, nor any other loyal members of my crew. I was especially concerned about Father Christophoros too, but he had disappeared without trace.

Eventually I managed to persuade Anatole to let my men have a go at capturing Whittle and a definite date was fixed. By the use of devious means we had managed to place a mole onto Whittle's staff at the Roman palace. He was able to keep us informed of Whittle's plans and also to describe Whittle's sleeping arrangements. Unfortunately I was not able to persuade Anatole to let me go on the trip.

The night of the kidnap attempt found me once again among those who only stood and waited while others fought; though in my case it was more a question of walking up and down and drinking endless cups of coffee. As I was in SAS headquarters, Fiona was not with me. Neither was Anatole. He was too busy putting another scheme into operation. He did 'phone me, though, and wished our force good fortune. As on the previous occasion there was a radio link with the attacking force, though we had decided that if possible radio silence should be preserved from the moment the troops entered the palace until they were back in their helicopters.

I must say I was beginning to feel very middle aged, even elderly, as I waited for news. The last message I had had was at one o'clock in the morning, just before the attack began. The plan was a two stage one. In the first stage a select group of eight men was to enter the palace to try to capture Whittle without arousing the whole palace. Meantime the reserve force, which was fifty strong and well armed, would wait at the back of the palace buildings. The first stage, of course, depended on various guards being immobilised silently. Should the reserve force hear any alarm or the sound of gunshots, the second stage would be put into operation. This involved an attack in two groups, ten men being left to watch the escape route. The forty men then attacking would storm the main palace building. Four men had been selected to get Whittle and take him to the waiting helicopters.

A final time for leaving the palace had been agreed. This was to be precisely adhered to and anybody not back at the homeward rendezvous would be left to find their own way "home". Home in this context referred to a further secret rendezvous at a private aerodrome where two planes would be waiting to transport everybody back to Britain. The planning had been very detailed and everything depended on careful timing.

So there I was in the small hours striding up and down and going greyer every minute. A row of silent computers stood at one end of the room. In the middle of the room was a scale model of the palace area which had been used in briefing sessions. Only three people were with me. One was the radio operator. The other two were officers with particular responsibilities. One was a radar expert and he had to follow our planes as they came home. At that point the radar was not switched on. The other was an air defence expert and he was ready to trigger our air defences if this should prove necessary. In the next room a dozen or so other staff were supposed to be sleeping.

A building in the park where our HQ stood had been prepared as a prison for Whittle. Guards were already there, ready to receive the prisoner if and when he arrived. The perimeter of the park was well guarded. Much of the park had been converted into a training area for SAS type fighting.

I must have checked my watch against the wall clock a hundred times in an hour. I was trying my best not to become too excited in case the plan fizzled out. But adrenalin was being pumped round my body at an alarming rate. I felt really hyped up. The trouble was there was no way of getting rid of the tension. I envied those who were part of the action. At least they had something to do. Time and again my mind went over the various steps in our plan. I looked at the model every now and again and tried to estimate what my men were doing. Had they got Whittle yet? Or had the whole plan been aborted like the last one?

It did not help my situation when the time for the evacuation of the palace came and went without any news. In fact it was several hours later before any contact was made with the commander of the operation. At eight fourteen precisely, when the sun had long since risen, the radio operator said, "I've got something, sir?"

His machine quickly printed out the coded signal. "We are over the Grand Canal. The bull has a ring in its nose. See you soon."

"Thank God!" I shouted gleefully, all the tension leaving my body. The Grand Canal was our codeword for the English Channel. Whittle was the bull, and he had obviously been captured. The planes would be landing within the hour at an air force base on the outskirts of the city. The radar was switched on and I left the two officers to their duties. I quickly wakened my helicopter pilot and we took off shortly afterwards, aiming to bring Whittle back to the accommodation prepared for him. As we rose in the air I wondered if this was the beginning of the end.

....

There was little opportunity to speak to our prisoner as he was brought back to the park at HQ. In any case, he was understandably surly and there seemed little point in trying to carry on a conversation in the circumstances. I decided to leave him for twenty four hours before interviewing him.

By noon on the day of Whittle's arrival a news item had been broadcast from the presidential palace in Rome. Our media in Britain soon obtained the news that one of Whittle's generals had seized control, not only of the palace, but of the whole political organisation of the empire Whittle had created. I managed to hear a few minutes of a speech the new president made that evening. It was the most depressing moment of my life. The man came out with the same sort of political gobbledygook that had taken Whittle to power and assured everybody that the status quo would be preserved. I almost wept. It looked as if our whole operation had been in vain. The only hope was that before the new president had warmed the seat of the presidential throne, some counter coup might establish a more liberal regime. Unfortunately it was not to be.

Nevertheless, on thinking about what had happened, I concluded that I had gained one important victory: I had removed the "aliens" from power. Whatever happened now couldn't directly be blamed on us, even though Whittle's wilfully evil actions would always be cited as the first cause of the planet's debacle into anarchy. The fight was now between the natives, as it were - or so I thought.

When I went to see Whittle the following day he was cheerful and confident. I was surprised at this attitude and thought it was a case of putting a brave face on things. However, I found that he was truly convinced that his capture was merely a temporary personal setback.

His quarters were quite well appointed, but he was as carefully guarded as Napoleon had been on St. Helena, or so I thought. I chatted to him in his sitting room, which looked just like any other comfortable sitting room. He was dressed in a sweater and slacks and looked very relaxed. His black hair was now flecked with grey. His swarthy face had a few more lines. Apart from that he looked like the same old Andrew Whittle. While I sat opposite him I found it almost incredible that this man, whom I had known professionally for a number of years, had managed to take over a whole planet.

"I'm sorry you have to be kept in custody," I said, trying to be friendly. I had taken care not to wear my military uniform because I wanted to create a neutral atmosphere in which I might be able to persuade Whittle to convince his former colleagues that they should capitulate to the Royalists.

He smiled enigmatically but did not respond. I said, "I hope you are reasonably comfortable."

I didn't address him as Andy because I felt that this would offend his awareness of his presidential dignity, but I was determined not to refer to him in any way as if he were a president. I think of myself as a tolerant person but that would have been too much for me to swallow, even in the interests of peacemaking diplomacy.

He said, "After being cramped in a space ship I could live anywhere, Bill. You should know that."

"Fair enough," I said. "I don't know how long you will be here."

Again he smiled, but this time with a hint of contempt. I continued, "And I don't know what the powers that be will do with you."

He said sharply, "Your so called powers that be are only in control of one tiny country. We shall soon retake it."

I saw then the reason for his confidence. He thought the Whitenik forces were so powerful that his early release was assured. At the risk of offending him I said, "One of your colleagues has declared himself President."

That certainly hit home. His face darkened with a scowl of anger. Then he visibly relaxed as he said, "He did the right thing. He'll hand back power in due course. I can guess who it is - it's Romero, isn't it?"

I nodded. Whittle said, "It figures. He's ambitious, but he's not a fool."

"Why don't you pack it in?" I said. "The Whitenik empire is done for. You could use your influence to persuade Romero to surrender."

Whittle laughed harshly. "I'll die before I give up."

I was certain he meant what he said, so I decided to leave things there for the time being. I thought that a few weeks in custody might change his mind, especially when he saw his old empire beginning to crumble. I knew that some of Anatole's plans were about to mature. I wanted to make sure that Whittle knew what was going on so I said, "I'll see you're provided with a television. But I must go. I have things to do."

He looked slightly surprised at my apparent generosity, but he didn't comment. Instead he said, "I'd like some writing materials. I want to get on with my next book."

Now that I did find frightening. Still, I felt that any further work was unlikely to be published, so I agreed to get him whatever he wanted for that purpose.

Before I left I said, "Do you want us to contact your wife?"

He said, "There's no need. She knows I'll be back."

....

It was shortly after we had captured Whittle that Anatole launched five simultaneous offensives in the name of the King in different parts of the world. The aims were to capture bridgeheads in New Zealand, the Balkan peninsula, Florida, Madagascar and the West Indies. When these bridgeheads were established it was then planned to expand as far as logistics would allow in the fastest time possible. In the event the invasions went like a dream and the first objectives were achieved easily.

I decided not to talk to Whittle once the invasions had started. I thought it wiser to wait until he asked for me. Besides, I wanted him to stew in his own juice for a while. That turned out to be a big mistake.

The third morning after the invasions had begun my adjutant came to me in a real tizzy. He was breathless when he arrived because I was out on a training scheme at the time. "Sir," he gasped, "Whittle's gone."

At first I didn't take in what he was saying. My rather foolish response was, "Gone where?" I didn't dream that he might have escaped.

"I mean, sir, that he's disappeared. And all the guards have gone too, except one who is bound and gagged."

"Show me," I said.

We got into a buggy and raced over to the main cluster of buildings. I strode into Whittle's quarters. There was absolutely nobody there.

"Where's the guard who was tied up?" I snapped.

"He's been untied and taken to the hospital unit for a check up, sir."

We hurried over to the hospital wing. Patients were quite often in the hospital because our training exercises were no lark. Broken limbs were not infrequent. When we arrived we found the guard with the medic. Jenkinson, the guard's name was. He was drinking a cup of tea.

Without ceremony I said, "What the bloody hell has been going on?"

The man paled and coughed as his tea went down the wrong way. He spluttered, "I couldn't stop them, sir."

"Explain," I said tersely.

"The others went with him, sir."

In a flash I understood what had happened. There was no way that Whittle could have escaped without help. He must have persuaded the guards to go with him. I cursed myself inwardly for not foreseeing such a possibility.

"You'd better start from the beginning," I said.

"He - Mr Whittle I mean, talked to us a lot. He really got us going, sir. But I wanted no part of it. He promised us all good jobs when he got back to Rome. He wanted to kill me, but my mates wouldn't let him."

"When did they go?" I said, hoping that we might be able to find them.

"Last night, as soon as it was dark, sir."

"Hell," I muttered. "They'll be miles away by now."

"They were going to steal a helicopter, sir. Not one of ours. There's a place down the road where people garage their helicopters."

"That's it, then," I said. "They're across the Grand Canal by now. It's not your fault. But why on earth didn't you come and tell me."

"They threatened to kill me if I did, sir. I was scared. I have three kids...".

"OK," I said.

I walked away, feeling slightly sick at the thought of what this escape would do not only to my reputation, but also to the aspirations of those aliens like myself who hoped to be allowed to remain in This World.

....

Four days after Whittle's escape the media vibrated with a startling piece of news. The new President of the Whitenik empire, Romero, had been assassinated. Ostensibly Whittle had nothing to do with this assassination and, indeed, he always disclaimed responsibility for it. For me, however, it was stretching the realm of coincidence too far to believe in Whittle's innocence. It is my theory that he persuaded one of his former lieutenants to arrange the placing of the fatal bomb. It is certainly significant that Whittle took over the presidency again almost within the hour.

It is to Anatole's eternal credit that he never once remonstrated with me about the matter of Whittle's escape. Any comments he made were to ascertain the facts and to speculate on the possible results. We didn't have to wait long for Whittle's attempt to recapture the initiative. He could see clearly that his worldwide empire was in danger of collapse if he didn't do something immediately. What he did astounded everybody. He surrounded the papal palace in Jerusalem and arrested the ancient prelate, now over one hundred and thirty years old. It is true that the Pope was allowed to stay in his palace, but nevertheless he was Whittle's hostage. It was announced that the Pope would be executed if the royalist invasions continued. Whittle allowed one week for the evacuation of all royalist forces from everywhere except Britain.

King William summoned a council to discuss this unusual situation. I was allowed to be present but only as an adviser. I did not have the right to vote in any decisions that might be taken. Anatole was a key figure, of course, because he was now a field marshal and was in charge of all royalist armed forces. The other people present were mainly politicians who hoped to have a say in running the world when it was once again under royalist control.

Opinions were about equally divided at the meeting, which took place in Buckingham Palace, now King William's residence. Those who wished to cancel the invasions argued that the Pope was too venerable a figure to put at risk. They further argued that the royalist forces were not yet strong enough anyway to defeat Whittle, so it would be safer to halt the invasions and to conserve our military resources ready for another try in a year or two. Propaganda, they argued, could be just as potent a weapon and it was now so obvious that Whittle was evil that spontaneous rebellions against his rule would take place anyway. Their final argument was a curious one. They said the Pope couldn't possibly live out the year because he was the oldest person in the world. When the Pope died in the natural course of events Whittle's blackmailing move would be frustrated.

The arguments on the other side were not apparently as strong because nobody wanted to put the Pope at risk. It was claimed that the invasions would succeed within the year and that Whittle wouldn't dare kill the Pope. The latter point was argued without conviction. Everybody knew that Whittle was unpredictable and that he might well carry out his threat. Perhaps the strongest argument used was that it was always wrong to give in to blackmail.

At the end of the day the two sides still hadn't agreed on a course of action. Anatole argued fiercely for the continuance of the armed struggle without let up, but his opponents were unconvinced. At last the King was asked to make his decision. To my horror he said to me, "Captain Stewart, I should be interested to hear your estimate of the situation. Will the man Whittle carry out his threat?"

All eyes turned in my direction. I felt that most people were hostile. I knew in that situation I had to tell the truth. I said, "Sir, Whittle will, I believe, execute the Pope as he has said."

There was a deathly hush. The wait before the King spoke again seemed interminable. At last he said almost in a whisper, "I think the invasions should continue. It is my opinion that the Holy Father would not wish us to give in to the power of Satan."

It was an opinion that had not been expressed by anyone else. I was surprised at the depth of wisdom behind the King's judgment. It was so obviously true. However the King hadn't quite finished. he continued, "I shall contact the man Whittle and offer to take the Pope's place. After all, I've been Whittle's prisoner before."

Anatole spoke up quickly: "Sir, we cannot allow you to take such a risk. Whittle has a clear motive for killing you. He covets your throne."

"It shall be done," said the King. He spoke in such a way that nobody was in any doubt that he meant what he said.

So it was that the invasions continued. Whittle was undoubtedly furious at the failure of his stratagem. He scoffed publicly at King William's offer to take the Pope's place. However, he didn't actually execute the Pope. He did something far worse and I hope he rots in hell for it. He stripped the Pope naked and put him in an animal's cage. Then the cage was drawn slowly round the streets of Jerusalem. As soon as he had done this Whittle realised that he had made a serious mistake. The tide of public opinion so rose against him that he was forced to release the Pope and make a public apology. After that, though, he bounced back to promulgate a series of draconian laws which were going to make a misery of life for everyone throughout his empire. He gave the excuse that he was only declaring a state of emergency because of the war. People including whites were arrested for the most trivial offences and placed in concentration camps. Uniformed police were everywhere and they were all paid to spy on each other. A regime of fear was made almost universal. Only in the free royalist areas, which were far too few even yet, were liberty and equality respected. The Whitenik armed forces were ruled by the same fearful regime and men who refused to fight were immediately executed.

I believe myself that Whittle had totally lost contact with reality. He had been on the verge of madness for some time, but now he had crossed the line from sanity into complete insanity, and I did not believe he would ever be brought back into the land of the sane. Unfortunately it was the sort of madness that operates within its own pseudo-logical framework.

It was at this time that two of my old friends surfaced from the anonymity they had cultivated for some considerable time. I refer to Father Chris and Professor Cherrington. It transpired that they had been released by the Whitenik authorities on a sort of parole basis. Essentially this meant that they were allowed to live within a restricted area provided they reported to the authorities at regular monthly intervals. Apparently they had been living in Provence.

What Father Chris and the Professor did was to break their parole. They decamped from Provence and finally surfaced in Rome. Then these two foolish and wonderful men started a two man campaign against Whittle by preaching sermons against him in the streets of Rome. Their actions were reported through our media, but apparently the severely controlled Whitenik media didn't allow any mention of the two itinerant preachers. They managed to avoid capture several times and their campaign became a focus of worldwide attention. I gathered that the bush telegraph in Europe spread marvellous stories about their exploits.

It was to be expected that the two would eventually be captured and it was announced on our television news that they had been arrested. However, no announcement was made by the Whitenik authorities and we were left in the dark to wonder whether they were dead or in some concentration camp. Fiona and I prayed fervently for their safety.

Chapter Eighteen

The expansion of the royalist forces continued inexorably for several months and then, perhaps predictably, it ran out of steam. The fact is that the more territory they took, the more logistically difficult it became to support further invasions. The result was a stalemate of sorts. Nevertheless, the royalists by then had conquered in the King's name about one third of the land surface of the planet. Much of the territory that President Whittle held was uninhabited and useless for human purposes. This meant that an approximate balance of power had been achieved. In these circumstances, no doubt because he was afraid of further invasions, Whittle sought a peace treaty.

The King and his new breed of politicians discussed this proposal for a long time. The politicians and the people were equally divided in their opinions as to what should be done. Those on one side of the argument thought it would be wise to agree to a treaty. The other side were for the unconditional surrender of Whittle's forces and an attempt to return to what used to be normality. What swung the argument was a foolish decision by Whittle. He started an anti-religious campaign in his territory, attempting to ban all religious faiths on the grounds that they were meaningless. He backed this campaign with a series of articles written by himself. The philosophical position he adopted was a simplistic version of logical positivism. He argued that the God concept was meaningless because God could not be perceived through the senses. On that premise he based a whole series of badly connected arguments to show that religion was harmful. Now it is true that some philosophers in past times have taken up a similar position and tried to persuade others to do the same. This they are entitled to do in a free society. However, what Whittle did was to attempt to force his view on the vast population of his empire. Such a policy was doomed to failure, of course, because people of strong religious conviction can never be persuaded that their beliefs are false.

This serious error on Whittle's part brought upon his head the wrath of Christians, Muslims, Sikhs, Hindus and a host of other religious groups. They had put up with persecutions of various sorts for some time. But now, opinions on the political questions were changed practically overnight. Royalist politicians, for example, voted overwhelmingly in favour of a policy of unconditional surrender.

What Whittle was likely to do next was a cause for speculation. He made several threatening speeches about continuing the war but did not specify what he might do. The world learned soon enough what further evil he was capable of.

One evening Fiona and I were out walking in the local park. It was a lovely summer evening and a thrush was singing its heart out somewhere among the trees. Only rarely were we together in this way, so we were full of romantic thoughts as we strolled, arms entwined, chatting about possibilities for the future. Only recently we had wondered whether a declaration of peace would allow us to resume a normal sort of life. The number of children we might have, despite her age, was very much on the agenda. We stopped by a stream to watch the water bubbling and swirling. I said, "I could teach the children to fish."

"You didn't tell me you knew how to fish," she said.

I was just about to say, "You don't have to know everything," when there was a flash of light across the sky. It lasted for a couple of seconds, I suppose. We waited for a peal of thunder, but none came.

"That's odd," I said. "It doesn't feel at all thundery."

"Perhaps it wasn't lightning," Fiona said. "I wonder what it was though. It could hardly be the northern lights, could it?"

"The northern lights don't look like that," I said. "Anyway, we're too far south in London to see them."

"Perhaps it was an electric storm, but a long way off," she said.

We strolled on, not dreaming that anything calamitous had happened. When we got back home, I switched on the three D television to see if there was any news about the political situation. The announcer was just saying, "...and the city has been so consumed by the power of the bomb that it is burned to a cinder. It is believed that half a million people have been destroyed, virtually blown out of existence by the fiery breath of atomic power."

Fiona was making some coffee. I shouted, "Come and listen darling. I think that flash we saw has been a bomb of some kind."

We listened together, holding hands to comfort each other as the news reader went on, "...the power of this bomb suggests that Whitenik scientists have created a new kind of atomic explosion not seen before on this planet. And now, I understand we have just had a news flash from Whitenik sources. President Whittle is supposed to have said that this is only the first of a number of hydrogen bombs which he intends to drop over Polyglot cities throughout the world. We'll come back to that later. In the meantime we shall try to make contact with our studio in Sheffield which is probably far enough away from Manchester to have escaped the worst of the effects of the blast. Yes, I have sound contact with Vernon Wilton. Unfortunately, we can't get a picture. What's happening, Vernon? Can you give us any information?"

"All I can tell you, Simon, is that we saw a huge flash about nine thirty p.m. The whole area was lit up momentarily as if the sun had come up again. Of course, it wasn't actually dark at the time, but even so the flash was brilliant. Then we heard a distant rumble several seconds after the flash. The north western horizon was lit up for several minutes afterwards and the sky was a mixture of red and purple. At the same time a searing hot wind came upon Sheffield from the same direction. Everyone is indoors and those who have cellars have been advised to shelter there. That's about all I can tell you really. There is no word or sign from the direction of Manchester at all. We have to accept the news that the whole city has been burnt to a cinder - but that I understand is as seen from a satellite."

"Thank you, Vernon, I have to interrupt you there because there is further information coming in which I must give to viewers. The news is that the Polyglot powers have responded immediately to the bomb on Manchester by directing a powerful atomic bomb by rocket to drop on Turin. The Italian city, it is understood, is now devastated, though I believe the bomb dropped there was not as powerful by any means as the one dropped on Manchester. We now have to wait to see what will happen next. All viewers in large cities are advised to take shelter, underground if possible, in case further bombs are dropped. In the meantime, I shall try to get in touch with our Swiss commentator to see if he can tell us anything about Turin...".

Fiona said, "Hadn't we better take shelter, Bill?"

I said, "You must, darling, but I have to try to contact Anatole to see if he needs me or my troops. It's my guess that there will be a pause now. Whittle will want to take stock. He'll be worried in case a bomb is dropped on Rome."

"I think I'll go to the hospital, in that case. They may be organising help of some kind."

I said, "There won't be anyone going anywhere near Manchester just yet. And when people do go in they will be properly equipped to cope with the fall out. My advice is to wait till morning."

"Wouldn't it be wise for you to do the same, darling?"

"I'll just try to get through to see what's going on."

I tried in vain to contact Anatole for over an hour. In the finish we decided to go to bed, after listening to an update of the news, which told us little that we didn't know already. Various politicians and scientists were being interviewed between news flashes, the idea being to try to guess what might happen next. Once we were in bed neither of us could sleep, so we talked for most of the night.

....

The following day I went to my military HQ as usual. However, I spent the whole of the day standing by and waiting for instructions which never came. In the meantime I listened to the news at frequent intervals. Whittle made a speech threatening to drop another hydrogen bomb if the royalists did not agree to a peace treaty. Our side made no public response at all, though I guessed that there would be a lot of talking going on. I assumed that Anatole would be deeply involved in any such discussions because I couldn't get through to him at all.

During the late afternoon His Holiness the Pope made an appeal for peace. Apart from that, the news consisted of descriptions of what was going on in the two cities which had been destroyed. There were some truly frightening pictures which showed deserts of smoking rubble. A few people who had miraculously survived were interviewed. One said he had been coming up the steps from the underground station when he was hurled back down the stairs by a gale of incredible force. He had remained unconscious for some hours. He looked completely dazed as if he hadn't taken in what had happened. His face was blackened, though apparently he had escaped with only severe bruising.

About six o'clock it was announced on television that the King was going to make an announcement. I waited, dying with curiosity to know what he was going to say. As always on This World television, it was almost as if King William was in the room with us. My secretary and adjutant were watching with me. There was no pomp or ceremony when he was introduced. The announcer simply said, "And now His Majesty the King is going to speak to us," and there he was. The King appeared to be quite cheerful, though he seemed tired. He said, "Good evening. I know there have been some terrible tragedies in the past twenty four hours and all our hearts must go out to those who have suffered, especially in Manchester and the surrounding area. However, I do have some good news which may help all of us to cope with the terrible times in which we live. I have agreed with President Whittle that there will be an immediate cease fire and that no more bombs will be dropped by either side. Furthermore, this cease fire is to be extended as soon as practicable by a peace treaty which is intended to be permanent. Politicians and others on both sides will meet in Paris to discuss the terms of the peace treaty, starting tomorrow. Everyone recognises the urgency of the situation and President Whittle agrees with me that there must be no further loss of life. I spoke to him on the telephone earlier today and I feel I can say with confidence that there will be peace in our time."

When I heard those words my hopes took a steep dive. I remembered only too well from my history lessons that a British Prime Minister in my own world had said the same words in similar circumstances and that it turned out that his words had been written on water.

The King went on: "That is my main news, but we now have certain priorities to fulfil. I'm sure all of you will wish to help in whatever way you can to comfort those who have been hurt in the bombing and to rebuild the city of Manchester. Then, of course, our long term priorities will be to bring our world back to its former glory. I know it will be a divided world, but nevertheless we must make the best of things. A divided world is better than no world at all. President Whittle assures me that there will be no interference in our rebuilding plans and, of course, I have given a similar undertaking to him. Our new world must be a strong one. We must educate our young people to be adventurous and to have courage...".

The King then went on for several minutes, exhorting people to face the future confidently. I didn't quite know how to react to this speech. On the one hand, I was reluctant to leave Whittle in such a powerful position, even though half of his empire had been taken from him. On the other hand I wanted to get on with my life and there was little chance that the aliens would be banished while Whittle held so much power. I also thought of my military career and decided that probably it was at an end. I could now resume my studies for the priesthood in Edinburgh. It was an inviting prospect, even though one half of the world was still enslaved under a cruel dictatorship.

The following day Anatole came to see me. We walked round the training area for about half an hour and discussed our respective futures. He was still as handsome as ever and as energetic. Perhaps he looked slightly worn, but I was sure he would soon be riding on the crest of a wave once he got going again. "What are you going to do, Anatole?"

"I have been asked if I'll become a politician, but I don't think that's my line really. I wish to persuade the King and the government that we need a standing army. I could do with you on my staff, Bill. How about it?"

I must admit I was tempted. Then I thought of how disruptive of family life it would be to continue with my military career. After a long, long pause I said reluctantly, "I'm sorry, Anatole. I must fulfil my vocation. If ever you need a chaplain...".

Anatole laughed. "I thought you might say that, but you haven't yet heard what I have in mind for you. I would like you to command a force of space ships. Ostensibly these will be for civilian purposes, but we shall ensure that they have military capability as well. How does that appeal to you?"

He looked at me expectantly. Now I really was tempted. I said, "How long for?"

Anatole knew then that I was his man. I didn't know how I was going to explain this decision to Fiona, but I felt deep in my gut that I couldn't refuse an offer like that.

Anatole said, "For as long as you like, Bill, but for a minimum of, say, three years. That should be enough time to get the project off the ground. Mind you, I have to persuade the powers that be that this is good long term strategy. I don't think Whittle has shot his bolt yet. Do you?"

I had to admit that I was almost certain that Whittle would try to recapture all the territory that he had lost. He would not be satisfied until he was master of the whole planet again.

Anatole went on, "There is so much to do, Bill. We shall need a proper espionage service if we are to survive. We must know what Whittle is up to at any given time. And then our atomic research must go on, and we need to train people for war. It's bound to come again. I think...".

His eyes were dreamy. I could see that he was under a sort of spell. He was naturally a man of action, but he was also imaginative. Events had brought him to a prominent position and this enabled him to work on a large drawing board. If he ever achieved his objective of defeating Whittle and regaining the world for the King, I wondered what he would do then. I concluded that he would dream more dreams and find new horizons to climb and worlds to conquer.

....

It was difficult to quarrel with Fiona, but we had occasionally crossed swords about important things. However, when I told her what I planned to do, at least for the next few years, we were thrust right into the middle of a good, old fashioned row. She really lost control. Her eyes blazed with anger. After about ten minutes of arguing and shouting at each other she finally burst into tears. Naturally I put my arms round her to comfort her.

When she had dried her tears I said, "I had no idea you would feel so strongly about it. I would still have time to study theology afterwards."

She looked at me with her mysterious, deep blue eyes. And then she smiled and said, "You don't know, do you? I thought you might have guessed."

I was puzzled and had no idea what she was getting at. She took my hand and placed it on her tummy. She seemed to be plumper than usual in that area. Then the penny dropped.

I gasped, "You... you're...".

"Yes," she said proudly, "we're going to have a baby."

This news made all the difference to my future. The next day I 'phoned Anatole to say that I had decided to turn down his offer of a job - and I hardly felt a pang of regret.

....

Fiona and I went to Edinburgh shortly afterwards. I was planning to complete the theology course which I had begun earlier. But to my surprise I was offered a teaching post in the Department of Space Research. My job was to teach the practical essentials of space travel. I had to build up my resources practically from scratch. My pride and joy was a space simulator which provided a fairly good imitation of space experience.

The birth of my son was an even greater joy. Between the happiness of my home and my intense interest in my job I was so fully occupied that I hardly gave a thought to Whittle and his machinations. However, about eight months after our arrival in Edinburgh I had cause to think of Whittle again. We had news that Professor Cherrington and Father Christophoros had died in mysterious circumstances in prison. It was never proved that they had been deliberately killed, but I have never been in any doubt myself that Whittle had deliberately caused their deaths.

It was Bernard Rawlins who brought the news. He had been released from supervision through the influence of his wife's uncle, who was a powerful politician. Shirley came with him. They were apparently very happy together. He had managed to carve a niche for himself in computer production. Apparently he had invented a new kind of micro-chip which halved the time needed to manufacture jet engines for military aircraft. The arms race was still going on and the two great empires were vying with each other to achieve supremacy for any potential future conflict. It was depressing to think that the peaceful world we had found when we arrived had perhaps gone for ever.

Bernard and Shirley came to dinner one evening. She was as shy as ever, but I grew to appreciate her qualities as I got to know her better. During the meal the conversation turned to the subject of our former shipmates. I said, "I wonder what's happened to Tom Adsworth?"

Bernard said, "Good old Tom. He was a great chef. Last I heard of him he was married to a Chinese girl and they were cooking for the army in South America."

I said, "Did you know Catchpole and Quigley were dead?"

"Yes," said Bernard, "and so is Kevin Oakley. He was killed in the war. He was a captain in the artillery."

"That only leaves three of those who didn't go with Whittle," I said. "Sorry, Bernard, I know you were with Whittle for a while. No offence intended."

"None taken, skipper."

It was very odd to be called "skipper" again. Fiona broke in with a comment about the weather. I suppose she was being tactful, but I wanted to ask Bernard if he had heard anything about Whittle's cronies and what had happened to them.

In reply to my query he said, "Kirkbride and Stevenson are high ranking officers in the Whitenik army, I believe. Do you remember them. Kirkbride was the red haired Irishman with a hot temper, and Stevenson was that big Cornishman."

"I remember them," I said. "They were right pair of bruisers, those two. But I must say I can't imagine them as colonels or whatever."

Bernard laughed. "They're both generals. I understand they're very popular. I heard about them from a Whitenik prisoner who came over to our side."

"There were two others," I said. "One was called Joseph Blenkinsop. I can't remember the other one's name now - but he was your assistant."

"You mean Ernest Clamp. He's something big in the Ministry of Munitions. I suppose I could have done something similar if I'd stayed with Whittle. I'm delighted to be where I am, though, I must say. I was becoming very unhappy with what was happening, even then. How are things going to work out, skipper?"

"I think we're in the game of keeping a balance of power, Bernard. I don't think there will be open warfare, but neither side dare back down. It's quite clear that atomic bombs are so destructive that they are a deterrent to both sides. I suppose we have to live with the situation. I can't imagine anything short of divine intervention which would alter things."

That evening after Bernard and Shirley had departed I went into our son's bedroom to have a peep at him. Fiona had already gone to bed. Paul was still a tiny morsel of humanity, but I was certain I could see strength of character in his tiny features. He was lying on his back and was fast asleep, cocooned in wool and silk and satin. His mouth was slightly open and I detected the faintest hint of a snore.

I watched him silently for a minute, wondering what fate held in store for him. Would he spend the whole of his life living under the shadow of a cold war?

Chapter Nineteen

The end of the Whittle era came with dramatic suddenness. He was found dead in his bed one morning. The doctor who examined him asserted that Whittle had died of a heart attack. There were those who disputed this diagnosis and all kinds of wild rumours were spread abroad. Some alleged he had been poisoned. Others swore he had been asphyxiated. Others claimed he had been gassed. The fact is, though, that nobody ever proved the doctor wrong. Still, the very fact that no other doctor was allowed to see the body served to increase the speculation which, as far as I know, may still be going on to this very day.

Everybody expected that one of Whittle's inner circle would seize power and that the cold war would continue. However, the contenders couldn't agree among themselves as to which one of them should become president, so there was a carve up of the empire. No less than four different mini-empires emerged. One was centred in Rome and covered southern Europe and a large part of Asia. Another was centred on Capetown and covered the southern half of the African continent. The third was in South America and the fourth one embraced parts of Australia and some adjacent islands.

Within three months two of these surviving empires were at war. They knocked hell out of each other for six months and then declared a shaky peace. The royalist empire remained intact and strong. On the face of it the Whiteniks could no longer muster enough power to defeat the Polyglot empire, even if they could agree. Very gradually these empires began to crumble and to split up into smaller units, each ruled by a petty dictator. Within a year of Whittle's death his empire was practically non-existent. It was just a matter of time before the massive royalist forces were able to take over the whole world.

The process of reunification did not come about without effort. In some countries small democratic groups rebelled and took power, after which they allied themselves with the Polyglots. In other cases the royalist forces simply walked in and took over. Eighteen months after Whittle's death there were only small pockets of resistance to royalist power and it was obvious that these areas could not stand alone for very long.

King William called a conference of politicians from all over the planet to decide how the world should be organised. It was called the Moscow Peace Conference. Several key decisions were made. Essentially these added up to a return to the status quo that had existed before Whittle decided to stir the devil's brew. However, it was agreed that security measures should be put in place to prevent any other group from starting a Whittle type of alternative society. The word "Whitenik" became a dirty word and the name of Whittle became synonymous with Satan's.

One important result of the Peace Conference was that a War Crimes Commission was set up to arrest and try those suspected of crimes against humanity. It was not surprising that the four surviving aliens who had stayed with Whittle were high on the list of war criminals. General Kirkbride and General Stevenson were accused of treason and mass murder. Joseph Blenkinsop and Ernest Clamp were to be tried for less important crimes.

To my surprise no mention was made of the other aliens, that is, Bernard Rawlins, Jack Gratton, Dryden Jenkins, Tom Adsworth and myself. There was no whisper of accusation against any of us in the media at that time. Whether we had been forgotten because we had merged into the background or whether it was judged that we were not responsible for what had happened, I could not say.

Fiona and I were ecstatically happy. I assumed that Whittle's cronies would receive some kind of punishment and that the matter would end there. Perhaps there would be a process of rehabilitation in which all the so called rebels were re-educated. I suppose I hoped that the world would return to normal and that everybody would live happily ever after.

A strange thing happened about that time. The whole idea of the young Prince Charles being the Messiah had been forgotten, it seemed. But now that the war was over speculation began once more. Prophets arose and they preached of a new era in which the Messiah would rule over a peaceful world. Noah Smith did not reappear, so I assumed he was dead. It was argued by these would be prophets that the war had been prophesied in the Scriptures. Whittle was characterised as the Abomination of Desolation, as the Roman Emperor Nero reincarnated, as the number 666, as the son of Satan by the Whore of Babylon and as the Beast Ruling the World for Seven Days. It was extraordinary. After much thought, I concluded that this was a way for the world to purge itself of the evil powers which had so nearly taken over the planet.

Fiona and I were invited to a select dinner party by the royal family while all this was going on. Anatole Bernatti was there. He told me that his space project was up and running and that there was still a place on it for me if I wanted it. I countered this offer by inviting him to send his spacemen to my faculty for specialised training. He laughed heartily at my cheek, but promised to look into the matter.

I didn't know anyone else at the dinner except for the royal family, and the only one of them I knew at all well was the King. Of course Fiona and I had lived on the Derbyshire farm with them for a while. In fact, Fiona knew the Princess Anne very well and I noticed that they were having a very intimate chat before dinner.

After dinner the King drew me to one side and asked how things were going. I explained what I was doing and he asked some very pertinent questions. In fact, he said, "I think my son Edward ought to come to you for twelve months. Do you think you could make a space pilot out of him?"

Of course, I assured the King that it would be a great honour to have the Prince, but I didn't commit myself as to whether Prince Edward would make a space man or not.

Fiona and I were overnight guests in the palace. The royal family was still in London, though plans were afoot for them to return to Rome as soon as possible. The next morning Fiona and I were invited to meet Prince Charles, now a toddler. I must say I was eaten with curiosity. Was this child really the Christ come again? Fiona and I discussed the prophecies before we went to bed and we concluded that there was no real evidence. Only time would show whether Charles really was the Christ.

The next morning, however, when we saw the child, we were very tempted to conclude that he was some one very special. The Princess Anne herself escorted us to the nursery where the boy was being entertained by his nanny. Even though I knew the Princess in some respects by now, I was still impressed by her quiet dignity. She had a deep, inner stillness which had the effect of creating an air of peace all around her, wherever she was.

When we went into the nursery the boy was intent upon his game with a soft ball, which his nanny kept throwing to him. He tried to catch it, but usually failed, in which case he picked it up. He then ran with it to nanny, not yet having acquired much skill in throwing. The boy's hair had darkened and he had a strong resemblance to his mother. After a while the Princess called his name. The child came over and threw himself into his mother's arms. Anne said, "Darling, I want you to meet Mr and Mrs. Stewart."

Charles looked at us calmly for a moment and then he smiled enchantingly and said, "Ball." Off he went back to his game. I went over myself to join in the game. I found that if I stood close enough to him when I threw the ball he could nearly always catch it. When he put out his hands to do so I noticed something quite strange. There was a small red blotch in each palm. The skin was smooth enough, but the marks were clear. I supposed they were birth marks.

When I rejoined Fiona and Anne I noticed that the latter had flushed slightly. We stood for a moment and then she said, "You noticed then?"

I said, "I suppose you mean the marks on his hands?"

"Yes," she said, "and he has similar marks on his ankles. We don't wish it to be generally known, so...".

"I shan't tell anyone," I said quickly. Fiona said the same.

(Captain Bill Stewart reports that he did not speak to anyone about this matter until he was back in his own world, at which time he felt he was released from his promise.)

Anne said, "It could just be a coincidence."

"Possibly," I said, but I was left with an odd feeling that I had encountered a mystery which could not readily be explained away.

....

When the four aliens on trial for war crimes finally came before the international tribunal, they were inevitably found guilty. I had always assumed that this would be the case and I had no pangs of conscience about it. However, like everyone else I was very curious as to what the sentence might be. In fact, sentencing was postponed for three months so that the politicians could have their say about the question. There was much speculation in the media and to my horror one politician was reported as saying that all the aliens without exception should be executed.

After three months the judges finally announced their decision, but it was something of a damp squib. They simply said that the four should be kept in custody until the new world council decided what should be done with them. Of course, this set off further speculation and I began to be a bit neurotic about my own position. Whether it was my imagination (as Fiona claimed) or whether people really were talking about me, I couldn't decide. Every time I saw two or three people gathered together I assumed they were saying I should share the responsibility for what the aliens had done and that I should share the fate of the guilty aliens.

When the decision of the council was made public I must say I was shattered. They resurrected the idea of banishing the aliens and recommended to the King that all the aliens, guilty or not guilty, should be put back on their space ship and sent off into space.

Without my knowledge Fiona 'phoned Anatole and he came to see me. Right away he assured me that the banishment would not apply to me. He said he had already agreed this with the King. I must say that this was at first a great relief.

During our conversation I remarked, "I suppose I can understand the decision. After all, if my space ship hadn't dropped out of the sky into the wrong world none of Whittle's machinations would have been possible. I suppose they are just trying to ensure that the same thing doesn't happen again."

Anatole said, "It won't. One of our scientists has already produced a secret weapon which will prevent anyone from taking that sort of action."

"I suppose I'd better not ask what it is," I said.

"I don't mind telling you," he said. "But keep it to yourself. It's a new sort of gas. It paralyses people for twenty four hours. There is no known way of stopping it from entering the human body. It can either be breathed in or it can enter through the pores of the skin."

"I suppose anybody wearing a gas mask and protective clothing would be immune," I said.

"Not at all," said Anatole confidently. "It will penetrate any protective material. The beauty of it is that the people gassed come to no harm at all. It has been tested on a variety of life forms, including human beings. While any would be rebels are under the influence of the gas they can easily be disarmed and put into custody."

"So who controls it?" I said. "Suppose it gets into the wrong hands. It could be used by unscrupulous people to do a Whittle."

Anatole laughed. "All supplies of the gas have been destroyed. Only the inventor knows the formula and there is only one copy of it in existence. This is printed on a metal disc which has been hidden. Only the King and the heir to the throne will ever know where it is."

"God forbid that it should ever happen," I said, "but suppose a future member of the royal family used the gas to gain more power?"

"It is so unlikely that it is hardly worth considering," said Anatole, "but anyway, we have to leave some things to God. Don't you agree?"

"I cannot disagree," I said. "But tell me, Anatole, when are my luckless comrades to be sent into space?"

"The problem of getting them back to their own world has been solved," he said. "The conditions will be just right in November, or so I am assured by our top scientists. That means that everybody including yourself can have a clear conscience about the matter."

At first I concluded that Anatole was right. There seemed to be no reason for me to worry about the former members of my crew. However, something deep inside me told me that I should go back with them. I didn't discover this until I had had numerous sleepless nights and several bad dreams. Once I realised what the trouble was I had to confess my thoughts to Fiona. She was very distressed for two days and then she came to me and said, "Darling, I have solved your problem. We'll all go together - the whole family. I'm sure we can be just as happy together in Transworld as we have been in This World."

Naturally I was ecstatic when this solution to our problem was proposed. I 'phoned Anatole and asked if this could be arranged. It was a full week before he got back to me. He told me that neither the King nor the Council would countenance such an arrangement. It had been argued that there was an element of risk in the journey and that it wouldn't be right to allow a woman and her child to be exposed to such a risk. Fiona and I were plunged once again into the depths of despair. What were we going to do? Personally I felt as if an immovable object had met an irresistible force in the centre of my being. I couldn't concentrate at work and I was moody and bad tempered at home.

About a month before the space ship was supposed to go I had a little note from King William asking me to stay in This World. I still have the letter and this is what he wrote:

Dear Captain Stewart,

I wish you to know that I have very much valued your services to me and to my family in the past and I very much hope that you will be able to stay with us to help to rebuild our world. You bear absolutely no responsibility for what happened and your good actions have more than made up for what that evil man Whittle did. I ask you also to think of your dear wife and child. Please stay with us.

Yours,

William R.

I didn't keep a copy of my reply but as far as I remember it went something like this:

Your Majesty,

Thank you so much for your very kind letter. My heart tells me to stay in This World but my sense of duty dictates otherwise. I know you will understand when I tell you that I could never live with myself afterwards if I let my space ship leave without me.

I know that you will recreate a better world and I only wish I could be of assistance in this great work.

With sincere regrets,

From your loyal subject,

William Stewart

....

My crew and I were gathered for a briefing the day before we were due to leave. Anatole came to say goodbye just before the briefing. We didn't say much. However, I knew he meant what he said when he told me I had been a good friend. His last words to me were, "I'll see that Fiona and the boy are OK."

I didn't know what to say in the circumstances, so I just smiled my thanks.

When we went into the briefing room I was allowed an hour with my men before the briefing officer joined us. I had deliberately arranged things so that we sat in a circle. I didn't particularly wish to create an us and them situation. Nevertheless, when they all sat down the Whittle group sat together. I looked around them, trying to see who had changed during the five years of our stay in This World. Most of them looked little different. One looked a little stouter. Another looked a little greyer. Another had grown a beard.

When we had all settled into our seats I said, "I believe all the survivors are here. I think I can remember all your names. let me see now, going round, it's Kirkbride, Stevenson, Blenkinsop, Clamp, Gratton, Jenkins, Adsworth and Rawlins. I note with regret that some of the ship's company have not survived - and that includes our Chaplain, that is Professor Cherrington. Andrew Whittle, of course, died suddenly. Jim Catchpole, and Daren Quigley and Kevin Oakley are also dead. I think I've mentioned everybody."

I looked round at their faces. Kirkbride and Stevenson looked very sullen. The others seemed calm enough.

I continued, "It is five years since we left our own planet. No doubt we have been written off as dead long since. There's going to be some explaining to do if and when we get home. I'm certain there will be a court of enquiry and I shall be asked to explain why some of our shipmates are not with us."

"What are you going to say?" said Kirkbride. I noticed the absence of the courtesy "sir" when he spoke.

I said, "I intend to tell the truth. I don't see how I do anything else. Whether I shall be believed or not is another matter. No doubt you will all be asked to give evidence."

"I shall refuse," said Stevenson.

"So shall I," said Kirkbride.

"I don't think you can be prosecuted in Transworld for what you've done in This World," I said. "Anyway, we've all been punished. Banishment is our lot. And I feel that's all we deserve."

"Balls!" said Kirkbride.

"Look," I said, "whether you like it or not the clock has been turned back in at least one way. You are all members of my crew and I'm the captain."

Neither Kirkbride nor Stevenson made any comment. "Incidentally," I said, "Bernard Rawlins is herewith appointed second in command."

Kirkbride said, "Bloody traitor!"

I said sharply, "Mister, you can either conform to the rules or be placed in custody. It's entirely up to you. Anyway, we have to forget the past. We're all facing an uncertain future and I didn't have to come with you. I wanted to stay and I could have done. But I felt it was my duty as your former captain to assume responsibility for getting us safely back."

That seemed to settle Kirkbride and Stevenson. "Any questions?" I said.

Gratton said, "Sir, how do we know we shall get back safely? We could be on a journey into nothing."

"That's why we're being briefed," I said. "I understand the boffins have solved the problem."

Bernard said, "Skipper, do we have to tell everything? Can't we be silent on certain aspects of what happened?"

I thought for a moment and then said, "Possibly, but I can give no guarantees. If pressed I shall have to tell the full truth. But I could say, for example, that there was a war going on here and that some of the crew were killed. That is near enough to the truth. I could also say truthfully that Andrew Whittle died of a heart attack."

Stevenson gave a sly smile when I said that. However, he and Kirkbride looked a lot more cheerful at the possibility of their misdemeanours being glossed over.

Nobody else wanted to ask anything so I went to the door and told the guard we were ready for the briefing. A youngish, scholarly man came alone into the room. "May I join the circle?" he said.

We made room for him and then sat apprehensively waiting to hear what he had to say.

He cleared his throat and said in a very quiet voice, "My name is Professor Montessori. What I have to say won't take long, gentlemen. Your space ship is refurbished and is all ready for you. My technicians have added one or two features, but these are to make sure you return to your own world safely. The space ship will be on automatic control. You will be sent into orbit at a very precise time. That is essential. You will make one orbit of the earth and after that the ship will be on manual control. It is expected that you will be back in your own world when you have completed one orbit. There may be a little bit of turbulence or spin, but it shouldn't be anything to worry about. After that it's up to you. Whatever landing procedures you normally use should be put into operation. The extra features we have fitted will disintegrate after twenty four hours so your space ship will be exactly as it was before. That's about it really. Any questions?"

I said, "Some of us are a bit frightened. Can you guarantee that we shall have a safe passage?"

He did not smile. Nor was his voice particularly confident. However, he said, "As far as I can ensure, my equations are correct. You could say that logic insists that I am right. Barring unforeseen factors there should be no difficulty."

"Bloody hell," said Joseph Blenkinsop, "does it all depend on a piece of algebra?"

Everybody laughed. Professor Montessori said, "All space travel depends on algebra and geometry, plus a bit of physics."

"What about our personal equipment?" said Bernard.

"It's all been worked out by computer and made to measure," said Montessori. "It's all laid out for you in a building near the launch pad."

I looked round at the men. Nobody seemed to wish to ask anything else. However, I wasn't quite satisfied that the ship would respond normally so I said, "Suppose something goes wrong with the automatic control. Is there any way I can change over to manual?"

The Professor said, "Adjustments can be made from the ground. You'll have to take my word for it that you won't need the manual control option until you are back in your own world. But if you are in danger we can bring you back to earth, provided you haven't passed through the grid."

There wasn't really any more to say. I had to trust the man's judgment.

Chapter Twenty

By the time Captain Bill Stewart had finished his story he and his old school friend, Carl Britton, were the only two people left in the bar lounge of the Coach and Horses.

Carl Britton said, "That's quite a story, Bill. I mean, we all know you got back safely - but it must have been quite traumatic to arrive back on earth five years after you left. Especially when everybody thought you were dead. Of course, some of your shipmates *were* dead. I feel sorry for that chaplain fellow. What was his name again?"

"Cherrington. Yes, if he'd come back the court of enquiry would have been more inclined to believe our story." At the mention of the professor a flood of sadness washed over Stewart.

"You didn't tell the whole story to the court, Bill, did you?"

"Nobody told any lies. I decided not to cause distress for the families of those who helped Whittle - and including Whittle's family, of course. I assume you're not going to blab to the newspapers, Carl."

"Cross my heart, old boy."

Bill Stewart was fairly sure his old school friend would keep his word. He said, "It has done me good to get it all off my chest." It was true. He felt much better for it.

"One thing really surprises me, Bill. And that is how you nearly became a parson. It wasn't really your thing at school, was it?"

Bill Stewart laughed. "No, it wasn't. But I'll let you into a secret. I've applied to Edinburgh University to do Theology. A place called New College. Later I hope to be ordained."

Carl Britton was silenced for a moment. Then he said curiously, "What really convinced you that you should follow a vocation, Bill."

Stewart paused for a few seconds before answering. "Well, if creation is complicated enough to have parallel universes, then God must be in the situation somewhere. But really, it was knowing Father Christophoros that convinced me."

"Do you believe there will be a parallel Messiah here, Bill. In the year of Halley's Comet, I mean." Britton was completely fascinated by the idea.

Bill Stewart smiled, his eyes seemingly looking far away into the distance, beyond the walls of the room where they sat. "I shall never know, shall I? After all, it is now the year of Our Lord 2020 and the comet comes again in 2061. Neither of us will be around at that time."

Just then, the outside door opened and a tall woman carrying a child walked into the room.

"Ah," said Bill Stewart, "Here's Fiona with the nipper."

Carl Britton gasped in amazement. "What...how...?"

Stewart smiled and said, "You don't think I was going to leave my family behind, do you. We stowed them away without any difficulty. Come and meet them."

POSTSCRIPT

Captain Stewart and the other survivors from the five year trip on the Leviathan were exonerated from blame for the deaths of those who had not returned. One of the key pieces of evidence was the report on the medical examination of Captain Stewart's wife, Fiona. The panel of doctors and scientists who carried out the examination all agreed that her genetical structure was unusual and was not paralleled anywhere on the Planet Earth as far as they knew. Moreover, Mrs. Stewart had talked with the doctors about methods of medical treatment previously unknown to them. These had proved to be effective when tried on selected volunteers.

Captain Stewart was ordained into the Church of England several years later and worked in a London parish for many years. He and Fiona had two more children. The first born child turned out to be a mathematical prodigy. Sadly, Fiona aged very quickly and died ten years after her arrival onto a Planet Earth which was alien to her.